LAUREL
NIGHT

VALKYRIE
FALLEN

VIKINGS & VENGEANCE
BOOK
1

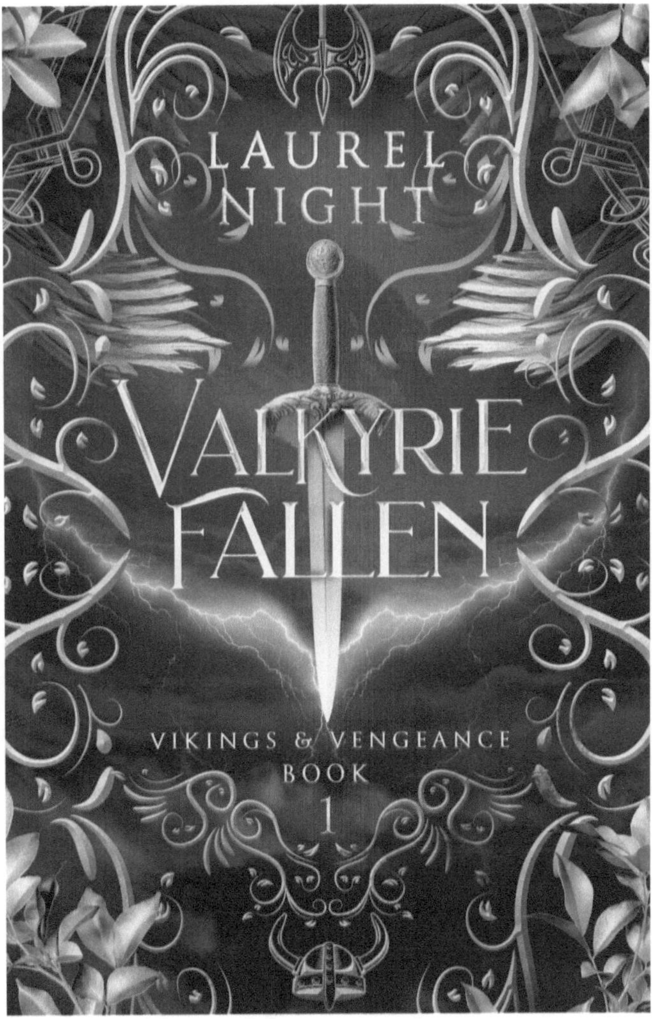

valkyrie fallen

VIKINGS & VENGEANCE DUET
BOOK 1

LAUREL NIGHT

note from the author

Dear reader,

This book was such a fun journey for me to write. Brenna is vastly different from other characters that I have written, and she deals with issues that my other characters have not.

Brenna suffers from a number of things that I know personally, including depression and alcoholism as a form of self-medication. This is not a trigger warning, as I don't believe these are triggers. I simply think these are everyday realities for many of us, and I hope you feel I've handled them with care and perhaps can relate to Brenna because of this. While Brenna may have a magical solution to help her with her problems, we don't all have that luxury. Please reach out to your family and friends if you need help, and know the world will ALWAYS be a better place with you in it.

LOVE,
Laurel

one

BRENNA

I KNEW my life was over the second I spotted the crow.

All crows have that beady-eyed, willing-to-peck-your-eyeballs-just-to-steal-your-sandwich look, but this one sent a shiver up my spine. I recognized this crow.

It wasn't every day you spotted a divine fucking bird.

This crow had haunted my dreams for the last thousand years. Ever since Odin banished me from Valhalla, and I turned his curse on its head. Instead of remaining in the village where he put me, destined to be his plaything for eternity when the mood struck, I earned my freedom by being the best damned shield maiden they'd ever seen. Even without my magical armor, no one could match me. I gained the Jarl's favor and eventually earned enough gold to strike out west. I still had stashes in banks all over the world: handfuls of trinkets that were treasured when they were made, but now were absolutely priceless to the people who collected such things.

I didn't stay put in any one place for too long. Five years in Amsterdam, four in Los Angeles. Moving around kept me from getting too comfortable, from being too easy to find. I colored my hair, changed my look, reinvented myself over and over. Right now I was rocking a hardcore grunge style, complete with holey jeans, a weathered old flannel, and a beanie on my dyed-black tresses. The 1990s were a great time, and I was legitimately happy some of the fashion trends had returned. Doc Marten's were way more comfortable than the spike heels popular in the early 2000s.

So, despite the way my heart skipped, I knew the crow wasn't certain I was Brenna the banished valkyrie. He stood out among the pigeons, but no one else paid him any mind. You saw a lot weirder things on the streets of New York City.

But this meant it was time to go.

Hughin had found me several times before, although he didn't know it. As soon as I'd spotted his raven feathers, I packed up and skipped town. Changing my hair color and clothing style, I altered my appearance enough, and the bird was fooled... most recently, a few decades ago in London.

He was a divine bird, but still just a fucking bird.

Hughin traveled through the nine realms at Odin's bidding, keeping his beady eyes on things and reporting back to the all-father. I knew, or at least suspected, that Odin wanted him to find me. Last time he'd followed me back to my flat, and I slipped out, disguised, right under his pointy beak.

Sighing, I trudged past and acted as if I took no notice of the giant black bird, just like the rest of the New Yorkers streaming along the concrete with me. A mental checklist was already growing in my mind.

I need to get new papers—hopefully Jimmy can handle the rush job.

I need to pick a new look and hair color... maybe more 80s? Big hair, sandy blonde?

I need to break it off with Andre... which is too bad. I had just gotten him trained up in bed the way I liked it, and now I'd have to start over.

I probably need to sell another trinket so I have the cash to hole up for a while.

Hughin wouldn't make a move until he was certain it was me. He'd follow me around for a few days as I made my preparations, and then one day I'd give myself a makeover and he'd be completely thrown when I gave him the slip.

Grinning to myself, I imagined the fury that would rain down on Asgard when Odin once again realized he lost. I slipped into the coffee shop, then sent a couple of quick texts to get things in motion before my shift started.

I didn't really need the money, but it was easier to

3

blend in when you were just another grungy 20-something working a shitty job with dreams of making it big someday. It was easier for other people to relate to me, and I needed to look like I belonged. Odin would expect me to be a loner, to avoid relationships at all costs, to preserve my secret.

So I had lots and lots of friends. Wherever I went, I was the most charming social butterfly anyone had ever met. I'd find a community that fit my new identity and insert myself in like a well-worn glove fit with the perfect hand. I was so good at it now, I scarcely needed to try.

While I pulled shots of espresso and added foam to cappuccinos, I mentally sketched out the basis of my new identity. She'd be the bubbly cheerleader type. Perhaps Jimmy could rustle up some sorority letters and a college degree, and I could negotiate a receptionist job at some boring, taupe-colored office. Maybe I'd try the Midwest again. I'd been nearly bored to tears in Omaha, but perhaps I should try Minnesota. There were still ten US states on my checklist, and it wouldn't be hard to affect the accent —I'd seen *Fargo*.

By the time I finished my shift, I had an entirely new life sketched out. I shoved the fistful of bills and coins from the tip jar into the pocket of my baggy jeans, locked up the coffee shop, and pretended not to see the crow now perched on a streetlight across the street, watching me.

And that is when fate—or perhaps Odin —intervened.

✳

I felt the energy in the air shift. It was just like before a battle: currents of electricity coursed through the wind, raising the hairs on my neck and electrifying my senses.

Someone was going to fight.

Someone was going to die.

I would need to choose.

No!

I fought the urge to seek the battle and send the winners to Valhalla. It had been over a thousand years, but it was still as difficult as the first day I refused to do Odin's bidding.

Choosing the Victorious Fallen was what I pledged to do. Selecting the best fighters, the most outstanding warriors, to join Odin's party and wait for Ragnarok was my purpose in Valhalla.

Until I just couldn't do it anymore.

But the instinct was still there. As much as I'd tried to fight it, it inevitably drew me to the fighting.

And oh, how many battles there'd been.

I thought the wars waged in Odin's honor were epic; I had no idea that men would continue to find newer, better ways to kill each other.

Throughout the dark ages, the Middle Ages, the great bloody battles over small tracts of land in Europe, I fought the urge to walk among the dead and test their soles with my magical Valkyrian blade.

It always seemed that as soon as I believed I'd adapted and overcome the urge, the wars grew again.

Fortunately, I couldn't risk traveling too far east, or too far south; my coloring would not have blended with the locals and I would have attracted too much attention. That spared me the bloody battles of Chinese and Turkish expansionism.

But there was plenty of war waged by pale-faced humans to keep me occupied.

I was drawn to the battles like a moth to the flame. It was just too much; the power of so many souls begging for afterlife. During the Great War and World War Two, I found work as a nurse to be near the newly dead. Most of these were not elite warriors that longed for Valhalla. They were scared boys, who took bullets within minutes of touching their feet to the dirt on a foreign land. Modern weapons ruined battle—there were no more epic sword fights, no true battling. Just sprays of metal and gases and other ways to kill a man that were too horrible to mention.

Nevertheless, the valkyries came.

I couldn't see them, not anymore. Odin had made sure of that. He swore I'd never see my sisters again.

I thought he meant I wouldn't be allowed among them any more. Little did I know, he meant he'd physically *prevent* me from being able to see them, as if I were just a regular human.

I still felt their presence on the battlefields as the bloodied and soiled medical teams searched for survivors.

The valkyrie were there, searching for the Victorious Fallen. Walking among the bodies, testing the souls with their magical blades. Occasionally, I felt the release as they sent one to Valhalla.

I cried for those men.

Because they were doomed. Doomed to endless days of battle, feasting and celebrating the end of the world, only to do it all over again the next day.

Odin sold this fantasy of his army built for Ragnarok, this glorious host that would feast with him and ride out to meet the end of the world.

Only the end never came, and they trapped those poor souls in a never-ending party of horrors.

They fought, they laughed, they feasted in the halls of Valhalla.

And at night, when they slept, they cried. They screamed in terror, in fits of loneliness and agony, missing the family that had long since died and gone to whatever heaven the new gods offered them.

This was no glorious host, no magnificent party of warriors and winners.

This was a million souls, doomed to endure the same torment every day for eternity.

And so when I felt the pull, the draw in my belly to go to the battle and select the Victorious Fallen for Odin's mighty host, I fought against it with every fiber of my being. My magical blade, concealed within a guitar case, shivered in excitement.

I continued my trudge down the street toward my apartment, careful to act normally under the penetrating gaze of the beady-eyed crow.

But it seemed the bird was smarter than I gave him credit for.

After so many centuries of slipping away right under his beak, he finally figured me out.

This time, he didn't wait for me to react.

This time, he brought the battle to me.

From the shadows of an alley between me and my apartment stepped four large, menacing men, forcing me to pause. At first glance, there was nothing unusual about them; they appeared like any losers that hung out on the street corners at night, looking for trouble. One casually cracked his knuckles and gave me a sly grin, while another leaned against the nearby building and leered at me suggestively. The third hung back, just making sure I didn't have a clear path beyond them short of hurtling myself into the street.

But the biggest wasn't looking at me at all. His stormy grey eyes focused on my guitar case.

And that's when I knew this was no coincidence.

New York was full of musicians. Students who attended elite music schools. Hopefuls who played troubadour in the subways or on the streets for donations. People who snagged small gigs in coffee shops and tiny bars, hoping they'd get talent spotted and hit it big.

As part of my cover, I learned to play just enough guitar to get away with the story that I was taking lessons.

But anyone looking at me would expect that I had

a crappy, cheap acoustic guitar in my beat-up case. It wouldn't be an item of interest to anyone but the most desperate tweaker who needed to get his next fix.

This man was a little too clean to be an average street thug. Although his clothes fit the bill, his body hinted at a generous, healthy diet. His face was neatly shaved. His grey eyes were sharp, calculating, cold.

"What's in the case, sweetheart?" The man smiled at me, but it didn't reach his eyes and his expression didn't match the menacing tone in his voice.

I tried to play it off.

"Uh, I dunno genius, what do you think would be in a guitar case?" Slouching, I snapped my gum as if I were bored and annoyed rather than on high alert. My cover was a tough-girl hipster trying to make her way in the world, and she didn't have time for this bullshit. I whipped out my phone and snapped a picture of them, then tapped at the screen. "Congratulations, I just sent that to my friend who's waiting for me two blocks up, and told her to call the cops if I'm not there in five minutes. Are you going to get out of my way, or do we have a problem?"

"Hey, we have no problems, girl. We just want to see your guitar. Why don't you play us something? Maybe we're the big break you're looking for."

I snorted. "Not likely. For one, talent scouts don't hang around in dark alleys waiting for their victims— sorry, *clients*—to wander by. Second, I don't play on the street. Third, you're pissing me off." I held up my phone with '911' entered on the dial screen and hovered my finger over the dial button. "Do you want me to hit this, or are you going to let me pass?"

The big one stared me down with cold eyes. "You're not going to hit that button."

"Try me."

"No need. I know you won't hit it because you don't want attention. You don't want to explain to the cops why you have a giant sword in your guitar case, which they will definitely want to see when we tell them about it."

I rolled my eyes. "You're out of your mind. I have a *guitar* in my guitar case. I realize that's a stretch for you to believe, but it's the truth."

"Oh, of course you do. But underneath it, in the false bottom, you have a sword. A sword, from what I'm told, that is precious. One might say *priceless*. So we're here to collect it, and then you can be on your merry way, with your guitar."

"Uh, pass. I'll be heading on my merry way with all of my possessions intact, because what's in my case is none of your fucking business." Tapping the button on my phone, I lifted it to my ear, tightening my grip on the guitar case. "Hi, yes, I'd like to report an attempted robbery at-"

The phone was snatched from my fingers and immediately smashed on the ground. I expected that to happen, and I was already swinging my guitar case at the culprit.

It was no ordinary guitar case, although it looked like one. I had it custom made from thin plates of steel, including the steel cables attached to the handle, then wrapped in the shell of a ratty old case to disguise it. The thug was correct: it had a false bottom that concealed my sword, complete with lead lining that prevented magical spill-over from being felt by those who recognized it.

Above me, Hughin's beady eyes burned holes in my back. I did not know how, but they definitely staged this little intervention to expose my sword and thereby my identity to the crow. I had to keep my secret under wraps.

The case hit the thug in the arm with a fair amount of force, but he parried the hit and it didn't knock him down. In the seconds since I'd hit 'call' on my now deceased phone, the others had surrounded me. A quick glance up and down the street told me there was no one to intervene nearby... the closest street with foot traffic was several blocks away.

I was on my own.

Gifted with eternal life, I had a certain amount of —shall we say—vitality that the average human didn't possess. I also hadn't wasted my time on this earth. I lived several characters who were deeply interested in martial arts. So I had some skills.

Now, if I pulled out my sword and used the magical power it possessed, I'd easily overpower these men. However, that was the last thing I wanted to do with Hughin watching.

I had to think smarter.

I crouched, prepared for a fight, when I heard a popping sound reminiscent of a giant soap bubble bursting.

Oh, for fuck's sake.

Turning my head slightly to glance at the thug over my right shoulder, I confirmed what I already suspected: The third man, the one who'd hung back, was no man at all.

It was Loki, and I was screwed.

Now, this was no hot, modern-era movie, Tom Hiddleston Loki, with limitless powers and a sexy smirk.

This was the real Loki, the freak born of a giant and—according to him—a goddess. A hulking, malicious bastard that cared for no one and nothing that didn't benefit him to care about. That he appeared in his actual form told me the game was up—he already knew it was me. Otherwise he would have appeared as some kind of sexy temptation and try to talk me into giving up the case first.

Instead he grinned, his wide, craggy face not improved by the gash revealing crooked brown teeth. At nearly seven feet tall, his sudden appearance should have surprised his companions. However, they didn't blink when he suddenly changed, which confirmed my suspicions they weren't your average thugs.

"It's so nice to see you again, Brenna." He spoke perfectly unaccented English as if it were his native tongue.

I tried to hold my ground. "Buddy, you have me mixed up with someone else. My name is Iris. Neat magic trick, though. Do you do shows around here?"

"You're not fooling anyone, Brenna. Odin knows it's you, and because he asked so nicely, I agreed to come collect you." His grin deepened. "However, I did promise to show proof to his pet first." He gestured to the ever-watching bird. "So why don't you bring out the weapon and we can get on with this?"

I was trapped. There was no way I could fight Loki's magic without my sword in hand. He could easily overpower me and just take it.

But pulling out the sword would mean I gave Hughin the proof he was waiting for. How long would it take for him to report back to Odin? Would I have an hour before he came for me? Less?

One thing was certain: If I didn't act fast, Loki would decide for me. At least if I took a stand, I might have a chance to run.

Sucking in a breath, I crouched to snap open the case and made a show of lovingly removing my guitar with one hand while the second felt for the flap underneath. I raised the instrument over the top of the case and offered it to Loki. "Here you go, sir. My weapon."

The others had stepped forward to see it, then reared back in confusion when they realized I was actually holding up a guitar. Loki laughed, a grating sound that resembled a choking bear.

"I do admire your spirit, Brenna. But that's not the weapon I meant."

My hand not occupied with the guitar slid under the velvet-lined flap, fingers circling the hilt of my most prized possession as the cold and hot currents of pure power ran up my arm.

"Really? I think you should take a closer look." I tossed the guitar at his face, tipping the case over and standing fully while my body charged with power. The confident, centered feeling filled me, and I grinned back at Loki while I calculated the shortest route I could take to dispatch them and hide before Odin came looking for me.

Overhead, Hughin flapped his wings and cawed, I assumed taking off to report to Odin. I had to have at least an hour to escape. There's no way he could be that fast.

What I had no way of knowing: It was already too late.

two

BRENNA

I HEARD the second burst of a bubble, and internally I cringed. I didn't know for certain who it was, but I had a fairly good guess.

Turning, I verified my suspicion was correct.

Odin had disguised himself as the main thug, his piercing grey eyes a trick of magic. Now, his single blue eye glared at me in victory, the empty socket on the other side concealed behind a dented metal patch.

"I told you I'd find you." Odin grinned ferociously, his long waves of silvery hair blowing in the light breeze. He also spoke in perfect, modern English. "It doesn't matter that you hid for a thousand years, here we are as if no time had passed at all."

"Why can't you just leave me be?" I hissed back at him. "You've already stripped me of my armor and my powers, and banished me to Midgard. What else can you possibly want from me?"

"Tsk tsk, Brenna," Odin chuckled darkly. "You pledged to serve me until Ragnarok. Just because you decided you no longer wanted to serve your purpose, it doesn't mean you get out of that obligation. Since you refuse to send the Victorious Fallen to Valhalla, you serve me by being subject to my whims. When I want something, you heel. When I snap my fingers, you obey. Heimdall!"

Odin lifted his face to the heavens when he shouted the last bit, and my knees began to tremble. Within seconds the rainbow descended out of the pure black night, surrounding us in glittering light, and I felt the distinct pull behind my navel as it whisked us off to Asgard.

I never thought Odin would come for me himself. As he dragged me back to his magical home between realms, I cursed the trap he'd laid. Maybe if I'd walked another direction, or...

No, it was pointless to go over the 'what if's' now. Odin had me; he must have known it was me, to come with so much backup. The feeling of flying while also remaining completely still as glowing rainbow colors whooshed by was enough to churn my stomach... it had been quite a while since I'd traveled the Bifrost. My body had become accustomed to the weight of Earth's gravity. Biting back the urge to gag, I waited for the moment when we'd stop, and my doom would be sealed.

It was an eternal moment and yet happened in a blink of the eye. One second I was on Midgard, the next riding a glittering rainbow, and then the next, I was back in the storied halls of Asgard. My pulse began to race, heat flooding my system as I desperately tried to convince myself there was a way out of whatever Odin had planned to punish me.

It was completely hopeless, of course, but I couldn't fault my subconscious for trying.

We were met by a host of guardians, who eyed first me, then the sword still in my tight grasp, with barely restrained curiosity. It wasn't common for Odin to bring a human—as I appeared to be—to Asgard, let alone one bearing a Valkyrian sword.

But it wasn't their place to question him, just to do his bidding. They surrounded Odin, Loki, and myself, along with the two guards, who had now shed their disguises as street thugs. With our escort, we marched toward the great hall.

Truthfully, Asgard was beautiful; nearly as beautiful as Valhalla. I'd only been here a handful of times, and it always impressed a sense of power upon me. Tall, gleaming buildings, cream-colored bricks and everywhere gold that sparkled in the sunlight. Lush trees and flowing brooks lined the neatly curving paths, everything rounded and smooth and majestic, as if it had grown organically from pure might. Long eggshell silks flowed from open window arches painted in gold with the names of Asgardian residents. *Óðinn, Þórr, Loki, Frigg, Baldr, Heimdallr,* and more, all decorated the residences in classic old Norse script.

We passed through several decorative arches laced with creeping ivy, and finally approached the massive pale wooden door where my fate awaited me.

Never one to draw out the excitement, Odin marched ahead as the guard opened the massive doors before him, and I followed. Ahead were several of the gods whose names I'd seen painted on silk just moments before. Bathed in beams of natural light, Frigg lounged on a chaise, her long pale blonde hair artfully plaited and draped over one shoulder. She wasn't surprised at our arrival, and it occurred to me she might have used her talent with *seidr* to weave this happenstance into my fate.

Heimdall had abandoned his spot at the entrance to the Bifrost in order to be present here, although his eyes were still turned toward his charge. Just as I remembered, his copper beard was thick and full, his shoulders wide and imposing, with muscular fore-arms and a grim expression. Heimdall had never been much of a conversationalist.

Thor, clutching Mjöllnir, appeared as if he would rather be anywhere else than waiting here. His brows, so blonde they were nearly invisible, were low over stormy eyes, with both arms crossed over his massive chest.

The only person whose presence was notably missing was Baldur, but I had a feeling if I inquired, they wouldn't be apt to tell me where he was.

When we reached the dais, I was unsurprised to see that Loki had given us the slip in the course of our little walk. *Typical Loki, shows up when it suits him but doesn't stick around to face the music.* I wondered what Odin had offered him in exchange for trapping me.

The most startling feeling came when I stepped up to the dais and waited for Odin to take his seat in the gaudy chair he preferred.

Of course I couldn't see them; Odin's curse held strong.

But I could feel them, and I could hear the air move as they landed delicately in the gallery of the great hall, passing easily through the roof like wisps of smoke and solidifying once inside, their wings carrying them to the ground.

The Valkyries.

Long ago, so long it wasn't even a memory so much as a legend, Odin had stolen us. Enchanted with our power, not to mention the legendary beauty of the two hundred Maidens of Valkyr, he destroyed every stone of our home. He rent a giant hole in the cosmos and reduced his power from ten realms to nine. One by one, he captured us like wild birds in nets, stripping us of the armor and swords in which we poured our power. He planned, perhaps, to surround himself with servants of a haunting, ethereal beauty. Clear, light grey eyes, perfectly symmetrical faces with full lips and delicately arched brows, and manes of wild hair like spun silver and gold. My sisters and I knew the differences between us, but outsiders could scarcely tell us apart. Odin thought he had found himself an eternal, immortal source of service and entertainment for his own pleasure.

However, he vastly underestimated the *Valkyrje*.

Without our swords, without our armor and our freedom, we could not, *would* not, do a single thing he wanted. We lay in heaps, spread out on the paths and floors of Asgard, lifeless.

Odin tried to use threats, violence, and anger to move us. Eventually, he discovered that torturing one valkyrie would not motivate her to act, but it would motivate another to end her torment.

But he swiftly discovered that was even more dangerous to his health than our inaction.

If he asked a valkyrie to scrub the floors, she would position herself in his path, attempting to trip him as he passed.

If he ordered a valkyrie to serve him food, chances were she poisoned it.

If he demanded a valkyrie help him dress, she likely would attempt to strangle him with the garment.

None of these things killed him, but Odin eventually learned that it was impossible to tame the Valkyrie. They would not serve him like slaves. Without our armor, without our weapons, we lacked the heart and soul that provided our legendary goodness and valor. Our hair dulled, our eyes lost the shine of vitality, and our hearts hardened.

Eventually, Odin came to his senses. Because our home was destroyed, he could not send us back, but he offered us a trade: We would become residents of

Valhalla, a beautiful place, with as much space and freedom as we could want. Odin would return our armor and our swords. In exchange, we would help him select the Victorious Fallen to join his host for Ragnarok.

And we agreed.

Reunited with our armor, with our souls, we were once again the creatures of heart and beauty we'd been before. The relief from the torturous emptiness was immediate; I still remembered how it felt when I buckled on my breastplate and the armor buzzed with recognition. My heart ached to remember it after all this time. It'd been so long since I'd worn it.

And we were happy to perform this one task in exchange for being whole once again. It wasn't as if we were killing the men; they did that very well on their own. However, we still had to walk among the dead and dying for eternity, and search their minds, sip their souls with our swords, to test their worth.

Their fear, their confusion, their agony wore on me. But I toughed it out; I survived, and performed my task again and again, sending more and more souls to Valhalla.

But soon, the reality of Valhalla wore on me as well. Because they weren't happy, the Chosen. They were miserable, locked in this never-ending fight and feast, and it was my duty to bring ever more and more people to this misery.

As eternity wore on, I grew tired of it. I knew I wasn't the only one who disliked the task, but when I put my foot down, none of my sisters stood beside me. I thought it would be a second revolution against the tyrant, but as it turned out, they were all satisfied with the bargain they'd struck and apparently didn't mind the suffering of the human souls as much as I did.

And so they had banished me, stripped me of my armor—but thankfully not my sword—and sent me to live among the humans on Midgard. Odin thought I ought to know what they were truly like, because I sympathized with them over him. Since I still had my sword, I kept a small amount of my power and just enough of my heart that I didn't fade away to nothingness.

But I was not nearly whole. I was hardened, calloused toward men and everyone I had cared about. Including my sisters, who now occupied the gallery, looking down on me with what I imagined was pity. Perhaps they thought Odin brought me here to give me a second chance, or to punish me for hiding from him. I didn't know what he told them, and had no way to ask them if I wanted to.

I stood before the 'gods' on the dais and regarded them with the same level of derision they aimed in my direction.

And I waited.

three

BRENNA

I STARED at Odin's cold blue eye, and he stared smugly back at me.

Abruptly, he switched from vengeful god to kindly father figure.

"Tsk tsk, Brenna, what are we going to do with you? You know, I scarcely recognize you—what have you done to yourself?" He gestured at me as if I were a naughty child covered in mud. "Come now, let's see if we can't do something about this..." Stepping off the dais, Odin reached for my face. I turned it away from him, and he snatched the cap from my head.

Pacing around me, the heavy plates of his armor clinked together. The hall was silent, everyone waiting to see what he would do.

There was no fighting it now; my power didn't compare to his, even with my armor. Without it, I was little more than a human with extra battle skills—no match for Odin of Asgard.

So when he stroked my dyed-black hair I cringed, and my knuckles tightened on my sword, but I did nothing.

"This color really doesn't suit you, Brenna. Let me see..." I felt both of his hands, palms and fingers rough, press along my hairline from behind, and he slowly dragged them down the length of my hair. A tingle on my scalp warned me he was using magic. I simply had no idea what he was doing. His hands pressed the bulk of my hair into a bunch and stroked slowly down as if he were squeezing water from my mane. When I no longer felt the tug, I risked shaking my head and sending a tendril over my shoulder.

With a swipe of his hands, Odin had restored my carefully colored black hair to its natural silvery blonde color. He strode around my side, pausing again to face me.

"There, that's much better, isn't it? Now you look like a valkyrie. An oddly dressed one, but we'll take care of that soon enough. So-" he turned to climb the dais again and resumed his seat. "As I was saying, what are we going to do with you?"

A bubble of bravado rose in my chest. "Send me back to Midgard where you found me and leave me the hell alone?"

The room was deadly silent for one long moment, then Odin chuckled and the others on the dais laughed with him. I heard no laughter behind me, only sharp inhales of breath from the invisible valkyries in the gallery.

"Ah Brenna, I missed your spirit. Even if it was sometimes a bit... irreverent... you were always entertaining. But no, I shall not be sending you back to where I found you. I feel as if I've missed out on so much of your life! You disappeared and left me worrying about you for over a millennium! That's such a long time to miss someone."

"Can't say I feel the same, sorry."

"Indeed. Well, the good news is that in your absence, my powers have grown. Time in Asgard is slower than on Midgard now, by a hundred-fold. It's much easier for me to monitor the realms, given that I have so much more time to observe.

"I also have the power to go back and adjust the timeline on a particular realm, if I want to... and this is how we're going to correct your little mistake."

"I don't understand. What do you mean 'adjust the timeline'?'" Something about this sounded horrific in a way I didn't yet grasp.

"I can speed up, slow down, or even reverse the timeline of a realm. Eventually we have to line back up, but this has allowed me to travel back, fix something, and then bring that realm back to heel.

"And that is exactly what I am going to do with Midgard. I'm going to rewind time—back to when I originally dropped you off—and this time I won't make the mistake of losing you. I'll have eyes on you at all times, and when I want you to do something for me, you will do it."

My stomach dropped to my feet. *Did I just hear that correctly?*

"Did you say you're going to rewind time?"

"Yes, you heard correctly. I'm returning you to the exact time I banished you to Midgard in the first place —although I think a different location, just for fun— so you have a chance to make the last thousand years up to me. The details of our agreement were that you got to live among the humans on Midgard in exchange for performing minor tasks when I asked them of you. You haven't held up your end of the bargain, disappearing in the dark of the night when I was occupied elsewhere. So you owe me those years, and I intend to collect."

Heart pounding in my chest, I considered the implication of his words. If he were really powerful enough to turn back time in a particular realm, I had no concept of how powerful he had truly become. Odin wasn't one to make idle threats, so he meant what he said. Memories of late-800's Norway flooded into my mind: the dark, smoky hovels, festering wounds with no medicine to treat them... so many things I'd become accustomed to in the modern world, about to be forgotten as if I'd never experienced them...

Desperately, I tried to bargain. "What if I go back to the time you found me and I agreed not to hide again? I would swear on it, on my sword."

Odin's eyes sparkled; he knew he had me and was

enjoying watching me squirm. "Well, the problem is that I will get those years, anyway. You have no more time to offer me than you already promised—eternity is eternal, after all. So the way I see it, you've cheated me out of nearly a thousand years."

"Then spin Midgard back to 1018. That's when I gave you the slip in the first place. You could catch me in the act!" I offered, panicked.

Odin grinned evilly. "No, I think you need a completely fresh start. A new village, a new beginning, to do things right. If the thousand years is what you owed me, we'll say the additional hundred fifty is your punishment for breaking our agreement."

I knew it was futile, but I couldn't help the physical response.

I turned and ran for the door. If I wasn't on Midgard, he couldn't rewind time and make me live it over again. The idea of being rewound, having my memory of so many things, so many people, wiped, and having to figure it out all over again, was absolutely terrifying.

It was only a few seconds before they caught me. Ghostly fingers I could feel, but not see, gripped my arms with irresistible force. I couldn't move if I wanted to. With light currents of air as the only clue that actual beings were the power behind the movement, they turned my body and marched me back up to the dais.

I had mostly ignored the others on the dais while I spoke with Odin, but now I cast my desperate eyes in their direction. Thor met my gaze, then looked away in dismissal of my plight. Frigg stared at me sadly, knowingly, but did not offer help or sympathy. Heimdall sent one disappointed glance in my direction before redirecting his gaze to the realms beyond.

They would not help me; and the valkyries, my sisters, clearly would not be of help to me either.

The last trace of hope drained from my body, and I glared up at Odin with renewed fury. "If you had no interest in striking a deal, why did you bother bringing me to Asgard at all? You could have just played your little trick and I would never have been the wiser."

"Well, I wanted to watch your face when you found out... to be honest, I was rather hoping for more of a reaction, but I still enjoyed it. Even so, I needed you here, on Asgard, while I spun Midgard back in time. I want you to know what I've taken from you."

And that is when reality set in: He didn't want to just rewind time and make me do it all over again with better supervision. He wanted to send me *now*, the me who had lived the last thousand years free of him through the ages of men all the way to the modern world, back to the barbaric time of the vikings.

I was so stupidly, incredibly, painfully screwed.

four

BRENNA

OF COURSE, Odin had to have his fun. He made a big deal of selecting which outfit he planned for me to wear when he dropped me off on Midgard in the 800s. At first he thought it might be amusing to just deposit me in my modern clothes, but then he decided that might give me an advantage with the locals. It was bad enough I needed my sword to be somewhat human—the humans would likely take notice of its craftsmanship, even though they didn't know how powerful it truly was.

In the end, Odin had a servant rustle up a basic rough spun gown in a dull grey color and a leather belt, then had me escorted to a chamber to change. The same servant accompanied me, likely to ensure I didn't sneak away or hide any modern items on my person to take with me to the past. If I thought she was my only barricade to freedom, I could have taken her out; however, I felt the movement of air beside us —at least two valkyrie were posted outside my room, ready to entrap me if needs be.

When I returned to the great hall it was exactly as how I'd left, but my arrival spurred them to action.

The first thing I noticed was a great rush of air, as if all the valkyries took to the sky at once, their powerful wings pushing their bodies away from the ground.

Odin, Frigg, Thor, and Heimdall all stood, and with an escort of guards, marched down the hallway to where I waited with my escort.

Passing us, they led the procession back along the delicate winding paths toward the Bifrost. A simple stone structure was the only marker for the magical pathway to the realms. It had to be activated first, then Heimdall would select the destination realm, and only then would the rainbow bridge appear. A shiver of excitement wound through the dread in my stomach. Part of me was innately curious to see exactly how Odin would turn back time.

We entered the humble building, crowding in around the wide circular table that occupied the center of the round room. Heimdall glanced at Odin, who nodded, then pulled a giant brass key from beneath his shirt. When he inserted it into the hole in the center, the table jumped to life.

The magic rose like a vessel filling with water

from the bottom. Glittering fragments of magic shivered into the air, pulsating with power as they formed ghostly renditions of the nine realms. They created a floating constellation of faintly glittering spheres, slowly spinning in the golden space above the table.

Heimdall nodded once more to Odin and backed away from the table. Odin reached for the sphere that represented Midgard, and I noticed a ring on his middle finger that sparkled with the same magical glow as the fragments on the table. He could encircle the ball with his fingers, and with an expression of intense concentration, he flicked one finger alongside the sphere, sending it spinning in the opposite direction.

Nothing else happened; everyone just watched Odin work a time reversal on Midgard like they saw it all the time. With a jolt, I realized I didn't know how many times he might have done this already... if I were on Midgard, I wouldn't even know it happened. I didn't bother to ask how it worked, or how he knew when to stop; I knew I wouldn't receive an answer.

At no signal I could see, Odin stopped the magical mini Midgard from spinning and replaced it to float among the others above the table.

"Well, darling Brenna," Odin smiled, resuming his paternal air, "it's time for you to go. I'll be in touch, of course, but I hope you like your new home. Heimdall?"

The other man appeared at Odin's side and leaned in to allow Odin to whisper in his ear. With a nod, he stepped away, avoiding my desperate eyes as he focused on the magical representation of Midgard.

Raising a small, ornate horn to his lips, Heimdall blew a short blast to summon the Bifrost.

The table glowed with dancing rainbow colors that concentrated on Midgard. Waves of magic thickened and brightened the light until it was too bright and impossible to look directly at it. Then, with a whoosh, a beam of glittering rainbow light shot out of the magical sphere and enveloped me, dragging me into the Bifrost once more.

I hadn't had time to panic. Truthfully, I'd felt more shock than any other emotion since Odin revealed himself.

But now, traveling the Bifrost over eleven hundred years into the past, panic rose in my throat and threatened to choke me.

I had nothing aside from the clothes on my back and the sword in my hand. I had nothing to barter with, nothing to trade or sell. I had no friends, no contacts, no one who would remember me at all. Odin had effectively wiped me and my memory from Midgard completely.

Even once I figured out where he was dumping me; even if I could reach the village, he'd banished me to the last time, they'd have no memory of who I was. I'd be starting anew there, just as much as I was starting over in a new place.

My heart, already a cold, withered thing, shrunk even more. I just couldn't do it again. It was too much; I shuddered to think of all the things I had survived the first time around. I couldn't live through those things again.

Valkyries were immortal, but not impervious to wounds. I had a way out through battle, if I was strong enough to take it.

Abruptly, the weight of my body crashing to Midgard hit me full force. My eyes closed, my hand gripping my only possession, I lay still for just a moment.

I was on my back, in a pile of something pokey that had a bit of give. Drawing in a deep breath, I sneezed. Yep, definitely hay. I was laying in a haystack.

I reached out with my senses, trying to glean information about my surroundings. I knew Odin wouldn't drop me in full view of anyone, so I had at least a minute or two to adapt to my new reality.

The earthy, damp smell of mud and horse drop-pings filled my nostrils beneath the sweeter scent of hay. It was dark beyond my closed lids, the night chill and damp... I'd need to find shelter and better clothing soon, or risk freezing in a damp heap of hay for the night. Sighing, I pried open my eyelids and stared up at a thatched roof, the sky dark and cloudy beyond. Nearby, a horse whinnied and other animals, likely pigs, rooted through wet-sounding slop.

But then I heard it: the sharp, metallic clang of sword meeting sword.

Nearby, someone was fighting. And if I wanted to

either earn my place, or find someone to end my torment, two fighting vikings were an excellent place to start.

five

BRENNA

CLAMBERING out of the hay pile, I paused a moment to pluck bits of straw from my person before hefting my sword and running in search of the fight.

It was a small, muddy village. The slick wet path squelched around my basic leather shoes, threatening to keep them forever and leave me barefoot, forcing my pace to slow. A few of the hovels had fires within, light leaking around the wooden doors. In the distance, I saw flashes of reflected moonlight and I knew that was my destination.

I still didn't know if I wanted to prove something or end my misery, but something pulled me toward this fight either way. Perhaps it was my valkyrie instinct, driving me to test the one who was bound to die for his place in Valhalla. All I had was my sword and my instincts, and I'd just have to see what came of them.

A chill wind blew from my right, and sparing a quick glance, I saw the reflected moonlight on water. The village was close to the fjord; I could just make out a few small boats and one ship pulled up on the rocky shore.

Good. At least Odin had dumped me off in a village with actual fighters, instead of just boys who played at swords.

My feet continued toward the *smash-clang* noises of fighting. To my left the ground was mostly level for a short way, then the hills rose dramatically, cupping the valley in rocky protection. Low grasses grew along the muddy path, and I racked my brain to figure out what season we were in. There was no visible ice: if it was spring, they'd be planning their raids for the summer already. If it were autumn, they'd be preparing to huddle down for the winter and there would be no more raids until the next year.

Obviously, the best-case scenario for me would be spring; it would give me an immediate opportunity to earn a place, if that's what I chose. Autumn would be much harder to eek out a position in the village with no raids to prove myself on. I might have to consider wedding some unwashed meathead just for a place to stay warm.

Perhaps I should let fate decide for me. If it was

autumn, I could let some moron end my misery. If it was actually spring, I would keep fighting.

As I drew closer to the fighting, I slowed down to observe. Now I could make out the combatants and hear their grunts and taunts as they fought.

Three men surrounded one and definitely appeared to be the aggressors. There was one giant of a man, who growled like a bear when he struck; A shorter man, but powerful, who made calculated strikes; and a third, leaner, with sharp features that made him appear almost as pretty as a woman in the moonlight.

The man in the middle was bleeding, and his eyes were wild; he was under no delusion that he would survive this fight.

That is until I intervened.

Darting into the center of the circle and inserting myself between the biggest man and their victim, I dug through my knowledge of languages, searching for ancient Norse.

"Kolme yhtä vastaan on tuskin reilua." Wait, was that Finnish?

The men paused, glancing at each other in confusion.

Hmm, maybe I got that wrong.

"Tre mot en er neppe rettferdig." As soon as I said it, I realized it was modern Norwegian, not Old Norse.

One actually reached up to scratch his head. Jesus.

"Þrír á einn er eigi… fair?" I couldn't remember the right word for fair, but that was as close as I could get to saying three on one wasn't fair.

Their heads tilted back with recognition. *Got it!*

"Hann's bastardr, andlát er too góð fyrir hann. En þat's allr vér haftilr gøra." The shorter one, the more clever-looking one, answered. "He's a bastard. Death is too good for him. But it's all we have to offer."

The ancient language came more readily to my tongue. "Why is he a bastard?"

The clever one pointed at the youngest, easily the prettiest of the three. "He killed Leif's brother."

I glanced behind me at the bleeding mass of man, who shrugged. "He challenged me and lost."

"He challenged you because you stole from him!" The youngest shouted, his voice a fine line between anger and pain. Clearly, this was a raw nerve.

"I still fail to see why that justifies three on one," I commented carefully.

This time, the largest man spoke, his voice deep. "Because Skarde is a cheat. It is the only way he could have beaten Leif's brother. Therefore we decided not to allow him-"

"What, not to allow him a fighting chance? It seems to me you all are the cheaters here. Leave now, or I will be forced to teach you a lesson." I glared at all three of them in turn, wielding my sword at the ready.

They burst out laughing. "Skarde, I had no idea you needed a *smár mær* to defend you," chuckled the biggest.

It took me a minute to translate those words, even though I knew it was an insult. Then it clicked into place. "A little girl, am I? Well perhaps to you I am small, but that is only because you are so fat." Truthfully he looked like a solid wall of muscle under his rough spun clothes and armor, but it was difficult to tell in the darkness. And it didn't matter if he was actually fat, only that the comment pissed him off.

Which it did.

He charged at me, and then the battle resumed. The injured man and I instantly positioned back to back, and I faced down the giant while he fought off the two smaller men.

My opponent was unbelievably strong, his attacks sending shock waves up my arm as I deflected the blows. If I held an ordinary sword, it would dent under the force of his hits. Fortunately, my Valkyrian blade was far stronger than viking iron.

I allowed him to press his attack, learning more about him and his fighting style, while I encouraged my body to remember sword fighting. It had been centuries since I'd actually wielded my sword as a weapon; mostly I had concealed it on my person or near me somehow, like in the guitar case. I could not be parted from it again; I would die first. But it was far too conspicuous to walk down a modern street carrying it.

My attacker grew tired of being unable to gain ground on me, and tired of fighting in general. He was a big man, who wielded a heavy sword and wore thick plated armor. He wasn't prepared for an extended battle; I was wearing him down.

I listened for the status of the fight behind me. My partner appeared to be in a good mood, issuing taunts to the other two, so I assumed it was going well for him.

It was time.

Pressing my attack, I beat back the giant of a man, setting him on defense under the fury of my swings. It helped to have the ball of frustration in my chest from my circumstances; I used the limitless anger and took my hatred for Odin out on the unsuspecting viking.

He was completely unprepared; in less than a minute I was kneeling on his chest with my blade to his throat.

In the black of night, all I could make out was that his eyes were dark and his hair light. A thick beard covered his chin, and he gazed up at me without fear. "Do it, then. I will see my brother in Valhalla."

That brought me up short. No matter what I did, I couldn't escape the legacy of the valkyries, and the last thing I wanted was to be the reason another good man spent eternity in Valhalla.

And he was a good man; my sword took sips of his soul and judged him worthy.

"Call off your friends, go on your way, and I will spare your life."

"I am not afraid of death!" His eyes were angry now, and he bellowed the challenge even though I was mere inches from his face.

"Who will look after your sisters, Björn?" The voice came from my side, where the other two attackers stood, watching somberly. It was the older of the two, the clever one.

"I will watch over them from Valhalla," the man beneath my blade insisted, but his voice trembled.

"Who will take care of them here, Björn? Who will protect them? You are all they have. Take the offer, our attempt has failed."

My gaze remained focused on the man beneath me, but his darted up to the faces of his friends. Sighing, he closed his eyes.

"Fine. I concede. Release me, and we will go in peace."

I stood and offered him a hand up, but he ignored it in favor of the arm offered by his friend. The three of them cast curious glances at me, but the one that pierced my withered heart was the gaze of the youngest, the pretty one. His eyes were wounded: the aching soul of someone grieving shone through his gaze. I may have saved a life, but I still didn't know if it was a life worth saving. This man clearly didn't believe so.

The largest man lay a heavy hand on the youngest's shoulder, and they walked off into the shadows together.

"Thank you," the bleeding man said in a humble tone. "I would be dead if you hadn't intervened. Can I offer you anything to show my gratitude?"

"I could use a place to sleep," I admitted.

"That I am happy to offer," he grinned. "My name is Skarde. May I have yours?"

"Brenna," I answered, accepting the hand he offered for a shake.

"My house is this way," he gestured back toward the collection of hovels I had passed, the opposite direction the other three had traveled.

As we walked along the squelching mud path, the thirst hit me. "Skarde, do you have any beer?"

six

BRENNA

AS IT TURNED OUT, Skarde did have beer, and plenty of it.

Which was a good thing, because the thirst was on me.

When I was banished to Midgard the first time, I developed a taste for alcohol. Beer, Meade, and eventually the stronger stuff. I spent entire years in a state best described as drunk, thanks to my misery at the hands of Odin.

Eventually, I got my act together and realized I was much more capable as a functioning adult. I still seemed to circle back around to it from time to time. No good reason, just because life became more difficult, and I struggled to find reasons I should do anything. I had entire years I passed as a lush that never left her house/apartment/condo save for partying or purchasing alcohol. Total party girl personality, which could be fun depending on the decade.

And why shouldn't I? When you'd lived as long as I had, it wore on a person from time to time. I had all the money I could want, and disguising myself as a ditzy party girl with daddy's money in Beverly Hills was genius—Odin wouldn't imagine I'd be that peroxide blonde, over-tanned barbie girl in a hundred years.

So I'd have my periods of debauchery, and then one day I'd be ready to move on to becoming someone else. Maybe a bookish college girl studying psychology at Oxford, or a starving artist in Paris.

It had been a couple of decades since the thirst took ahold of me, but the dramatic turn my life had taken in the last few hours brought it on with a vengeance.

Fortunately for me, as a valkyrie I had a robust constitution. It took a lot to get me drunk.

Two beers in and I was willing to listen to Skarde's version of the story. Apparently, he did not agree that he'd cheated in the fight with Leif's brother. He was cocky and not what I would call 'smart', but he wasn't horrible.

I finished my third beer during his explanation.

After a fourth, I'd shrugged off his half-hearted

attempts to learn anything about me aside from my name.

After my fifth, I started feeling a little more relaxed, and helped Skarde clean the blood from his face. He'd removed his armor when we walked in, and now just wore a simple woven shirt and pants, but hadn't bothered cleaning up.

He wasn't too unfortunate looking under the gore. In fact, once clean, he was almost attractive. Light blue eyes, a flat brow, thick reddish-blonde hair with a dense, wiry beard. And the man was muscular; not as large as the one he'd been fighting, but not small. Not hot by any means, but doable.

And fortunately, I'd had enough alcohol to make that seem like a good idea.

I straddled his lap and moved in for the kiss— Skarde was more than willing, the appreciative groans that rumbled in his chest encouraging.

He was a rather sloppy kisser, but I'd had worse.

Fortunately for me, Skarde was the type of man who liked to get right to business.

Personally, I was not interested in a romantic experience. I had enough drink in my system that a nice orgasm would help to knock me out and give me a few hours' release from reality.

I just really needed to fuck, and Skarde apparently felt the same way.

I freed his dick from the rough-spun pants and was pleasantly surprised by what the man was packing... I knew from experience the size of a man was not necessarily a clue to the size of his equipment. I slid myself onto him in the seated position and groaned my enjoyment of the sensation... this was definitely the distraction I needed right now.

Unfortunately, this position was clearly a novel experience for the man. He kept trying to move his own way and didn't understand this was meant to be my show.

Our movements were so disjointed, it was almost humorous. He kept trying to pull my hips closer when I was moving away to my own rhythm.

Finally, I was frustrated enough to stand and tug him to his feet, asking how he wanted it. If he needed to be in charge, it was probably better to let him do his thing.

Skarde definitely took the invitation to lead, pushing me toward his fur-covered bed with a grin.

Sigh. Missionary wasn't my favorite position, but hopefully it was one he could master.

I stripped off my dress and settled back into the soft furs to wait while he pulled off his shirt and shed his pants.

And when he finally joined me in the bed and slipped back inside me, his performance did improve. Skarde was an aggressive thruster, and I could work with that. I lifted my hips to meet his thrusts and, finally, I felt the building sensation that would bring on my orgasm and eventual release. I shut all mental activity down and focused on the purely physical moment, which was the point of the entire exercise.

Take copious amounts of alcohol, mix with physical pleasure, and create a circumstance in which it's impossible to focus on the dire reality of my life.

But, of course, I should have expected disappointment. Skarde started moving in a frenzy, and I'd experienced enough male orgasms to know the end was near.

"Fuck, don't finish yet! Think about baseball or something." In my distraction, I slipped into speaking English. I tried to wriggle a hand between us and help myself along.

"Hvat er 'baze bol?'" He grunted, then with a final thrust, groaned and poured his Neanderthal seed into me.

Skarde collapsed on top of my body, panting and sweating and supremely pleased with himself.

Great... all of that and I didn't even get an orgasm out of this deal. I tried to work my fingers, but my arm was pinned between us, and the budding sensation of pleasure died.

This was officially the worst day of my several-thousand years-long life.

I lay as still as possible and tried to pretend this wasn't my new reality.

After a few moments, Skarde rose and climbed from the bed, heading directly to his impressive supply of home brew to pour himself another horn mug. Some of the liquid escaped his mouth and dribbled through his beard onto his chest, which he pummeled with a fist when he finished.

"This turned out to be a great night, after all. I'm happy I met you, Brenna." He grinned at me.

Well, if I was out of luck on the orgasm, at least I could drink some more.

Rising, I strode naked over to where he stood and helped myself to another mug as well. I clanked my drink against his and downed the cup in one pour.

To your health, Skarde.

seven

BRENNA

FORTUNATELY FOR ME, Skarde wasn't a one-and-done kind of viking and I was eventually able to get off. By that time, I was ripping drunk and fell blissfully into a deep and dreamless sleep.

The waking up part was a lot rougher.

My valkyrian body may be ever youthful, but I'd never been great at getting over hangovers. It'd been years since I drank that much, and there was bound to be a price to pay.

That price caught up to me sooner than I'd hoped.

"You should get dressed," Skarde grunted in my direction, slamming the wooden door and cutting off the eye-searing beam of daylight that had woken me. "It's midday. My wife will be home soon."

"Your wife?" I struggled to grasp the concept over the pounding sensation in my skull. "Why did you invite me to stay if you have a wife?"

"She was gone, you were here." He shrugged. "But now she will be back and it's better if you go before that happens."

Typical fucking egotistical asshole. I almost cussed him out, but I realized my favorite insults were in a language he wouldn't appreciate and I would waste it on him. I found my dress and my underclothes and slipped on my shoes, wondering if I should treat him to my steel after all.

These thoughts fled when I looked up and saw what he offered: a fresh mug of beer, and a handful of silver pieces. "I can't let you stay here, but as a thank you for your help, please accept this silver. It should be enough to help you survive until you can start earning your keep. Several of the farmers up the road are looking for help. And the beer will help with the headache." Skarde grinned, and I let the resentment slip from my face as I accepted his gift.

"Thank you, Skarde." I threw back the warm beer and accepted one more mug before I left. Outside, he showed me to a rain bucket where I could wash up, and even let me use his bone comb to tidy my hair.

Even though he was showing me the door, Skarde watched me brush my mane with hungry eyes. I knew my hair was unusual, even among the fair-haired vikings. Its silvery tones appeared almost like the chunks of metal I hid in a pouch tied to my belt, and no one on earth had hair quite like it. To be honest, it was nice to be back to my natural color again. I suppose I could thank Odin for that. No matter how many times I dyed it, nothing felt as good as the way I was meant to be.

Face freshly scrubbed, hair combed and loosely braided, I was a good deal more presentable than I'd been the night before, with straw in my hair. I'd left my sword propped against the side of his house, and now Skarde held it, examining the ornate hilt and pommel. When he caught me watching him, he handed it over, grinning.

"That is quite a sword, Brenna. How do you have such a weapon and nothing else?"

"I'd give up any possession in order to keep it," I answered. "And I have, many times. It's worth more to me than its weight in gold."

Skarde nodded. "You are a good fighter, but a fighter is nothing without a sword."

My link to this weapon was beyond his ability to understand, but I nodded as if I agreed. "Where did you say I might find a place to stay and work?"

"Further up the hill, away from the harbor, are several farmers that have no slaves, so they may be willing to barter work for pay or lodging. If you go back into town, the chieftain's house is right in the center. You should go there and ask for help. He may allow you to stay there, or he may direct you to someone interested in accepting your silver for food and lodging. He will want to know how you came to be here... I suggest you have more of a story for him than you gave me," he raised a brow with intent.

51

"You may give my name as a recommendation, if he asks."

"Thank you, Skarde. I appreciate your help."

"Consider my debt for your help paid," he grunted, then pushed off from the side of his house. "Goodbye, Brenna." And with that, he turned and walked back into his house.

Fucking infuriating vikings. Gruff and rude as all hell, and yet thoughtful and generous and almost endearing. The sooner I wrapped my mind around these people and their habits, and forgot the civilized society of the twenty-first century, the better off I'd be.

Speaking of mind... the beer had helped to ease my headache, but it was still a dull throb in my temple. The sun was high in the sky, warm on my exposed face and neck, and the air temperately cool enough for my grey rough spun dress. But I knew it would only be a few hours before the sun dipped behind the jagged mountain walls of the fjord and the temperature dropped dramatically.

Skarde's home was on the flat of a hill overlooking the small collection of houses that huddled around the harbor, forming the village. The path he'd pointed out split, one lane going to town and the second heading up toward the farms where he said I might secure work.

I chewed over my options. On one hand, it might benefit me to throw myself on the mercy of the village chieftain and use the pity angle. It could get me hooked up much faster, and much easier, than I could do on my own. Plus, I had Skarde's name to use as a reference, which he seemed to believe would help me.

On the other hand, I'd never been the type to ask for any kind of handout. I chafed at the idea of what a chieftain might expect in return for granting me favors, and it would be difficult for me to prove myself a warrior and convince him to give me a ship to captain if he saw me as some pathetic near-slave.

No, it was probably better for me to lie low, put in some work, and start making connections in town. Once I was more known, properly clothed and armed, I could get on a raiding party and start earning a reputation.

My feet followed the narrow rocky trail where it angled uphill toward the looming walls of stone.

Day labor for now, but it wouldn't be long before I was earning my keep at the tip of a sword.

eight

BRENNA

THE FIRST THREE farms were a total bust. Because of my feminine stature, the first two were unconvinced I could do the work they needed done, and the third leered at me so openly his wife kicked me out. Judging by the sympathetic gaze she gave me, I think she was doing me a favor.

There was one last pitiful farm in the valley, edged right up against the mountain where it caught the last of the afternoon light. A smallish parcel of land, with a barn, a paddock that contained very few livestock, and a decent-sized wooden longhouse with a thatched roof. I could see a woman sitting outside in the distance, combing wool from a basket beside her as a young girl played near her feet and another tended the animals.

The sun was dipping behind the mountains now; if I didn't secure a place here, I'd have a long chilly trudge back to the village. Girding myself for disappointment, but putting on my most confident expression, I shouldered my blade and marched directly toward the woman.

As I got closer, I realized she was not so much a woman as a teenage girl, perhaps fourteen. There didn't appear to be anyone older nearby, so I continued my trajectory to where she sat.

The girl's appearance was neat, spun-gold hair clean and carefully plaited in decorative braids. Flashing blue eyes, a full mouth, and a stubbornly pointed chin came together in a very pretty visage. Her cornflower blue dress was rough spun, simple but neat, with some hand-woven decorative elements. The child nearby was perhaps three, with white-blonde hair and the same cerulean eyes, a sweet round face and ruddy cheeks. She was happily slapping at a mud puddle with a stick, laughing in high-pitched peals every time a spray of mud hit her.

"That's close enough, traveler," the older girl called out when I was still several yards away. "What do you want?" She moved her skirts, revealing an enormous sword propped against the bench beside her.

"I mean you no harm," I answered. "I was told you might need help on your farm. I need shelter, food, and pay. I am stranded here and have no people of my own."

The girl gazed at me with a shrewd eye. "What kind of work can you do?"

"I can do almost everything—I'm stronger than I look," I added. "I can plough, plant, harvest, clean, cook, sheer sheep, haul water, weave… if it's something you need done, I guarantee I can do it."

Her sharp blue eyes landed on my sword. "Is that yours? Can you wield it?"

"Yes, it is mine. Yes, I can fight. If you need protection, I can provide it." Licking my lips, I padded my story to really sell it. "You've heard of the Shield Maidens of Valkyr, haven't you?"

The girl hesitated, unsure whether she should admit she'd never heard of such a thing, since I stated it in a way that I assumed she knew. "That sounds familiar," she hedged. "That's you?"

"Yes, I was one. But I grew tired of killing men at the orders of other men. And now I have no one." That's *basically* how it happened.

The girl's eyes narrowed as she considered. I waited patiently, with the most pleasant smile I could muster despite my headache.

"We can't afford to pay you a wage. But we can provide shelter and food in exchange for your help here. And if we have a good harvest, and my brother does well in the summer raids, we may provide you some compensation in autumn. Is that acceptable to you?"

It was by far the best offer I was likely to get.

Surely, opportunities would present themselves for me to make some more silver and get outfitted properly and start proving my value on the battlefield. Even if it took a year or two, it didn't matter anymore. I had all the time in eternity.

"You will provide food and lodging, and I will provide labor. In the autumn, we can discuss any compensation we agree I have earned." I stepped forward and offered her my hand.

She shook it once, firmly. "Agreed." Throwing the combs back onto her basket of wool, she pulled her skirts further aside and revealed a roughly carved crutch. Standing with obvious pain, she gestured to the wool and her sword. "Grab those things and follow me. Astrid! Time to go inside." The little girl abandoned her puddle and dashed toward the house. The other girl I'd seen from the distance had disappeared, no longer in the paddock with the pigs and goats.

I kept pace with the elder girl. Clearly, her right foot was lame. She did her best to avoid putting weight on it, and every step was delicate.

"My name is Brenna, by the way. Thank you for offering me a place. The others would not."

"I broke it, my ankle. It never healed right." She stated matter-of-factly through gritted teeth, attempting to disguise her discomfort. "My name is Signe, the little one is Astrid, and my other sister is Yrsa."

"Where are your parents?" As she was clearly the

spokeswoman for the household, I had to assume her parents were gone.

"They died in a fire a couple years back." She used the same unemotional tone with which she'd explained her debilitating injury. No self-pity, no tears. Just facts.

"I'm sorry." I knew my condolences did little for her, but I offered them anyway.

She ignored me, and we slowly approached the house. "We will need your help with tending the fields, mostly, and helping to carry heavy things. Also to defend us. Neighbors who want to take our land, or men who wish to claim Yrsa or myself in order to take our property, sometimes set upon us."

"How have you survived this long alone?" Truly, it was pretty incredible for this teenage girl to have held her household together for two years on her own.

"They're not alone," a deep male voice growled behind me.

An icy shiver of dread poured down my spine. I knew that voice.

Turning, I saw the giant of a man whose throat I'd nearly slit last night.

In the light of day, I could see he was far more handsome than I'd given him credit for last night. His thick golden hair, the same color as Signe's, was pulled back on top and loose below his ears. The eyes beneath his low, blonde brows were a deep, ocean blue, and his golden beard was thick but neat, extended in a gradual curve below his chin. He wore simple clothes, a woven tunic with the sleeves folded up, belted over wool pants. Farming clothes.

Beside him stood the third girl, barely reaching his elbow, even though she appeared to be around nine or ten years of age. She didn't have the delicate features of her sisters, but appeared more like a miniature female version of her enormous brother.

"Brenna, this is my brother Björn. Björn, this is Brenna. I've hired her to help us while you are out raiding."

A dark red flush had crept up Björn's cheeks as soon as he recognized me, and the anger emanated from him in palpable waves. "Yrsa, my sword," he snarled, and the girl ran off to retrieve his weapon.

Striding toward me, he used all of his nearly seven feet to tower over me threateningly. "Give me my father's sword, set down the basket, and leave. Now."

I could hardly blame him. My heart dropped to my stomach, but this was not a fight I wanted. Sighing, I held out the sword Signe had asked me to carry.

"No." The firm challenge had come from Signe, standing tall without her crutch, carefully balanced on her one good leg. "We need help, and I trust her. You don't trust any of the men in the village to protect us while you're gone. She is exactly the answer we needed."

"I don't trust her!" He bellowed directly in my face. I stared back at him without reaction.

"You don't trust anyone," Signe accused. "We are out of options, and she is here. What more do you want?"

"Anyone but her." The low, deep growl threatened violence. It tore at my heart in the smallest way, but I brushed it off. I was used to people not wanting me around.

"Oh, anyone? What about Knud? Or Toke?"

"Well, obviously not them." Yrsa returned, hauling Björn's massive sword.

"Yrsa, stop." Signe's command brokered no discussion. Yrsa stopped in her tracks, still several yards from Björn.

"Brenna, please go sit on the bench for a minute. I need to speak with my brother."

I glanced back and forth between the two. Equally stubborn, it appeared. However, I was willing to bet I knew who actually ran this household.

Nodding, I set down the basket and Signe's sword, and carried my own blade over to the bench where I sat.

Björn snatched his father's blade from where I'd left it and assisted Signe inside their home, with Yrsa close behind, dragging her brother's massive blade.

The door closed, and I waited.

nine

BRENNA

I DON'T KNOW if they thought I wouldn't be able to hear them from outside, but their voices carried loud and clear through the wooden structure.

"She is not staying," Björn roared. "You can't just invite any stranger into our home. You know nothing about her!"

"You have to leave, and it will leave us with no one to protect us. She is a far better option than the men here who aren't going on the raids." Signe's voice was thick with implication. "Would you leave us at their mercy? Or the mercy of our neighbors?"

"Of course not. I will stay."

"You can't stay, you have to earn gold and favor with the Jarl. It's our only hope of keeping this place.

If you don't serve him, he could take away our home and give it to someone else."

"That's not going to happen; he wouldn't be that stupid. The entire village would revolt."

"You don't know that, and he has the power. Whether he should do it is a different matter. And don't count on the village to take care of us; you haven't done a good job of ingratiating yourself with the chieftain or his family. You should try to make friends with the right people."

"I have no interest in Åge's daughter. He only wants me to take her because he figures a man caring for three girls would have no trouble with a useless wife. I will not marry someone who would expect my sisters to wait on her hand and foot. He raised Åse to think she was a princess hoping to shunt her off on the Jarl's sons, and none of them would have her."

"You don't have to show him how much you dislike her. You can at least be friendly. Go on some raids, drink beer with Åge, make friends."

"No," the reply was stubborn. "My responsibility is to take care of you three, and that is what I will do."

Signe's sigh was audible. "Brenna is exactly the answer to our prayers. Why can't you see that? Frigg must have seen how much we would need a shield maiden and sent her to us, and you sneer at her gift."

"She will not set foot in my house."

"This is *our* house, not your house. And we outnumber you three to one. We need someone to protect us, and you need to go on the raids. The decision is made, and you have no reason to argue against it. Do you?"

The silence was long and painful. Would Björn actually admit he hated me because I'd already beaten him in a sword fight and spared his life? Or was that just too humiliating for him?

I could just picture the fierce, proud face of Signe staring down her much larger, much older brother without mercy. The girl was a force, to be sure. Despite her injury, or perhaps because of it, she was as hard as the granite walls of the fjord.

"Fine," Björn sighed, breaking the silence. "I will allow it, for now. So long as she pulls her weight and gives me no reason to doubt her honor, she can remain here until the autumn."

Their voices lowered, and I could not make out what was said anymore. A few minutes later, the faded wooden door creaked open, and Björn strode out. He closed the door behind him and marched in my direction.

The shadows had stretched with the setting sun, and it grew quite chilly as the damp clouds of mist rose from the water below. I stood to meet him, intent on not revealing any weakness.

Björn stopped a few feet away and crossed his thick arms over the barrel of his enormous chest. "We will not pay you, but you can stay and eat, as long as you work. Understood?"

I nodded solemnly. "That is the agreement I had with Signe. I don't want handouts, I will earn my keep."

He grunted and nodded by way of agreement.

"And I will protect them. You have my word. After last night, you should have no doubts of my skill."

At that, his eyes flashed, and he moved in until he was mere inches away, bending down to place his angry visage nearly nose to nose with mine. His voice was deep and deadly serious when he said, "Neither of us, not you nor I, will speak of last night, ever. Do you understand me?"

I nodded, my hand tightly wrapped around my sword pommel. This man was begging me to take him down again, but right now, I needed to be smart, not strong.

And the smart play was to let him have his way, so long as it didn't cause harm to anyone.

Apparently satisfied that I understood, he straightened and sighed, then held out one massive hand. "I'm Björn, as Signe said. Your name is Brenna?"

I accepted his shake. "Yes. It's nice to officially meet you Björn."

"That remains to be seen." Withdrawing his hand from mine, he waved toward the house. "Go on inside and help Signe with supper. I'll be in when I've finished." He strode off toward the barn without elaborating on what he needed to finish.

Relieved that I had a place to stay and, hopefully, a warm meal ahead of me, I headed for the house. I wasn't sure whether to be pleased or insulted that he'd just addressed me like one of his younger sisters, but I was in no position to do something about it either way.

The irony—that this man offered me shelter after I beat him in a fight—was not lost on me. I knew it had to burn his pride, knowing I could have killed him and instead let him live. Now my presence here would remind him, constantly, of that fact.

However, some part of him had to be grateful that I was a capable fighter, and not a predatory man who might harm his sisters while he was away.

Now it was just up to me to prove how useful and honorable I could be.

I stepped up to the door, and feeling awkward, unsure of how to handle it, I knocked.

Signe's voice rang out from inside. "Come on in, Brenna. This is your home now, you are not a servant." I pulled the rope handle and let myself inside.

Heat from the fire in the hearth immediately smacked me in the face, chasing the chilly dampness from my skin. The timber longhouse was neat, clearly well-kept by Signe and, to some degree, Yrsa. Solid wooden platforms lined the walls, topped with stuffed cushions and pillows. In the center of the room, a stone fire pit contained a carefully constructed fire, with an iron kettle suspended over it on a three-footed structure. Various household materials were hung from racks around a doorway, through which I could make out another sleeping platform. That must have been the parents... perhaps Björn slept there now?

A rough wooden table was at the far end of the room, and Yrsa was busily setting it for five. Immediately inside the door to my right appeared to be the location to drop weapons, as several shields hung on the walls like decoration, and pegs for hanging swords were partially filled with the two I'd already seen and one I hadn't: a slim, decorative blade, obviously made for a woman, was among the others. I hooked my sword beside it and searched for Signe beyond the glowing fire.

She was sitting on a padded bench to my left, attempting to bathe a wriggling Astrid. Of course the child thought it was a fun game, and Signe struggled to remove the mud from her hair, occasionally wincing as her injured ankle took a blow from a tiny foot.

"Would you like me to help?" I offered. I knew little about caring for children, but I had a few tricks I knew distracted them.

"You don't have to," Signe replied quietly. "We need your help with the farm, and with protection, not babysitting."

"I just thought I could get her to sit still for you. I know nothing about bathing a child," I laughed. "That's on you."

Signe smiled. "It couldn't hurt, thank you."

I sat in front of Astrid and pulled a silver piece from the pouch at my waist. "Astrid, do you see this silver?" Little girls like shiny things, and she was immediately entranced. "Do you want to see me make it disappear?"

"Yes yes!" She clapped her little hands, ignoring Signe, who sluiced water over her corn silk hair and scrubbed to remove the mud.

"Okay, watch carefully!" I did several complicated hand motions, waving the fingers with the silver piece in front of her face repeatedly before slipping it into my other hand when I formed fists. I hit both hands together three times, then opened the fist she expected to contain the silver, showing her it was empty.

"Where did it go?"

Signe had finished cleaning Astrid's hair and was scrubbing her back, but had paused to watch my magic trick as well.

Astrid pointed to my other fist with a chubby finger.

Slowly, I opened the hand to reveal it was also empty.

The shock on her cherubic face was adorable. Signe frowned, trying to puzzle it out.

"It disappeared!" I grinned at their matching expressions, then glanced at Signe and schooled my features to confusion. "Wait a minute, what is this?" Reaching behind Signe's ear, I retrieved the chunk of shiny metal. "Now, how did that get there? Signe, I think you need to wash better behind your ears."

Astrid erupted in peals of delighted laughter, and Signe chuckled. Yrsa had crept up behind me to watch, and now reached over to look behind Signe's ear for more treasures.

"Very clever." A deep male voice came from the

doorway behind me. I hadn't realized there was even more audience for my performance. "Where did you learn this trick?"

I turned to meet Björn's eyes. "It's magic, Björn. I learned it from a witch."

Returning my gaze to the girls, I gave Astrid a wink, and she giggled. Signe had finished cleaning the child, and was sliding her into a clean dress. She pulled the girl onto her lap and started combing her damp hair.

"Signe, is there... something else I can do? Check the food, or prepare something?"

She shook her head. "No, it's all done. But you should go wash up for supper. There's fresh water and soap outside."

"Okay." I headed for the door and squeezed past the giant, who apparently didn't feel it was necessary to make room for me. Just to the right of the door was a barrel with a large ladle and a brick of soap laced with lavender on an attached wooden shelf. I pushed my sleeves back and poured water over my arms and hands, then splashed some on my face and soaped up with the hard bar. After a rinse I was definitely refreshed, and the night had almost completely fallen. When I let myself back inside, the entire family was already seated at the table, waiting for me.

"I'm sorry, you didn't need to wait." I hustled to the spot where an empty bowl and full mug waited.

"Of course we did," Signe answered. "You are our guest, and basically a member of our family now. Family eats together. Yrsa?"

The younger girl collected the bowls and carried them to the steaming pot suspended over the fire. Some instinct in me cringed, watching the child handle the scalding iron lid and spoon the bubbling mixture into the bowls, carrying them carefully back to the table. But she performed her job perfectly, proudly executing it without spilling.

Once everyone had a bowl, Yrsa took her seat, and everyone tucked into their food. Signe drew small spoonfuls from her own bowl, blowing on them to cool the stew and feeding it to Astrid. It made me sad to see this girl who'd taken over as a mother when she was still essentially a child herself.

I turned my attention to my own bowl. The steam rising from it was fragrant with fennel and onions, and there was clearly meat and potatoes as well. A hearty meal, although I didn't want to know what kind of meat it was specifically. I chose to believe it was beef. My stomach rumbled in appreciation, and I realized it had been over a day since I'd eaten. Skarde had been generous with the beer, but he hadn't offered me food.

Aside from the chattering of a happy three-year-old, the ensemble was quiet. The loud crackling and popping of the fire was the most prominent sound, the scraping of wooden spoons on bowls the second. Mixed with the scent of stew, the smoky fragrance of fire combined with an earthy pine fragrance from the longhouse and created a warm, homey atmosphere.

I'd become so accustomed to living alone in my sparse, modern 'pretend' lives that I'd forgotten how comforting these rustic homes could be. I didn't want to think too deeply about the lack of sanitation, or the likelihood of critters living in the cushion I'd be sleeping on tonight. It would be better for me to just shut down all memories of the lives I'd lived over the last millennium; this was exactly the torture that Odin wanted for me and I was determined to deny him the satisfaction of seeing me long for the future that was so far removed.

But perhaps I didn't need to close it all out. The magic trick I'd learned from a street magician had been helpful. Perhaps there were things I knew, things I'd learned, that could help people now. Nothing too crazy, of course. But some things...

My thoughts drifted to Signe's ankle. Maybe I could help her with that injury? I'd spent several life-times as a nurse. I knew human anatomy intimately and if the bones weren't shattered, I might be able to set it. Likely, anything I could do would cause her a good deal of pain before it healed, but she was already living in so much pain anyway... and what if I could end that for her?

I scraped the bottom of my bowl, claiming every drop of nourishment I could get. It was probably best to table that idea for now. I would have to earn her trust first, and there was so much work to be done.

ten

BJÖRN

OF ALL THE strangers to show up at my home seeking help, it had to be her.

I didn't recognize her at first. Last night she came out of the darkness like a banshee, waving her sword with straw in her hair. She looked almost like a crazy person, and I didn't think she'd be a challenge to take down.

Clearly, I'd been wrong. I should be dead. She had bested me fairly. But she allowed me to go, and Søren had reminded me that dying honorably for a chance at Valhalla would leave my sisters unprotected.

The humiliation of accepting her mercy still burned in the back of my throat, scorching my cheeks whenever I looked at her.

It was best for me to keep my eyes away. Yes, she was beautiful, far more so than I realized last night. Her unusual silvery hair and heart-shaped face, full lips and clear, pale skin all formed a pretty face.

But it was her eyes that tore at my heart. Clear, stormy grey eyes that looked as if they'd seen a thousand lifetimes. There was a deep, wounded soul in those eyes.

I wanted to hate her.

I wanted to hate the humiliation she caused me.

I wanted to hate the fact that Signe was right, and she was exactly what we needed.

I especially wanted to hate that she could protect my sisters better than I could.

But something about her eyes held my hatred at bay. There was no mocking, no shrewd trickery or judgement in those eyes.

Just a painful history, buried deeply behind layers of protection like scars over broken bones.

And so I allowed her to stay in our home, and part of me was quietly relieved that we had a solution to our problem. Because Signe was right, I needed to curry favor with Åge—without making him think I wanted to marry his daughter—and I needed to capture the Jarl's attention. If Leif, Søren and I could get our own ship ready and start finding success with raids, the Jarl would offer us gifts... perhaps he had someone in his court that could help Signe.

It killed me to see her hobbling on her broken foot, and unable to do anything about it.

It was my fault she'd gotten injured. She was

trying to do too much after Mother and Father died, and I hadn't been there to help her. Stubborn thing that she was, she refused to wait for me to help her reach the thing she wanted from the loft, and she fell.

We were lucky it didn't need to be removed, but it never healed well and she'd been unable to walk on it ever since. I knew she was in pain every day, and it was my job to protect her; I failed.

And so it was imperative that I caught the attention of the Jarl, got him to like me. There were no guarantees, of course, but once the Jarl favored someone, every door was opened.

So, Brenna had come to us at a crucial time in our lives. I knew she was a capable sword woman, but that was all I knew about her. The magic with the silver was a mysterious element... the girls had enjoyed it, but she worried me when she said she learned it from a witch. I thought she was joking, but I would have to check tomorrow. I certainly didn't want witchcraft in my home, around my sisters.

Something about that moment had warmed my heart, just a bit. The magic had delighted even my serious little bear of a sister Yrsa, and she rarely smiled. As similar as Signe and Astrid were, that was Yrsa and I. Signe was more serious now, taking on the role as mother to the other two. But before our parents died, she'd been such a happy, carefree girl. She loved to sing, making up her own songs or repeating ballads she heard in the village, picking flowers and dancing circles around our mother.

Now Signe looked far too old for her thirteen

years, with a tight jaw and hunched posture from her injured leg. She deserved far better than the life she'd had the last two years.

It was up to me to give her better.

And that started with the Jarl.

BRENNA

I settled into the lumpy cushion-covered bench that was now my bed. There were several thick pillows, covered with woven wool threads, to cradle my head and give me something to hold. It was close enough to the fire to feel the warmth on my back, but still cool enough to sleep.

As if I could sleep.

After the last couple of days I'd had, sleep should be my priority. It was disorienting and exhausting to find myself suddenly nearly twelve-hundred years in the past. Not to mention that I'd spent the previous night dead drunk... that wasn't exactly a recipe for a restful night's sleep.

Guilt and embarrassment filled my chest. I knew better than that behavior, but I'd fallen so rapidly into the darkness it took my breath away. I'd lived so many life-times, I knew the cycle. Right now, I was teetering on the edge of a deep depression. I could let myself fall into it, wallow in my self-pity, and lose sight of the way out. It would be so easy to do, so comforting, to slide back in the destructive behavior I knew like the back of my hand.

Or I could try to turn things around before it was too late.

Of course, that was the pipe dream. We all liked to think we were in control of our own minds, our own hearts, our own bodies. Odin had just reminded me I had absolutely no control in the face of his all mighty self. And just as I'd slipped into bouts of depression before, despite fighting it valiantly, I knew it wasn't entirely in my control.

But I also knew that I would absolutely lose the battle if I refused to fight at all.

And so my decision became: give in or try to fight it, knowing I might still lose, anyway.

Landing here, at Björn's farm with his three younger sisters, almost felt like a thread woven into the tapestry of fate by Frigg herself. Here were four good people, people who had already lived through difficult times, but from whom goodness still radiated. Even little Astrid was a happy, sweet child, despite having lost her mother so young. Signe with her broken ankle, saddled with caring for younger siblings and managing a home at such a young age; it would have been understandable, reasonable even, for her to be angry and bitter with her lot.

And yet she was strong, and fierce, and so very good. I knew it without the help of my sword.

These people needed me. I could help them. And they could help me.

But I had nothing to offer them as a self-destructive, depressive drunk.

If I stayed here a year, earned my keep and perhaps a little extra, I might join the raids next year and start working on a way forward to a new life.

But that meant I had to be valuable, and helpful, and earn their trust.

Clutching the woolen pillow to my chest, I vowed to try, just to try, to stop my downward spiral.

It was the best promise I could make for the time being.

eleven

BRENNA

IF BJÖRN THOUGHT I would be useless, or weak, or unhelpful, he soon learned how wrong he was.

He shook me awake at first light and I helped build up the fire and prepare breakfast before we set out into the fields as the girls took over the household duties.

From the looks of it, he'd just begun plowing the field in preparation for harvest. The ard plow was far too large for Yrsa to help steer, and clearly Signe wasn't able to, so the work had fallen to Björn to manage himself with his team of oxen. Of course, he had many other responsibilities, and this one had fallen behind.

But I didn't know what day it was, let alone which month. I had a fairly good guess, but...

"Björn, what is the date?"

He paused in hooking up the oxen to look up at me curiously. "You don't know the date?"

"No." I didn't feel like going into detail about why.

He stared at me without expression for nearly a minute, then sighed. "Tomorrow is the new moon of Harpa."

I'd forgotten vikings didn't use the Roman calendar. They assigned names to months and tracked from moon to moon. I racked my brain to remember where Harpa fell...

It was nearly May, and his field wasn't even plowed yet.

"What are we planting?"

"Barley here, rye in that field there," he pointed to the next field over, "and oats in the field behind me. We also need to prepare the vegetable garden for the girls to plant."

For fuck's sake... we had less than a week to get these fields plowed and planted, or we'd be incredibly behind and might not have a mature crop come autumn.

Björn watched me think through this realization with his arms crossed, daring me to say something about how far behind he'd fallen. These fields should have been plowed weeks ago, seeds already planted.

Instead, I asked, "Do you have all the seeds?"

"Yes, we save it in the barn from our previous harvest."

"Perfect. Why don't you and I trade off running the plow, with the other person following behind to sow the seeds and cover them as we go. That way, we can each get a break from the plow work and be sowing at the same time?"

Björn barked a short laugh. "You think you can manage the oxen and the plow?"

I shrugged. "Yes, I've done it before."

The giant of a man stared me down with disbelief plain on his expression. "Okay. Show me."

I marched up to the oxen and double-checked their harnesses, making sure they were secured and the ard plow was attached correctly. Then I grabbed the leather whip that rested on the handle of the plow where he'd left it, gripped the handle to right the simple machine, and snapped the whip at the oxen. "Yah!"

With a disgruntled groan, the oxen tugged forward and began dragging the blade of the plow through the dark soil.

A few more whips and vocal encouragement, and we were rolling smoothly. I glanced back at Björn's begrudgingly impressed expression. "So, you're sowing first, then?"

He glared at me for a moment, then marched toward the wooden barn to retrieve the seed.

I couldn't help but notice the barn was new. It was a long-roofed structure similar to the longhouse, but the timbers and threshing on the roof were notably newer than the dwelling. Obviously, this is where his parents had died, and Björn, perhaps with the help of his friends, had rebuilt it. It must be painful for them every time they looked at it. As fortunate as they were that the fire was not in the house, it was never easy to count yourself lucky to have *only* lost your parents and not your entire family. A loss of that magnitude still hurt deeply.

Björn returned with a canvas bag tied around his waist, bulging with seed. He began at the rows he had plowed previously, sprinkling the seed and kicking hardened clumps of dirt over them.

I continued to forge ahead with the oxen team, reaching the end of the field a few minutes later and carefully steering the stubborn beasts around to plow the next row. It was hard, back-breaking work. The plow took a lot of strength to hold steady, and the oxen were not keen to continue on a straight path. I had to manage the heavy plow and keep the animals to a direct line that followed our previous row.

By the time I'd finished three entire rows, my dress was soaked with sweat. I whistled and tugged on the reins to stop the oxen, then tipped the plow to the side and hung the whip on the handle.

Björn was just reaching our freshly plowed rows, having neatly and efficiently seeded the older ones.

"Björn!" I waved. "I'm going to get a drink. Would you like one?"

The burly man just scowled at me and shook his head, then returned to his work.

I stretched my tense arm and back muscles as I

marched past the barn, vegetable garden, and animal paddock toward the barrel of fresh water by the house. Once I slaked my thirst, I splashed my sweaty face with a handful before I began trudging back toward the field.

As I rounded the corner and the field came into view, I saw that Björn had taken over the plow and left the bag of seeds waiting for me.

Well, I guess he has accepted my plan after all.

Whistling, I scooped up the heavy bag, tying it around my waist and following the line of the plow, sprinkling seed into the divot and kicking dirt back over the top to provide a small amount of cover. It shouldn't be too heavy, or the seeds wouldn't germinate. But it had to be enough that the birds didn't think the field was a great place to get a tasty snack.

Björn managed the plow for quite a while. By the time Yrsa came to fetch us for lunch, we'd plowed and seeded two-thirds of the field. The serious little girl said nothing, but the roundness of her eyes told me she was impressed with our progress, and that was good enough for me.

We finished the row we were working on, and Björn freed the oxen from their harness to lead them to the paddock and rest while we ate. I tracked his footsteps, but he didn't offer conversation and I had little enough to say for myself, either.

After washing up we settled in to eat the simple meal the girls had prepared: smoked herring, blood sausage, pan-cooked rye bread, and a few slices each of withered apple.

The memory of five-star restaurants I'd dined at in New York formed a hard lump in my throat. It would be—literally—a thousand years before I got to experience that again. I forced down the reflex that wanted to push my plate away and demand something else, instead casting a grateful smile in Signe's direction.

"Thank you for preparing this meal."

She returned a small smile of her own, and the family and I tucked into our food quietly. Clearly, mealtimes were not a chatty occasion for them. I wondered if it had to do with memories of their parents around this table, or just their habit.

For my part, I needed all the muscles in my jaw to work on the tough food on my plate. The beverage Signe served me was beer, and while I knew it was customary for vikings to drink it with their food—it was often safer than water—I didn't trust myself to drink just one and not wake up my thirst.

So I focused on finishing my food and planned to get water when we finished. I could talk to Signe after and explain, so she would skip the beer next time.

Unfortunately, Björn felt the need to comment.

"Is my beer not good enough for you, Brenna?" The threatening notes in his tone immediately put me on edge.

"I'm sure it's very good. I just prefer to stick to water when I'm working outside in the sun."

"Why? You need the strength to keep working."

There was no way I could explain the truth of my situation in such a way that he'd understand it. Instead, I just answered, "I have plenty of strength from the excellent lunch Signe, Yrsa, and Astrid have prepared."

Signe, perhaps sensing that I didn't want to continue this conversation, stepped in. "Yrsa says you've made a lot of progress on the field already. We are happy to provide whatever food you need to keep it up. If the two of you can continue at this pace, we could be caught up within the week."

Björn grunted. "She probably won't be able to move tomorrow. Don't count your plowing done yet."

I glared at him, but said nothing. Arguing would only antagonize him, and I just needed to prove myself. Words wouldn't make him trust me, only work.

twelve

BRENNA

AND SO AFTER LUNCH, we went back to work. I took over on the plow for several rows, then switched with Björn to finish the barley field. We led the oxen over to the vegetable garden and made quick work of the much smaller parcel of land before he announced we were done plowing for the day. Björn led the oxen to the paddock, then disappeared into the barn, dismissing me to help Signe with household chores.

I tried not to be insulted that he treated me like a servant. In his mind, I was hired help, certainly not a friend or partner. Of course, he'd treat me accordingly.

Signe showed me a modicum more respect, requesting help with tasks rather than ordering me around. They used a good portion of the separated room in the longhouse as a sort of pantry. It was further away from the fire so it stayed cooler and kept the food from spoiling as fast. She sent Yrsa off to tend their small menagerie while I assisted with preparing dinner and fetching ingredients.

But once the stew—made with smoked strips of pork belly this time—was cooking, there wasn't much to do. I built up the fire and collected more firewood to add later on, and then I sat and stared at the flames.

"Brenna?" Signe's voice was hesitant, and it surprised me. She was seated with a basket of clothing that Yrsa had brought in from the drying line, checking the garments for spots in need of mending. Astrid napped in a pile of pillows to her side.

"Yes?"

"There's a basket... of clothing... in the other room. Would you get it for me, please?"

"Sure." I stood and retrieved the basket, placing it at her side. "Is it more mending? I could help." I felt bad, watching her continue to work while my hands were idle.

"No, it's not mending." Her voice was faint, and she reached into the basket, pawing at the fabric until she tugged a garment from the neatly folded pile. "Here, take this."

The item was grey, nicely woven with soft wool fibers. I unfolded it to discover it was a very fine dress, the sleeves and collar decorated with delicate needlework flowers in a rich plum color.

Heat rushed to my cheeks. "I can't accept this." It was clearly something of her mother's, far too big for Signe, and she had saved it since her mother's death.

"You can't live and sleep in the clothes you wore to plow the field. You're just leaving mud on everything you touch," she snapped. "And no one else is wearing it. You need clothes, and we have them. Wear it." She reached into the basket and pulled out a pair of clean leather and wool slippers. "Wear these in the house, please. Leave your other shoes by the door." She held the basket up to me but avoided meeting my eyes. "Can you put this back? Then I imagine you'd like to get cleaned up and change."

"Of course. Thank you," I added, then took the basket in the smaller room. The bowl and pitcher she'd used to wash Astrid the night before was also in this room, on a rough wooden shelf. I grabbed the pitcher and took it outside to fill it, leaving my muddy shoes at the door when I returned with the water and soap. The slippers were warm and incredibly comfortable after a day of hard labor.

I ducked into the more private room, grabbing a clean rag from the shelf, and gave myself a quick wash. Once my body was clean and dry, I slipped on the new garment. It was heavenly soft and warm, compared to the rough, ugly item Odin had given me. Careful not to soak the dress, I wet and soaped my hair, using fresh water from the pitcher to rinse it before I sluiced the water off and dried it with another clean rag.

When I reemerged from the back room, Yrsa was busily setting the table. She took one look at me, wearing her mother's dress and slippers, and stormed from the building, leaving palpable fury in her wake.

Signe smiled sadly in my direction, unshed tears lining her eyes. "Don't worry about her. She'll get over it. The dress fits you. I'm glad. Do you need a comb?"

My cheeks flushed again. How did this girl, scarcely more than a child, manage to be more patient, kind, and thoughtful than I could with all of my lifetimes behind me? Her absolute goodness shamed me.

Swallowing my pride, I answered. "Yes, I do."

"Here, you can use this." She held out an ornately carved ivory comb, and I accepted it with thanks.

I sat and set to work, combing out the knots from the long tail of my hair.

"Brenna?" Signe's voice was light, a note of embarrassment in her tone.

"Yes?"

"Just so you know, we have a bathhouse. The next time you want to wash up, you might prefer it to the basin."

"Oh, okay, thank you. I... didn't know." I'd forgotten that most vikings had an actual bath house. She probably just bathed Astrid inside when it was convenient.

We worked quietly side by side; she mending

clothes and I untangling my hair. After a few minutes, I decided to ask the question on my mind.

"Signe, how old are you?"

"This is my thirteenth summer," she replied quietly, eyes on her work.

Wow, she was even younger than I thought. Despite her small stature, her relative maturity led me to believe she two years older.

"When did you hurt your foot?"

"Last summer."

"Do you mind if I ask, how did it happen?"

As if my questions reminded her that the injury bothered her, she reached down to adjust her mangled limb.

"Björn was away. I was trying to reach something high, and I fell. I was here alone with the little ones. We had no way of getting help. Björn was gone over a week, and by the time he returned, it had healed poorly and the local healer couldn't help. He said it would never be normal again."

"Would you mind if I looked at it?"

Signe's eyes flashed to my face. "Why?"

I knew I had to answer this carefully. "Where I come from, we know a little more about healing injuries, and I have some experience in this. I'm just wondering if I could help you." I held her gaze for a long moment, trying to radiate calm confidence.

"Okay, you may look at it." She set aside her mending and let me help lift her leg onto my lap, slowly peeling down her stocking.

Signe valiantly maintained a stoic expression, but

the pain caused by my lightest touch was clear in her rigid posture.

The ankle was swollen, red in some spots and purple in others, and her foot turned in toward the other at a sickening angle. I touched the sole of her foot lightly. "Do you feel that?"

"Yes," she answered through clenched teeth.

"Okay." I helped to replace her sock as gently as I was able and helped her lower it to the floor.

"Signe, would you say your ankle hurt more the week after you injured it, or now?"

"I would say it was not painful at all for several months, but lately has slowly gotten worse," she admitted. "Björn won't say anything, but I know he's afraid we will need to cut it off at some point."

I nodded. "Signe, I don't think your ankle healed poorly. In fact, I don't think it healed at all. I think it is still broken, or perhaps was healing, but walking on it is keeping it from healing. Which could be a good thing or a bad thing, because it hasn't set."

"I don't have a choice. I can't just sit in one place and wait for it to heal. Besides, it's clearly not going to heal right."

"Well, I think I can help you with that. I might manipulate the bones back into the right place... and with some luck, there was no serious damage to muscles that connect to them. We could make you an adequate brace to hold everything together, and with me here to help you so you don't need to be on your feet as much... we might be able to heal it, properly."

She looked at me coldly, her expression clear she

thought I was trying to sell her a fairy tale. "That's not possible."

"I can't promise it will work, but… even if your foot isn't ever perfectly healed and completely functional again, if we can get the bones the correct position, it won't pain you as much. Otherwise, if you keep on this way, you will definitely lose it. Those purple spots mean blood is pooling in those areas. They aren't getting enough fresh blood flow to keep the flesh healthy. Just think about it, okay?"

She glanced down at her foot, once again concealed beneath her skirts, and nodded before picking up her work.

I supposed that was the closest I would get. I set to work braiding my freshly combed hair back in a neat plait and waited for supper.

BJÖRN

When I entered the house, I thought I was seeing a ghost. Across the fire sat Signe, working on her mending. Beside her sat our mother, only twenty years younger, also working on mending.

I blinked twice to clear the haze from my eyes, remembering that of course it wasn't our mother I was watching. It was Brenna, clean and neat, sitting quietly with Signe. Wearing our mother's dress.

Of course, Mother had coppery-gold hair, not the silvery color Brenna possessed. And she had dark blue eyes, like mine and Signe's, not Brenna's stormy grey.

Our mother never had the haunted depth to her eyes, either. They were stern, solid as stones.

Even though I knew it wasn't her, I let the smoke and heat from the fire distort my vision for just a moment longer so I could pretend. Signe wasn't the only one who'd had to grow up sooner than her years. I was scarcely a man, preparing to head out on my own, when our parents died and I gained my three orphaned sisters. Of course, a few local families offered to take them in, in exchange for claiming three-quarters of our land and possessions. But they were my sisters, and I knew my parents would want me to protect them at all costs.

So I enjoyed a moment to imagine the woman on the other side of the fire was our mother, and any moment our father would come through the door, and we'd sit down to dinner and listen to Signe regale us with her day's adventures.

At that moment Yrsa came through the door, having just finished washing up. Signe glanced up and realized we were all assembled. Instinctively rising to check the pot suspended over the fire, she was immediately forced to sit again.

"I can check it," Brenna offered. "You should stay off that foot as much as possible."

She used a rag to lift the heavy lid and stirred the stew with a wooden ladle. "It's ready," she confirmed, then crossed to Signe's other side to wake Astrid, who wrapped sleepy arms around her neck and let Brenna carry her to the table. Yrsa knew her job; she'd already collected the bowls she set out previously and headed for the pot.

Suddenly realizing I was the only one not making myself useful, I crossed the room to help Signe. In a fit of guilt, knowing that I shouldn't have ever let her walk on her injured foot, I scooped her up and carried her to the table as well.

"Björn, really, this is completely unnecessary," she protested. "I can make my own way just fine-"

"Brenna is right. You shouldn't be walking on that foot. And it's much faster for me to carry you, and more pleasant for everyone not to have to watch you hobble painfully down the length of the house, Signe."

Color rose in her cheeks, and she looked away. I immediately felt terrible; it was cruel to imply that watching her struggle was more painful for us than her leg hurt her.

I set her gently in her chair, then took my seat as Yrsa delivered our meal.

Once we had finished, I helped Signe back to her spot by the fire, on the bed where she slept with Astrid. Yrsa preferred to be further away from the heat, and Brenna had settled on the bed across the fire from Signe.

When I knew they were all settled in the house, I

stepped out to the barn with a glowing log from the fire for light. I just had to check that everything was safe and secure before I could rest. I'd put in too much work to lose it now, and it would only take a moment. Glancing up at the nearly full moon, I drew in a deep sigh, then pulled open the door and slipped into the pitch-black barn.

thirteen

BRENNA

THAT NIGHT I slept even better. A full day of work, warm, comfortable clothing, and a full belly really worked wonders on a person's neurosis.

Once again, Björn shook me awake at dawn and we set to work, stoking the fire and preparing porridge for the family. I slipped away to put on my work dress, that was already looking distinctly shoddy from wear compared to my finer garment. With a vow that I would wash it well after I changed this afternoon, I strapped on my belt and tried to ignore the itch of dried mud on my legs.

This time Björn didn't waste energy taunting me; clearly, we'd achieved a level of understanding yesterday. And while I was sore from the hard labor, I was certainly not about to let him know.

Besides, I'd experienced far worse.

This time we hauled the ard up to the rye field, and working together made quick work of hooking the oxen to the plow and beginning the furrows. Björn handed me the seed and took the first shift at the plow.

Our day went much the same as it had yesterday, with the two of us occasionally switching roles to allow for a break from the more arduous work, and Yrsa collecting us for lunch.

I was on the plow, and Björn was seeding when they arrived.

My back was to the path, and the noise of plow cutting through hard soil and the grunts of oxen were more than enough to disguise the sound of men arriving on foot.

I didn't realize Björn wasn't behind me until I reached the end of the row and turned the plow, only to see him at the edge of the turned soil, speaking to two other men.

It was the men from the night I'd met him, I'd be willing to bet. I monitored them while the oxen continued forward, but the closer I came, the more convinced I became.

The taller of the two was more slender, with shiny, pale golden hair that was cut just over his shoulders, tied back with a strip of leather that left a few strands swinging to frame his face. And it was an exceptionally pretty face, with high, full cheekbones, a square jaw, and lush lips that curled up at the edges. A neatly cleft chin, straight nose, and elegant brows over cornflower blue eyes completed the package. Clearly the youngest of the three, as I'd imagined, Leif would have put Parisian catwalk models in tears.

The shorter man, more muscular, was older than the other two. His face was unlined, but definitely more weathered. It wasn't the age of his skin, so much as the wisdom he wore on his brow. He was the clever one in the fight, and everything about him said 'danger' in flashing neon lights. His darker sandy hair was shorn below the ears, braided back from his face down to a thick tail that reached his mid-back. Low, sharp brows that angled up at the edges were barely set above piercing, predatory eyes. His nose might have once been straight, but someone had clearly broken it more than once. The sharp cheekbones were prominent above a neatly sculpted beard, trimmed close to his jaw. The moustache did little to disguise his thin upper lip.

As I watched them talking, the shorter man's sharp, hawk-like green eyes turned in my direction as if he knew I was watching them. The other two turned their faces in my direction also, and now I knew they were talking about me.

Of course it made sense; I just hoped I wouldn't need to make a mad dash to the longhouse to retrieve my sword. I hadn't picked it up since I hung it on the wall that first night.

I continued my slow trajectory toward the three men, occasionally whipping the oxen or issuing a command to keep them in line. Their conversation was heated with stern expressions and sharp hand gestures, but I couldn't make it out over the sounds of the animals and the ground breaking before me.

The closer I came, the more concerned I became that Björn's friends were making a case to get rid of me. I certainly had done little to endear myself to them when we met, and Signe notwithstanding, I had little standing between me and the door as far as Björn was concerned.

A few dozen arguments formed in my mind to combat his prospective reasons for telling me to leave. Clearly, these men were his partners for raids, and they were used to fighting together. I knew Björn recognized my ability to protect his sisters while he would be away during the summer... I had no doubt he blamed himself for being away when Signe was injured in the first place.

I just had to get him to trust me. Trust was the missing element here. I was a stranger who showed up with nothing but a really nice sword, and the first thing I did was get into a fight and stop them from killing someone they believed deserved it. I had no basis for establishing trust.

The men continued their terse conversation as I approached, the occasional pair of eyes darting in my direction.

My heart pounding, I finished the row and turned the beasts to begin the next row, then set the plow and whip down, and marched toward the men with an outward confidence I didn't feel.

Wiping my sweaty, sore palms on my dress, I decided to play the 'misunderstanding' angle.

"Hello, I'm Brenna. I didn't get the chance to introduce myself the other night. You're Leif, right?" I approached the younger one first, whose name I already knew, hoping he'd be too surprised to deny my outstretched hand.

Leif stared at me as if unsure of what he was seeing. "Hello... it's nice to meet you, Brenna." He accepted my handshake, but continued to wear a confused expression when his eyes darted to Björn.

Pulling in a breath, I turned to the other man. "Hello, it's a pleasure to meet you." I knew it was oddly formal, and perhaps not how they introduced themselves, but for the life of me I couldn't remember how I was supposed to do this after so long and I figured better to err on the side of being polite.

His predatory green eyes narrowed, searching my face for something, before he slapped a thick, rough palm in mine.

"Søren. What are you doing here, Brenna?"

"Plowing," I answered simply. "And planting, and cleaning, and any other work Björn or Signe need me to do."

"I can see you are plowing. But what I want to know is why you showed up here in the middle of the night, in our village, looking for work."

My eyes darted to Björn, but he'd crossed his arms over his chest and waited as if he wanted answers as well.

I swallowed, running my tongue over my lips to wet them. God, I missed chapstick.

"I'm not a criminal, if that's what you're wondering. My... chieftain liked to take advantage of my skills to force me to do work for him I didn't want to do." My mind spun rapidly, trying to spin my issues with Odin into something non-celestial. "He held me hostage to his whims. My only escape was to leave my life behind in the middle of the night, and hope to find a place to start over."

Søren's shrewd eyes examined my every move as I spoke, and I did my best to appear embarrassed but honest.

"So how did you get here?"

Shit. I still did not know where I was. On foot was not likely, most of these villages were remote and they likely knew most of the people in the next village over. There was clearly a storm the night I arrived...

"I had a small boat, but I got caught in the storm and crashed it. I only managed to save my sword and make it to shore. I don't know how long I walked until I reached your village." My heart beat against my ribs as I waited to see if he bought my story.

Søren's eyes narrowed again, then he nodded. "That storm was rough. I know many whose fences or homes got damaged near the water."

I stopped myself from breathing the deep sigh of relief my body wanted, allowing only a slow breath instead as I tried to calm my racing pulse.

"So what is your plan, Brenna? You'll stay here and help Björn for the summer, and then what?"

I needed to tread carefully here. If I erred on the side of caution and didn't mention my plans of joining the raiders, they would likely never think of me again and they would safely relegate me to household duties. But if I admitted to having some plans, perhaps they could help me...

"I plan to help Signe here, as agreed. I hope by autumn I will have secured a place in your village, and that by next spring I can join a raiding party. I can work, and I don't mind it. But I'm a warrior, and that is where my talents lie."

Søren's eyes darted to Björn, who scowled, and Leif glanced between the two of them. When Søren's gaze returned to me, his eyes held a sparkle of challenge. "I wish you the best of fortune in that endeavor." He nodded, then turned his focus on Björn and gestured for the barn. When all three of them started walking in that direction, I realized I'd been dismissed.

If I wasn't more concerned about having a meal in my belly and a place to sleep tonight, I might have been annoyed by his rudeness. Then again, I was still digging the memory of customs from this era out of my mental archives. In their minds, I was a nameless, penniless wretch, barely above a slave. No doubt they'd witnessed my skill with a sword as I'd bested Björn, but I had no power or influence to back it up.

Sighing, I returned to my plow.

One step at a time.

fourteen

LEIF

I STOLE a glance back at the woman, Brenna, as we hiked up to Björn's barn. She was a far cry from the mud-caked she-demon who'd stood between us and Skarde. That night I'd screamed my fury from the cliffs above the churning fjord; this woman had come out of nowhere and prevented me from fulfilling my sworn duty of avenging my brother's death. It was as if the gods were mocking me, to have everything so well-planned, and then this unexpected hindrance flew in from nowhere and ruined it all.

Now, of course, she appeared to be a different person completely. Clean, for one. Beautiful. Silverly blonde hair and deep, soulful grey eyes. My heart throbbed so loudly I couldn't hear her words over the blood rushing through my ears. Even now, even from this distance, I could see an almost glittering sheen that emanated from her skin despite the dirt and labor.

She was no ordinary girl like the others in this village. Of that I was positive. I started cataloguing a list of excuses I could use to visit Björn, and Brenna, more often.

Like what he'd hidden in the barn, for starters.

We reached the new structure—Søren and I, along with most of the village, had helped to build it in the wake of the fire that took Björn's parents. The wooden sides were showing a bit of weathering, but for the most part, it was still clearly newer than the house. Cool, welcoming darkness greeted me in the door-way, but Björn strode to the windows on the opposite side of the structure and threw open the wooden shutters, allowing wide beams of sunlight in.

And there it waited: the project Björn had been working on in secret for over a year, that we were pinning all of our hopes for glory and wealth on.

A ship.

A boat, really, small enough for four to manage, but with room for more if we added to our team.

The plan was to have it ready to go before the summer raids began, but Björn had fallen behind, trying to run everything that needed to get done on the farm. Guilt flooded my chest: we were meant to be helping him with it, but there always seemed to be something else that needed to get done.

It wasn't a proper *drakkar*—it was far too small. At

the most, this ship would carry fifteen, but ideally less than ten. Most drakkar carried as many men as possible, some large enough to accommodate nearly fifty.

This ship was a secret because we knew it was a risk. It wasn't how things were done, men forming their own raiding party. Typically, each village provided a team, and they might be their own party or they might be joined with another village at the behest of the Jarl.

But after everything that happened with Skarde, my brother, and the rest of the village, we couldn't put our trust in our team. They'd already betrayed us in favor of Skarde and we had no reason to believe that would change.

And so our plan was to go to the Jarl with our own ship, prove that we could bring him just as much wealth without the others, and gain his permission to do things our own way.

But we still needed a fourth. There were a couple of men we hoped might be interested after we dispatched Skarde, but now we didn't have the option—they wouldn't leave a cushy spot on Skarde's party for one that was likely to get them laughed out of the Jarl's presence.

And here was this woman, who declared herself a warrior…

"…, Leif?" Søren's voice was stern, as if he knew he'd caught my mind wandering, as it tended to do. Both he and Björn were glaring in my direction.

I swallowed the lump in my throat. "Sorry, what were you saying?"

Søren's jaw flexed, his teeth clenched against the insults he was probably tempted to throw at me. My drifting thoughts were a constant pain to his calculating, focused mind.

"The ship needs a good deal more work before it's seaworthy, and we only have a week. Can you commit to helping Björn finish it this week, and actually show up this time?"

"It looks mostly ready to me," I answered sheepishly. "It only needs a few more planks, right?"

Søren sighed. "It needs more planks, and then the spaces between need to be filled, and then sealed, and the entire thing needs to be sealed, and we still haven't worked out how to get it down to the shore. Plus, it still needs a figurehead for the prow. If you have any ideas for that, by all means, please contribute. You're welcome to carve it yourself. I know you're handy with woodcarving."

I nodded. "Yes, I'll get to work on an idea, and I will be here the afternoons for the rest of the week, I promise. We'll get it finished."

"Good. I'll continue trying to work out a way to get it to the shore."

"I'm sorry, Søren," Björn added. "Sten backed out of his promise to let me use his oxen when I refused to sell him my sister, and Knud is his brother…"

"No one blames you," Søren replied curtly, cutting him off. "We just need a new plan. I'll figure it out."

We walked around the boat and examined Björn's work, praising the quality of his craftsmanship. It was impressive how he'd taken the design of a *drakkar* and shrunken it without sacrificing the function. A mast and plain canvas sail lay along the side of the barn, waiting for the ship to be finished so they could be mounted. I couldn't help feeling the sail ought to have something painted on it, but until we had a seaworthy ship it didn't matter what we painted on the sail, it wasn't going anywhere.

Björn sealed up the shutters, and we exited the barn. I promised to return in a few hours to help him install more planks after he finished seeding the field with Brenna. My eyes drifted to the woman, every part of her seeming to shine while she balanced the plow and whipped the oxen along.

An image came to my mind just then, her standing triumphantly on the prow of our ship with long flowing wings of fabric on her shoulders, hair whipping in the salty breeze...

Grinning to myself, I bid goodbye to Søren and rushed home to sketch out the picture my mind had given me.

fifteen

BRENNA

AFTER WE FINISHED the rye field, Björn once again dismissed me and disappeared into his barn. I had no idea what he did in there—did vikings have a 'man cave'?—but either way, it didn't affect me. We had a comfortable working truce, but it wasn't as cozy as working with Signe and the other girls.

They'd been outside for a while; Yrsa started on planting the vegetable garden, then tended the animals while Signe watched Astrid and combed wool. When I finished with sowing, I hauled in the basket of combed wool and helped Signe keep her weight off her injured foot. She hadn't asked me about my offer to help, and I didn't dare bring it up again. If she wanted to try it, she would ask.

I got her settled in front of the fire with her clean wool and a drop spindle, where she would spin the thread she'd eventually use to make fabric. Having tended to Astrid, I cleaned up and headed out to wash my dirty work garment.

A shallow tub sat outside, beside the rain barrel, with the heavy bar of lye soap. I ladled a few scoops of water into the wooden tub, carefully tucked up the sleeves of my fine dress, and made sure the dirty one was truly soaked before I began attacking it with the soap.

I'd forgotten how difficult this was. How difficult everything was… or *is*, now. For me, at least.

A bubble of despair rose in my chest and erupted from my eyes, streaming tears down my cheeks as I scrubbed and slapped at the filthy, sodden rag that was the only article of clothing I had to my name. All the frustration that had been building in me since Odin sent me back, all the fury I had nowhere to unleash, now channeled through my hands as I attacked that dress. With everything I had, I swore I would make sure it was clean.

My mind drifted to piles of treasure I'd squirreled away in a future that no longer existed. The fabulous parties I'd attended. The mouthwatering meals I'd eaten, the absolutely incredible sex I'd had through the years. All of that was just gone in a snap of Odin's fingers. That reality just erased as if it never existed, everywhere except in my mind. To punish me. To make me feel insane. To make me suffer.

And it was working. I was hopeless in the face of

everything I'd lost. The thirst was on me, burning in my gut with a need to make myself forget. Hard work in the sun all day was an excellent distraction. I'd avoided drinking the beer Signe offered me the last two nights, but I felt so weak now I didn't know if I'd survive a third night. Maybe it was better if I just gave in and stopped trying to be something I wasn't: good. I should stop trying to be good, pretending to be good. I wasn't good; I was a valkyrie who abandoned her sisters. Who backed out of the agreements she'd made. Who'd run away and hidden, swinging wildly between being an insatiable seeker of vice to someone who desperately tried to make amends with the universe for my past behavior. It was insane—I could never make amends for that.

Finished beating the dress with the soap, I set myself to the task of squeezing water from the woolen garment. It was difficult; the dress was heavy with water, the fabric seemingly designed to retain as much as possible. My hands and arms were shaking from exhaustion, from emotional turmoil, from cravings for the substance I knew I needed to avoid if I wanted a chance to start again.

I tried to methodically sluice water from the dress one handful at a time, but halfway it slipped from my fingers back into the several inches of muddy water at the bottom of the barrel, quickly soaking it back up. That was the moment that broke me, and I hunched over with my face in my arms, allowing myself to dissolve in tears of absolute self-pity.

"Brenna?" Björn's rich baritone shocked me out of my tears.

Immediately drawing the emotion down, I wiped the tears from my cheeks and reached for my dress. "Yes?" I asked, as if he hadn't just seen me sobbing into the barrel. The last thing I needed was for him to think I was a useless, weak, tear-sodden female. I avoided meeting the gaze I could feel burning a spot on the back of my head.

"Here..." he reached a beefy hand over my shoulder and grasped the dress, folding it in half and twisting the entire garment in one go. The filthy water poured from the grey fibers in a river, and I tipped the barrel to dump it onto the grass. Björn replaced the dress for me, and I ladled clean water on top, swirling and swishing it to rinse out more filth. As soon as I pulled my hands free, Björn fished the dress out and wrung it dry for me again.

This time, I turned to meet his eyes. Björn's expression was still hard, distrustful, but something in his eyes had softened. Perhaps my moment of vulnerability had helped me after all.

"Thank you," I said softly, accepting the bundle of damp wool from the enormous man.

"It's not a problem," he replied gruffly. "I always helped my mother with the laundry, then Signe when she took over. They both have small hands like you, and wet wool is heavy."

"I can manage it," I snapped, and immediately regretted it. He was being kind, not insulting me.

Fortunately, he didn't rise to the bait. "I know you

can, Brenna. But I don't mind helping with something so small. You've been working all day. It'd be a miracle if your arms weren't tired after pushing that plow for so long." He turned to leave, then hesitated. "I appreciate your help. I hope you know that. Another day or two and we'll be caught up with the fields. I don't know how long it would have taken me on my own. So, thank you."

Emotion welled in my throat again; I hadn't expected any thanks from this man, and with everything riding so close to the surface for me right now, I was far more emotional than I was accustomed to.

I nodded, not trusting myself to speak, and Björn seemed to understand. He lingered for another moment, then turned and went inside, leaving me to my own thoughts in the fading light of evening.

sixteen

BRENNA

I SAT OUTSIDE LONGER than I really should have. There was work to be done, preparing the meal, helping with Astrid, anything to keep Signe off her broken ankle.

But the interior of the spacious longhouse felt too crowded to me right now. After being mostly alone for a millennium, I just needed space from time to time.

The wet dress was still bundled in my hands and I was just staring into space, lost in my thoughts, when I heard the animals.

The pigs made a racket of startled oinks, along with the deep, annoyed brays of the oxen and aggravated clucking from the chickens.

Abandoning my dress on the side of the tub, I stood and walked around the corner of the house to investigate.

Standing there, cooing at the horse, who looked as he was considering biting his tormentor, was Loki.

My first emotion was absolute terror that Björn would come out and see him here, blowing my secret wide open.

My next was annoyance at his nerve. Hadn't he helped Odin trick me and cart me back to Asgard, only to disappear as soon as we arrived?

"What the hell are you doing here?" I snarled, marching up to the god of questionable loyalty.

"I wanted to see how you were doing. Aren't you happy to see me?" The hideous half-giant grinned at me smarmily.

"No, I'm not. I'm pissed that you helped Odin capture and dump me here, actually. Then you slipped off as soon as we got to Asgard, so I couldn't call on you for help. Are you here to gloat?"

"Not at all. In fact, I feel bad about this whole thing. I didn't want to help Odin, but he made me an offer I couldn't refuse, so I agreed to do it. However, I didn't agree *not* to help *you* as well."

Well, that changed things. "Help me how?" I leveled my best suspicious glare at Loki's bulging brow and waited.

"I've brought you a present. Would you like to see it?" He indicated a roughly woven sack at his feet that I hadn't noticed in the tall grasses.

"Depends on what it is," I hedged.

"It's something you want very, very, badly. Something Odin took from you, and has kept under lock and key for over a millennium. Something I could only sneak down and steal when everyone in Asgard was distracted by Odin parading you through the great hall."

My heart leapt. Surely I was dreaming. I tried to keep my excitement down.

"Loki, is this real? Not a trick? Did you really get it?"

"Maybe... you'll have to tell me you want it first, before you can know for sure." His eyes glinted mischievously.

"I want it," I breathed. "Please Loki, may I have the gift you've brought me?"

He pretended to consider it, then reached down and grabbed the bag. "Okay, here you go."

I snatched the bag with eager fingers and peeked inside. Sure enough, it was my armor.

Tears stung my eyes when I looked back up at his hideous face. "Thank you, Loki. I can't thank you enough. I don't know how you kept it hidden this entire time from Odin and his servants."

"You forget, Brenna, time flows differently on Midgard than on Asgard now that Odin likes to play with it. On Asgard, Odin had just returned to the great hall from sending you here when I visited Heimdall."

"I-" my response stuck in my throat. Odin had said as much. I just didn't think about it. Which meant that the several days I'd just spent on Midgard

Odin hadn't even been watching, because he wasn't even back to the great hall yet. This felt important. It could definitely be something I used to my advantage. I just needed to keep it in mind.

"Never mind. Thank you, Loki. It's been a very long time since I had my armor."

Loki shrugged. "I thought it was unfair of him to take it from you in the first place. I know how you valkyries get without your armor. I can imagine it was difficult for you the first time. It seemed unnecessarily cruel to make you go through that again."

I stifled a giggle. Loki could be so kind, even profound, when he wanted to be.

He could also be a downright dirty asshole if it suited his needs. I just needed to remember that before I started getting all soft about him.

"Is that the only reason you're doing this? Because it seemed unfair? Or was there something you wanted from me for doing this favor?"

Loki gave me his best benevolent grin. "I told you, Odin made me an offer I couldn't refuse... I literally didn't have a choice. So consider this a repercussion for him that benefits you as well. Deal?"

"Deal." If this was not really for my benefit, then I didn't owe him anything, and that was exactly how I liked it.

"Brenna!" Björn's baritone voice sent a flutter of nerves through my gut.

"You'd better go, and I need to find a place to hide this before he comes looking for me."

"You don't want to introduce me to your friend?"

Loki feigned a hurt expression. "After all we've been through, Brenna, I'm crushed."

"Ugh, get over yourself. Thank you for the armor, now pull a Loki and disappear!"

Grinning, Loki darted around the side of the long-house where he'd be out of view if Björn came looking for me. I imagined he'd wait until we were inside to summon the Bifrost.

I stashed the bag behind a pile of hay near the horse paddock and scampered back to the door to the longhouse. Björn was standing in the doorway, glaring out into the darkness.

"Where'd you go?"

"The animals were making noise like they were startled. I went to check on them and calm them down." That was actually true. After retrieving my damp dress from the washtub, I followed Björn inside, ignoring his suspicious expression.

Once again, everyone was at the table and waiting for me. I quickly draped my dress over a wooden rack and set it near the fire to dry, then claimed my seat, heart positively thrumming with excitement.

I'd have to wait until everyone was asleep, but hopefully, then I could sneak out and slip on my armor with no witnesses. The idea of reconnecting with a piece of my soul I'd thought lost forever was making adrenaline course through my system uncontrollably. My face flushed, heat dappling over my skin at just the idea of wearing it again.

My heart was soaring, and soon I would be, too.

seventeen

BRENNA

IT SEEMED LIKE AN ABSOLUTE LIFETIME, but eventually the entire longhouse was asleep. Even Björn snored lightly, his back to the door.

Drawing breath as silently as I could, conscious to keep my every movement quieter than the crackling fire, I slowly lowered one foot at a time to the packed-earth ground and crept to the door. The good news was that my bed was closest to the door. The bad news: that door was noisy. They didn't have the benefit of modern tools when they built this place, and the doorframe no longer had ninety-degree corners since the house had settled somewhat during its lifetime. The door, however, remained stubbornly rectangular.

First, I lifted my sword gently from the pegs on the wall. Immediately, a rush of soothing energy spread through me. It was pure stupidity that I hadn't handled it since I'd been here. I knew I needed the contact to keep me sane; it's like I was punishing myself by not touching it.

Now, sword in hand, I reached for the latch on the door. Lifting the handle, I slid my sword between the door and the jam, attempting to create space so it didn't scrape loudly when I pulled it open.

The spirits were with me tonight; the trick worked and the wooden door scarcely made a peep when I opened it. I crept through, waiting for just a moment to ensure no one woke, then pulled the door behind me. I didn't shut it all the way, just enough so it stuck and wouldn't move with a light breeze. Hopefully, I'd be able to slip back inside silently when I was done.

My heart danced in my chest, and my feet were swift as I walked around the longhouse to claim my treasure. I had to sneak another peek—just to be sure I wasn't dreaming—before I shouldered the sack and climbed the hill to the barn.

I didn't dare take a torch from the hearth, but my eyes adapted quickly and the moon was almost full. However, the interior of the barn was black as pitch. I'd seen some window frames from the backside of the building when I was in the field, so I stumbled my way around an excessively large object to the back wall and, finally locating the first shutter, unlatched and opened it. I moved to the second to let in more light, then turned and gasped in absolute shock at what I saw.

Björn was building a ship. An incredibly fine, compact raiding ship. This is what he'd been working on instead of plowing the fields. Given how late into spring we now were, I imagined he was in a panic to finish before the raiding began.

I walked the perimeter of the ship and could find no flaw in the design. He still had a few more planks to attach, and it needed to be sealed, but it was nearly done. It had a nice, deep hull for the deeper waters of the sea between us and the rest of Europe, perhaps even Iceland. There was space for only ten oars and shields, five on each side.

Perhaps this was why it was a secret: my memories were pretty sharp where the ships were concerned, and they were typically much larger than this one.

I wondered why he wanted such a small ship. Was there a strategic advantage I wasn't seeing?

Like getting struck by a lightning bolt, I remembered my purpose for being in the barn in the first place. My armor!

The legendary warrior maidens of Valkyr were renown throughout the ten realms, back in our time. We gave up the hope of love and families in order to serve as protectors of our world; there was no higher honor. As part of that sacrifice, we took place in a magical ceremony that bound us to our sword and armor for eternity. By imbuing our heart to our sword, we could never use it for evil. By imbuing our soul to our armor, we would live for eternity.

When Odin stripped us of both, it left him with soulless, heartless shells of women who had lost all the characteristics that made them legendary. When he banished me, he was clever enough to not make that mistake again. He kept my armor—it was by far the most powerful piece, and by keeping it, I was still bound to him—but he allowed me to keep my sword so I wasn't completely empty inside.

I had my heart, so I could feel how empty it was without my soul.

Now, I finally had them both.

With my heart in my throat, I pulled back the flaps of the woven bag and pulled out the first piece. It was the breastplate, with the collar that attached to my shoulder pieces. Despite over a millennium in Odin's dungeon, the metal shone as if freshly polished. As soon as my fingertips touched the piece, warmth spread throughout my body in a coursing river of sensation. I held it, let it fill me as much as it was able, then gently set it aside and reached for the next piece.

First the gardbrace for my shoulder, then the rere-brace and vambrace for my sword arm. Then the fauld for my hips, beautifully decorated to match the tasset below; the two cuisses and greaves, and finally the sabatons.

I wasn't accustomed to don this myself, but I had no other choice. With trembling fingers, I slid out of my cozy wool dress and pulled on the fauld. It was designed as one piece and sort of fit like a pair of metallic underpants, with pieces that rose to protect the soft flesh of my hips and stomach. The air was chilly in the barn, but my armor was warm and comforting to put on, like my favorite pair of worn-in sweatpants back home.

Once I strapped the cuisses and greaves on my thighs and shins, I attached the tassets to the fauld. I'd been putting off the breastplate—it caused a rather dramatic moment—but there was enough room in this barn and my bare breasts were freezing.

I attached the gardbrace before I put on the breastplate, then pulling in a deep breath, I slid the whole thing over my head and attached the silvery hooks in the back.

A rush of energy flew through my body, beginning at my toes and culminating in pressure along my spine. With a brief burning sensation, my wings erupted in a gust of wind, extending to their full fifteen-foot span and flapping to lift me from my feet before settling back on the ground.

Pure, unadulterated, glowing *joy* filled every inch of my body. I felt complete for the first time in over a thousand years. *Finally*. My eyes welled with tears, and I strapped on my rerebrace and vambrace through the blur, chuckling to myself in a slightly delirious level of happiness. I was no longer cold. I was no longer vulnerable. I was no longer thirsty, or depressed, or broken. I was *whole*.

I tucked my wings as tightly as I was able, reveling in the warmth of soft feathers at my back once more. They were no snowy white dove wings, and that suited me. I was not a perfect, pure person. My wings appeared brown in the darkness, but when lit with the sun on Valkyr, they were astounding. As if made from the precious metals, my feathers were a shimmering bronze, flecked with speckles of gold to complement my silver hair.

I stuck my head out of the barn door, watching for any signs of movement on the farm or nearby under the bright waxing moon. After watching a few moments, I was confident no one was around and I stepped out into the moonlight.

Even though the air had been chilly when I left the longhouse, now it felt like a warm summer breeze wherever the air touched my exposed skin. My sword pulsed joyfully in my palm, and my body, now complete, hummed with the power of the valkyrie. A faint glow, like a dusting of moonlight, lit me from head to foot, and I admired my sparkling body for a moment before I set my sights higher.

Spreading my eager wings, I shot into the air with a single, powerful thrust, tucking my sword into the scabbard on my hip to free my hands completely. In mere seconds, I was so high I'd be only a speck to those on the ground. I soared for the simple joy of it, flipping, spinning, and rolling through the air like a seal in the ocean. Even after so long, my wings hadn't forgotten me, and I hadn't forgotten how to fly.

Tears stung my eyes once again; tears of happiness. My heart felt so full, where I had felt so hopeless just hours ago. I had nothing but joy filling every cracked and broken place within me.

I considered trying to go higher and determine where exactly we were, but it would be too difficult to be sure in the night. I might have to sneak a flight at dawn or dusk, where there was enough light to make out landmarks, but not enough for me to be seen by anyone on the ground.

Keeping the mountain ridge against which Björn's farm rested in sight, I indulged myself in joyous flying for another hour before I reluctantly returned to the ground.

In Valkyr we only removed our armor for bathing and sleep, during which it remained in our sight. I would have slept in it if the wings weren't an inconvenience.

Although it pained me to take it off, having been without it for so long, I knew I possessed it again, and that was the most important piece. It was mine again, and I would not lose it. I removed each piece with care; the warmth remaining in my skin even as I undressed and donned my woolen clothes. Once every item was lovingly stowed in the humble bag, I climbed the loft of the barn and found the most secure spot to stash my treasure behind a surplus of hay.

I returned to the longhouse and slipped back inside undetected, hanging my sword gently back in its place.

As I drifted off to sleep on my padded bench, I could feel the glowing wholeness within my chest, and I couldn't help the smile that curled my lips.

eighteen

BJÖRN

FINDING BRENNA SLUMPED over the washbasin, pouring out tears over a dirty dress, tugged painfully on something in my chest. Since the moment I'd met her, she'd been a hard, confident, superior-acting woman who seemed as if nothing could ruffle her feathers. I realized in that moment it was just an act; bravado, showmanship, for her to behave that way. She pretended to be cold and unbothered, but there was more beneath the surface.

She came in for dinner with flushed cheeks and shining eyes. For someone who'd appeared in the depths of her despair just moments before, the sudden shift was remarkable. I observed her carefully for the rest of the evening, but her mood didn't shift again. She was quietly neutral in demeanor, but something bubbled just beneath the surface... something good this time.

The following morning, there was a new light to Brenna's eyes. Her past clearly haunted her, and yet something new existed in their stormy depths: hope.

She hummed a tune I didn't recognize as we prepared breakfast and headed out to collect the oxen. We made our way to the highest field, the last one we needed to plow and sow with oats, and Brenna smiled to herself all the while.

I observed her more closely; there was a glow about her. Perhaps it was just a trick of the morning light, but her skin appeared to shimmer. Maybe it was just a few nights of good food and rest had restored her vitality.

She certainly looked healthier. If you compared this woman to the mud-soaked wretch that had appeared at our door just a few days ago, you wouldn't believe it was the same person. Natural smile, hair and skin shining, eyes lit from within... even her presence felt different. Whereas before she was just a person, perhaps a little pathetic, now she seemed to radiate positivity.

I did not know what had wrought this change, but I doubted it was just that I squeezed some wet fabric for her. Something had happened, and she wasn't saying a word. Perhaps I needed to ask.

"Brenna, you appear in good spirits today," I commented.

"I am, thank you. It's a beautiful day, isn't it?" She

grinned in my direction, squinting in the early morning light.

"Much the same as yesterday, if you ask me. Is the weather the reason for your good mood?"

"No, I guess I just woke up feeling more... positive than I did yesterday."

"I'm glad." I paused, choosing my next words carefully. "You seemed rather upset last night."

"It was a long day."

We'd reached the field now and set about hooking up the plow and oxen. Brenna took the first row with the beasts, cheerfully shouting, 'yah!' And encouraging them forward with a few slaps of the whip.

By the time I visited the barn and returned with the oats, she was already circling back on the second row. She must have been feeling extremely energized after her rest. I hurried to catch up, sprinkling the oats into the furrows and kicking soil over the top.

Brenna continued with the plow for the entire morning without stopping. Her brow scarcely broke a sweat, and she grinned every time she passed me. I'd long since given up catching her. She was moving too quickly for that to happen.

When Yrsa came to call us for lunch, Brenna had already finished two-thirds of the largest of our three fields. I was sweating, my back aching, by the time I finished sowing the rows she'd dug, and she looked as fresh as she had at dawn.

I ate my lunch quietly, and Brenna joked her way through the meal with Signe and Astrid. She even drew a smile from Yrsa, my serious little bear cub of a sister. The instinct that things were happening in my home without my knowledge grew; a person didn't just change overnight like that. From proud warrior to begging laborer to a distraught woman crying in a washbasin, to this... this glowing image of happiness and vitality.

It didn't make sense, and my head hurt just trying to puzzle it out.

After lunch we finished the field; Brenna insisted on taking the plow again, leaving me the easier, and yet still back-breaking, work of sowing. Leif arrived mere moments after I'd set down my nearly empty sack of oats. He'd appeared much later yesterday, but at least he'd shown up to help for an hour.

Leif's gaze stuck to Brenna as soon as she was in his view. The kid was not subtle; his entire face turned in her direction as she moved. Brenna greeted him with a warm smile, and his eyes were glassy as he stared back at her, clearly admiring. A tiny bubble of anger rose in my chest when she accepted his attention rather than telling him off.

I dismissed Brenna and pointed Leif toward the barn. As far as I was concerned, she could go help Signe and stay out of our hair—we didn't need the distraction.

"If there's more work to be done, I'm happy to help. I'm feeling very... restored today." Brenna grinned as if enjoying a joke that I didn't know.

"No thank you, we have it in hand," I replied sharply, but regretted my tone as soon as I'd said it.

There was no reason to be rude to her for offering to help.

"Well, if you want that ship to be seaworthy by the end of the week, I think you really need my help."

My earlier regret disappeared immediately. "What did you say?"

"Your ship," her head tilted to the side slightly. "It's very good craftsmanship, but it still needs a lot of work. I'm impressed you could adapt the proportions so well. Did you design it, Björn?"

"That was all three of us," Leif stepped in eagerly. "Søren had the concept. I helped sketch it out, and Björn figured out how we could build it."

"Impressive," she nodded. "I happen to be rather knowledgeable in the art of ship making, if you could use another set of hands."

"Of course, we-"

"Is there anything you *can't* do, woman?" I didn't mean to growl at her, but the frustration was building and fit to boil over. It felt as if she had arrived in this town just to prove she was better than me at every task I prided myself on. Sword fighting, plowing, caring for my sisters, and now shipbuilding?

Brenna tilted her head in the other direction, as if thinking about it carefully. "No, I really don't think there is." Grinning, she added, "Thank you, by the way. That was quite the compliment."

I did not mean it to be a compliment, but I didn't feel the need to correct her. "Thanks for the offer, but we're fine. We can take care of it ourselves."

"Now just a minute," Leif interjected. "Just yesterday, you and Søren were complaining about how far behind we were, and you want to refuse an offer of help? That seems foolish." Turning to Brenna, he said, "We'd love your help, thank you. This way," and gesturing forward, encouraged her toward the barn.

LEIF

Sure enough, the room was almost too dark to see after the bright light of day. However, Björn found the shutters just fine, and once they were open, the room flooded with light.

Brenna made her way to the pile of curved planks still waiting to be attached to the exposed ribs of our ship. She studied the wood, and I studied her.

Something had changed. I did not know what it was, but it wrought the most magnificent change on Brenna. Yesterday she had been pretty, but today she was absolutely striking. I couldn't pull my gaze from her, fingers itching to draw out my charcoal and sketch. The figurehead I'd imagined yesterday wasn't nearly as beautiful as Brenna in real life. I'd need to sketch it all again, with the details I was currently memorizing.

She finished her examination of the work before us, and we got started.

If I had expected that she wouldn't be up to the task, I would certainly admit to being surprised. Brenna helped lift the heavy planks and hold them in place for hammering. She could also wield the ungainly iron hammer and nails, beating the rough metal pins through the hardwood with no more difficulty than Björn or myself.

And while we were pouring sweat and grunting—Björn more so than myself—with the difficulty of the work, Brenna seemed to handle the tasks with much more ease. A light sheen of sweat coated her brow, making her, impossibly, more beautiful. A few strands of silvery hair escaped the single braid, falling to frame her face and highlight the high cheekbones and narrow, rounded chin. The more I was around her, the more I saw her, the harder I fell.

I'd never seen such a woman; none of us had. Goodness and positivity practically shone from her, even bent under the heavy weight of oaken beams. My heart swelled with admiration in a wave I couldn't possibly stop, and I felt it crest over and drown me.

I couldn't say anything to Björn or Søren. They treated me like a silly younger brother, little more than a child, and I'd learned after pining for Gertrud, not to mention romance to either of them. Björn was far too concerned with taking care of his sisters, and Søren... well, Søren had his share of pain in his heart.

We finished building the ship in a few hours; Björn had expected it would take us at last two more days to complete, but with Brenna's help, the work flew by.

"Do you have the materials for sealing? We'll need to fill the gaps between planks with something— wool, moss perhaps, anything we can mix with tar and cram in." Brenna wiped her brow, grinning with enthusiasm for the next task.

Every muscle in my body hurt, and I wanted to flop on a pile of hay, but I couldn't show that weakness in front of her. Instead, I stood as straight and wide as I could make myself, crossing my arms over my chest. "Søren is bringing tallow to use for sealing. I'll let him know we're ready for that step, and I'll collect moss tomorrow. I can be here at midday?"

nineteen

BRENNA

ONCE AGAIN, as soon as the household was asleep I snuck out, donned my armor, and took to the sky. I allowed my mind to wander as I floated in and out of the clouds, just enjoying the wholeness once more.

The warm, complete feeling stayed with me for most of the day, fortifying my body as well as my heart and mind. All of my struggles, the demons I faced for so long, were nothing now. I was no broken person, subject to the incredibly low lows of a depression for which there was no cure. My armor fixed what no bottle could. There was no liquid in the world that could substitute for a missing soul.

But as the day turned into evening, I still felt the chill creep in. The dark, bitter sadness at the edges of my mind, picking at my peace and happiness, eroding my calm.

On Valkyr, we only removed our armor for bathing and sleep. We wore it for thirty-six of the forty-nine hours that made up Valkyrian days. There was never a point where my cup was empty. I wore the armor more than I was without it.

Here the days were shorter, and it appeared an hour was what I required to sustain me for a twenty-four-hour period. More would probably be better, and perhaps I would do even better if I could sneak out in the morning instead.

However, Björn's habits were still too unpredictable. I was risking a good deal by sneaking out directly after bedtime, but I also needed to sleep at some point. I didn't have any way to wake myself without disturbing everyone else in the single-room house.

No, for now, my best option was to stay up and take advantage of the quiet night to steal my peace.

My thoughts turned to Björn's companions, Søren and Leif. Apparently, Leif was only three years younger than Björn, although I would have guessed it was more like a decade. Søren was only two years older than Björn, although even at twenty-five he seemed to have lived a lifetime longer than the other two. It was sometimes difficult for me to see age differences for people so young, but perhaps the harsh living of the vikings emphasized these differences more than the softer life of the youth that surrounded me in the future.

Because even to me, Leif was so fresh, his heart and demeanor so pure and unassuming. His cornflower blue eyes always filled with optimism and goodness that seemed to surround him like an aura. Boho girls in Venice Beach would have doted on him... I could just picture him running through the waves with a giant surf board and unassumingly setting hearts ablaze all along the beach.

Björn watched me carefully all day. I knew the change between what he saw last night to today was stark. He didn't ask me for an explanation, and I didn't offer one; I hoped he would simply draw his own conclusions. If he wanted to blame it on woman's troubles, that was fine with me. Valkyries don't have those issues, but I could pretend for his sake.

I should have tried to ease into it somehow, acted less joyful or more withdrawn. But I simply couldn't... I wanted to celebrate my reunion with that missing piece of me as loudly and flagrantly as I could. I settled for humming and working cheerfully.

It would likely take Björn, as stubborn as the oxen that pulled his plow, more time to accept my new, sunnier personality. And that was fine. He shouldn't take it for granted.

In the back of my mind, I was working on a plan, and I needed time to bring it to fruition.

But I needed to bring Søren on board. Leif was clearly already a fan, and Björn begrudgingly appreciated me, if nothing else, for my strength and swordsmanship.

Søren was a different story—the one time I'd seen him in daylight, he was impossible to read. I got zero feedback from him during our terse conversation; I couldn't tell if he was impressed, or interested, or even repulsed. His features were completely neutral, like the best poker professionals in Vegas.

Perhaps Björn thought me ignorant, but I knew the secret they still weren't telling.

There was no way the three of them could pilot that ship alone.

They needed at least one more person, if not three. Especially once laden down with treasures, it would be a heavy, unwieldy craft to steer through the rough landscape of the open water. Larger craft weren't just convenient for holding more men; there was a balance to be struck between being nimble and being sturdy. Björn's boat was toeing the line—with enough men inside, enough weight, but also enough oars, they could be heavy enough *and* fast.

Too few of either and they would get tossed at the first rogue wave.

Either they hadn't calculated correctly, or they were planning on bringing in more crew.

I didn't believe it was the former. Søren was too clever for that, too careful. So I could only conclude they were weighing their options and trying to pick who would join their raiding party.

Obviously, I intended to claim one of those spots.

It would take some planning. Signe had asked Björn about his trip over dinner. Apparently, they were required to attend a planning meeting with the

Jarl next week. Björn would be gone for seven days, which could be enough time, if everything worked according to my plan.

But first, we had to finish their ship.

And I had to show them I was an excellent candidate for their raiding party.

Which started with impressing Søren.

twenty

SØREN

WALKING around in the bright midday sun with a wagon full of stinking animal fat was not my idea of a pleasant time.

I'd been collecting it for months, from every source I could, rendering it in small amounts so as not to be suspicious. If I suddenly accumulated a large amount of tallow, people would question what I needed so much for.

Until we were ready to reveal our plan, I had to make sure no one suspected a thing.

Which meant that some of it had soured. It was just animal fat, after all, and that stuff didn't keep forever.

Once it was boiled down again and coating the

ship, it would be fine; it'd harden and provide a nice, waterproof seal for the planks.

I just didn't expect it to be this unpleasant before we reached that point.

When Leif stopped by and said they'd finished the construction, he had honestly impressed me. He had a tendency to flake off, so I hadn't really taken him at his word he'd show up and work.

Of course, he then confessed that Brenna had assisted, and then I understood. Leif had the heart of a poet, and he was just searching for a woman to write a ballad about. The light in his eyes, the excitement that radiated from him, suddenly made more sense.

I'd never been a romantic, even at his age. Before I asked a woman to devote her life to mine, I intended to have a name I'd earned, recognition, wealth I could offer her. There had been one I was interested in, but she wasn't content to wait for me to make my name first. I refused to wed a woman and leave her and my child without comfort while I took off to seek my fortune.

This season, I was sure, would make all the difference. In Skarde's ship, we could not shine. Despite the accomplishments of many, he only praised himself and a single other when he had the Jarl's ear. To his mind, his entire ship existed to make him wealthy, to help him look good in front of the Jarl. After two seasons of sending more men to Valhalla or whatever gods they worshipped than anyone else in that boat, I would no longer spill my blood for Skarde to suck up to the Jarl.

Of course, Brenna had prevented us from dispatching him, which was both infuriating and fascinating. She didn't know what a bastard he was, so it made sense for her to intervene if her intuition took issue with the scene she found. There was no way we could explain to her in a satisfactory way what a despicable human being Skarde truly was. Then she bested Björn at sword, but didn't want to kill him.

That told me two things: she was both incredibly skilled to have beaten such a large, powerful man, and she had a distinct sense of honor. Both nuggets were fascinating, and I stored them away for later use.

Then, to discover her on Björn's farm seemed like quite a coincidence. Björn explained how she'd come to stay with them, and she certainly seemed dedicated to performing her duties while I'd observed her. She was far heartier than most women of her stature; the plow was difficult to steer, heavy, and straight rows required complete mastery of oxen who were notoriously stubborn beasts and keen to wander whichever way the wind blew.

That she'd essentially completed all three of Björn's fields in three days, with little help from him, was nothing short of miraculous. She'd certainly appeared at exactly the opportune time; Björn was behind on his farming, behind on the boat, and didn't want to leave his sisters without someone he could trust who could defend them properly.

This mysterious woman had appeared out of the storm and, with one broad stroke, solved all of his problems.

I was cautiously curious, but something about her felt off. Just her presence rose the hairs on the back of my neck, alerting me to something out of the ordinary. She was not some regular, unfortunate stranger that washed up on our shore looking to start a new life.

There was more to this story, secrets she was keeping.

And I intended to get answers.

BRENNA

When Søren appeared with his horse pulling a wagon of tallow mixed with piles of raw fat, I honestly didn't know what I was in for. Maybe I didn't know, or maybe I had blocked the memories from my conscious mind.

Either way, I could definitely say now that cooking sour animal fat for sealing a boat was absolutely foul, and I hoped I never had to do it again.

The first part wasn't too bad. Leif had shown up with two large bags of dried moss to fill the cracks between the planks on the ship, and a handful of fragrant pale purple blossoms, which he presented to me with rosy cheeks.

It took me aback at first, but I accepted the gift and his delicate attempts at flirting throughout the day. I placed the flowers in a cup and they soon filled the longhouse with their fragrance. Leif seemed determined to stay by my side, work where I worked, and tried to attend and anticipate my needs.

Which is how he ended up stirring the stinking vat of tallow with me. His shoulder length hair was half-tied today, the golden strands brushing his collarbone while his bare arms and shoulders worked. The youngest, and leanest, of the three, Leif was no light-weight. He appeared slender compared to the other two, but I could appreciate the fine musculature of his form. He'd eagerly offered to take a turn stirring the tallow for me and soon discovered it was far more difficult than expected. When sweat had soaked through patches of his shirt, he opted to dispense with the garment altogether, and I got to enjoy the view.

I'd imagined him as a catwalk model when we first met, but he was far too muscular to fit that mold. Wide, powerful shoulders, keenly developed pectorals lightly dusted with fine golden hair, tapering to absolutely astounding abs that glistened with a sheen of sweat as he worked. I focused on shredding the dry moss and tried not to get caught staring, or drooling, in his direction. The image that kept popping into my mind was Michaelangelo's David. Aside from the curls, I felt as if I were looking at a Norwegian version of the pinnacle of male perfection.

Leif glanced up from his stirring and caught me looking. His cheeks colored under the scrutiny, but held my gaze as if to say, *"Do you like what you see?"* And then it was my turn to blush. To be honest, I liked it very much.

Part of me felt like a dirty old woman. Here I was, thousands of earth years old, ogling a man who had barely lived twenty of those. The comparison was even more disturbing when I considered how sweet and innocent he was, truly. There was a purity to his soul that shone from his eyes, and it drew me in like a moth to a flame. I yearned for that kind of innocence.

Men I'd dated in the last few decades before Odin sent me back had seemed far more worldly, far more jaded, even at Leif's age. They'd already had and lost their first love, grown cynical in the face of global warming and corporate greed and manipulative politicians.

In this world, at this time, Leif was of an age where he should have started a family already, or at least be working toward one.

Truthfully, it was interesting that all three of them were without wives. Life was brutal and short in the viking age, and people here were considered adults at an age when they weren't even paying their own bills in the future I'd left behind. There was something more to these three men than just friends. The spread of their ages, clearly different backgrounds and interests, would seem to make them all unlikely to band together.

And yet, here we were.

Björn and Søren were busily cooking the fat that still needed to be strained, working the delicate process together. We'd set the cook fires up in the dirt patch outside the barn, as close as we dared to avoid setting the entire structure ablaze. Søren, the shortest of the three but by far the most muscular for his size, had his back to me. He held a tightly woven cloth over the pot while Björn poured the cooked fat over it, slowly straining out the bits of animal meat and fur that had still been attached. Björn had also shed his shirt; although he didn't have an impressive display of defined abdominals, it was clear his body was solid muscle. His wide back flexed under the strain of leveraging his giant ladle to pour the liquid slowly through their straining cloth. His body was turned sideways, revealing the sheer girth of his barrel chest and solid core. A slight depression ran down the center of his body from bulging pectorals to his naval, dividing his belly into two solid walls of muscle. As I watched, a trickle of sweat dribbled down his body, appearing below his sandy tuft of chest hair and running the gauntlet of muscles until it soaked into his waistband.

My mouth watered, and I swallowed down the lust that suddenly flared up in my gut. In a different time, a different place perhaps, I would climb that man like a tree. I knew without a doubt he'd never experienced the things I could do to a man... it was easy to see in his stern expression. He hadn't known great sex in his lifetime. *Yet*.

Leif either. I was almost willing to bet he was a virgin. Someone that sweet... I just couldn't imagine him rolling in the hay with the local milkmaid for kicks. He'd be hopelessly in love with the first girl who bedded him, and devoted to her forever.

Søren... there was a depth to him, a darkness. After so many years judging men's souls, and then a thousand years living among them, I could read him plain as day. He was a hardened man at the tender age of twenty-five. Perhaps he'd lost his first love tragically—something had made him the way he was. And yet something told me he would be a fantastic tumble in the sheets.

After the hundreds of lovers I'd had in my lifetime, I could absolutely say I'd experienced it all. Granted, there were some kinks I was simply not interested in throughout the years, but for the most part, I had an impressive list of check marks on my 'been there, done that' list. I enjoyed a wonderful variety, and I usually picked a lover that suited the personality I'd assumed.

My fingers were numb with shredding dried moss, and there was still so much more to do. I amused myself by imagining each of these three in bed. Leif would definitely be the sweet, attentive lover. Eager to please, begging for direction on how to satisfy his partner. Björn would be the more traditional 'get the job done' type. It would take a firm hand, but someone could definitely teach him a few things. And Søren…

A shiver ran down my spine, complimenting the clench in my belly. Søren would not be the gentle, romantic one. He'd be aggressive, commanding… absolutely a take-charge type.

Even as lovers, I imagined them all so differently. My curiosity was growing; I really wanted to know what bound these three together.

And what it would take to bind them to me.

twenty-one

BRENNA

ONCE THEY'D STRAINED the fat and rendered it completely, we mixed it with the tallow Leif had been warming and then filled the smaller pot with my shredded moss. Björn ladled the tallow over it until the pot was once again filled, stirring to incorporate it well, and once it was cool enough, we set to work.

This was definitely the dirty part of the work. The sour meat odor had cooked out of the tallow, so it wasn't nearly as foul smelling. However, the texture of cooling fat mixed with soggy moss was... gross. The grease coated my hands and squished between my fingers with unpleasantly fibrous bits.

One handful at a time, we stuffed every gap in the ship. The four of us worked in silence, each turning to grab another scoop from the pot we'd set in the middle of the boat. Hair that freed itself from my braid tickled my forehead, and I wiped my brow with the back of my wrist, hoping I wasn't smearing fat all over myself.

Even as careful as I tried to be, I somehow ended up with globs of tallow dotting my dress. It was a relief to know I had a second dress to change into, so I could wash this one again… by hand.

Fucking dresses. I longed for buttery soft leggings, tank tops, fitted hoodies and oversized sweaters that sagged off one shoulder while I sipped a giant mug of coffee laden with syrupy sweet creamer…

I'd tried so hard not to wallow in memories of the long-distant future that was now in my past, but sometimes they caught up to me.

Fuck it, it's not like I have anything else to think about. The men worked quietly, occupied by their own thoughts, and I decided to indulge in memories of my favorite moments that wouldn't exist for so many lifetimes. I felt tiny stabs in my chest when I considered them.

Warm, melt-in-your-mouth croissants, served with tiny cups of rich espresso. I pictured myself on a café patio in Paris, springtime, the fragrance of summer blossoms in the air. Strolling the cobblestone streets, the Eiffel Tower in the distance while a street musician played 'La Vie En Rose' for tourists.

The hot, dry markets of Marakesh, spices poured in gravity-defying, rainbow piles on wide shallow plates, their scents filling the air and combining with the mouth-watering fragrance of grilled meat. The clang of my bracelets as I adjust the scarf concealing my hair and face. Stalls filled with colorful silks, embroidered with golden threads in delicate floral patterns. Smoking hookah on satin pillows with a wealthy merchant who offered me piles of riches to join his harem.

The steaming volcanic springs in Iceland, a brilliant aquamarine color against the glimmering snow-covered ground. Bundled in fur and wool, watching dazzling displays of northern lights from the warm circle of Helgi's arms.

The stinging prickle of tears rose in my eyes. I hadn't thought about Helgi in a long time. After I made my way west, escaping the scrutiny of Odin and setting off on my adventure, I traveled around Europe for a few hundred years before I escaped the dark ages and landed on the shores of Iceland. And I'd been happy there.

Helgi was a giant of a man, not unlike Björn. He was strong, and fierce, and proud, and so very good.

And I'd loved him. I'd loved him enough to spend far too many winters in Iceland. I told Helgi I would never change, I could never bear him children or grow old with him; that I could never grow old, period. I told him I could stay only as long as he never asked me why.

And he never did. I stayed with Helgi for nearly thirty years until his heart finally gave out. He wasn't an old man by modern standards, barely in his fifties, but that was a long life for the mid-1300's. I gave him a traditional Viking burial at sea—he descended from Vikings that had settled Iceland and still held firmly to the culture. When his burning ship disappeared on the horizon, I left Iceland and never returned.

That was a dark time for me. I'd given more of my heart to Helgi than I thought possible, and when he died, he took it with him. I vowed from then on to never let another man to get so close I'd break when I lost him.

Because I would always lose them. I would live forever, and they would wither like summer fruit.

Despite my best intentions, I came very close to making that same mistake again and again. In fact, I could tie my depression-fueled benders to leaving behind a lover to whom I was far too attached. As I got older, it got easier; the walls of my heart thickened, and I knew belief in magic and gods had faded. People were far too curious, and no longer worshipped many gods. They wouldn't accept my explanation that I simply wouldn't age without asking questions... at least, that's what I told myself. It was better to not let anyone in again.

Now, with the core of my soul returned to me by my armor, I could revisit these memories without drowning in alcohol. I'd been far too weak to face them as a broken, empty person. Now restored, whole, the memories still ached. But it was a sweet ache, equally sad and happy. I remembered Helgi's boisterous, booming laugh that always made me grin despite how angry I'd been. The cozy home we'd made far away from the village, so there were fewer people to question my astounding youth. Curled up in furs by the roaring fire, still panting from our lovemaking, my face resting on his burly chest.

Helgi had been such a lovely gift in my life, and now that I could think about him with a grateful heart, it was nice to mull over those memories.

I was still lost in my own mind when I reached the prow of the ship and finished stuffing the cracks with sticky lumps of tallow-soaked moss.

Turning, I saw the others were nearly finished as well. Leif's deft fingers were plugging the very last slats on the back of the starboard side, and Søren was at a similar spot on the port side of the stern.

And Björn—Björn, who reminded me so much of Helgi I didn't know how I avoided realizing it this long—Björn was right beside me, watching me with an inscrutable expression.

"Brenna, are you okay?" His face was stern, but his deep blue eyes were concerned. I realized I'd been crying slow, silent tears as I pored over my memories.

"I'm fine." I faked a smile. "Never better."

His eyes narrowed slightly. "It's okay for you to be sad, if that's how you feel. You know that, right? Clearly you've gone through something, and you've lost everything you had. It would make sense for you to be sad from time to time."

My heart throbbed in my chest, and I bit my lip to reign in the emotion threatening to flood me. That's exactly what Helgi would have said.

"Thank you, Björn. I appreciate that you understand. I try not to dwell in the past, but sometimes it creeps up on me."

Björn nodded sagely. "Yes, but our past made us who we are. It's impossible to separate your past from your present or your future. It's part of you. Perhaps it would be easier to accept it and mourn your losses, than to try to forget them." His gaze was filled with meaning, and I remembered that he'd lost both of his parents barely two years ago. If anyone understood the pain of tragic loss, it was this man.

"Perhaps," I agreed softly, lost in the depths of his open, emotion-laden gaze.

Leif's bright voice interrupted our intimate moment. "You guys finished over there?"

Resuming his gruff demeanor, Björn stood and turned away. "Yes, we're finished."

I brushed the tears from my cheeks quickly, then rose to face the others. "What's next?"

twenty-two

BJÖRN

BRENNA CONTINUED TO PUZZLE ME. Her rapid shifts from joy to despair tugged at my heart. Clearly her bright, chirpy exterior hid a well of pain, and she was quite practiced at hiding it.

But she didn't have to.

Given what she'd told us, she'd clearly experienced some dramatic losses in her short life. Her entire family, her village, her home—she'd left them all behind to live a life free from her chieftain's control. We may not know the full story, but we could certainly sympathize with her struggle.

Particularly me. I knew better than most what it felt like to have your family ripped apart, and she knew that.

I wanted her to open up to me, but part of me didn't blame her for withholding. I was never good at drawing people out, as Leif or Signe could do. I stayed within the confines of my own mind, so I was not a great example of opening up to another person. And since sharing first was usually what led to someone else being willing to share, it was rare that anyone opened up to me.

Brenna was full of secrets... I was under no delusion that her sad history was the only one. There was precious little she'd told us compared to the amount she already knew of our plans.

As we set about coating the ship in tallow to seal it completely, I considered how I might delve deeper into the mystery of this woman I'd allowed in my home. Søren and I would leave for Ravndal in two days, and I needed to feel confident that she would protect my sisters and be here when I returned. We'd be planning the summer raids, and I had to know I could leave for weeks at a time and things would be fine here while I was gone.

I knew Signe was astute, and she would tell me if something felt off. What worried me is that I could be gone long enough for things to fall completely into shambles while she had no way to contact me.

Signe, if she weren't broken, could handle things on her own. Even though she preferred to pose with Father's sword to threaten unwanted visitors, she was actually quite good with our mother's weapon that currently collected dust on the wall. I think she left it there out of mourning... since her injury, she hadn't been able to fight with it.

Her fall had happened during our last raid the previous summer, just before autumn, and while it appeared to get better for a while, her leg was rapidly getting worse. I hoped having Brenna here would help her stay off it and perhaps heal again, but unfortunately she'd spent her days helping me get caught up on my work instead.

Guilt flooded my chest; Brenna shouldn't be here helping me tallow this ship. She should be helping Signe with the household duties. She appeared to have knowledge of shipbuilding, as she had done well running the oxen and the plow, and that was why I hadn't argued. Someone who had the skills, let alone the strength, was valuable. Particularly when that person expected no pay for the work. We needed the fields planted so we'd have stores for winter, and we needed the ship finished so I could finally earn my place in front of the Jarl.

Gritting my teeth, I focused on spreading the warm liquid tallow over the boards. There was nothing for it. We needed her here now more. But once the ship was finished, Brenna was going to be attached to Signe's hip. I would make sure they both understood that before I left.

I couldn't allow Signe to suffer any more. Some way or another, I would get her proper help, and that started with the Jarl.

❄

BRENNA

We finished the first coat on the ship before dusk, and Søren bid farewell with a few stern commands on how to keep the tallow for the second coat tomorrow. Leif lingered behind, fixing me with dreamy smiles while he dawdled, until Søren's shout sent him running.

Björn and I had our work cut out for us, first cleaning ourselves of the greasy tallow and then our clothing. With his help to wring, I was able to scrub most of the fat from the fabric without too much struggle.

Once again, Björn carried Signe to her seat at the table and we ate in a peaceful silence.

Signe put up a stern front, but she was pale, exhausted, and looked far older than her thirteen years. It had shocked me when Björn told me the actual ages of his siblings... Astrid I wasn't too far off, but Yrsa and especially Signe I had believed to be much older than they actually were. It saddened me to see these girls who'd grown up far too quickly when their parents died.

In Signe's case, I knew it wasn't all the weight of responsibility. After dinner Björn went out to the barn and I insisted she let me examine her foot. What I saw wasn't good. The purple areas were spreading and darkening. Honestly, it was a miracle she hadn't lost it already. I carefully restored her stocking and met Signe's hopeless eyes.

"I still have the runestones, but I think they stopped working," she whispered.

"Runestones?"

"The healer in the village gave them to me to heal my leg. She told me to keep them with me at all times and the magic would heal me."

She withdrew a small woven bag from her pocket and handed it to me. Inside were a handful of ivory pieces—I assumed bone—with runes carved on one side of each piece.

Oh Signe.

"Signe… magic can only do so much to help these kinds of injuries. You understand that, right?"

She nodded, eyes cast downward, but didn't speak.

I racked my brain for details on what I remembered about viking-era medicine. "Was Björn, or your father, ever wounded in battle?"

Signe's eyes rose to my face. "Yes, many times."

"What kinds of injuries?"

"Cuts mostly, some small and some deep."

"And the deep ones, did your mother have to treat them?"

"Yes. She used a blade heated over the fire to stop the bleeding, then coated them with honey and wrapped them in cloth. She showed me how to do it so I'd be prepared…" she sighed, then added in a lower voice, "to care for my husband."

I knew why this memory was so difficult for her.

As beautiful, and clever, and capable as she was, the likelihood that a man would want a hobbled wife was very low. Vikings expected their women to fight. To defend their homestead while they were gone. A girl who couldn't walk was not an ideal wife.

"So," I encouraged, "you understand that there are some injuries that need help to heal. Have you thought about what I told you? If I can move your bones back into place and we can encourage them to heal by keeping you off your foot, there's a very good chance you'll heal properly. You could walk without a crutch in weeks, Signe. With much less pain, at any rate."

Silent tears tracked down Signe's porcelain cheeks. She collected the runestones and packed them away in their pouch, then restored them to her pocket. "I... I'm afraid it will make it worse," she admitted. "If we try, and then I lose my foot completely, things will be worse."

"Signe, you're already about to lose your foot," I said as gently as I was able. "It's very close and I'm not absolutely certain we can save it. But I know we need to act quickly to still have a chance. I know it's scary, but... I guess the best thing I can tell you is that it can't get much worse, but it could be so much better."

Her body shuddered with quiet sobs, and I wrapped an arm around her shoulders in comfort. She was strong, but she was still just a thirteen-year-old girl facing the genuine possibility of losing her foot. Where I'd sympathized with her before, now my heart lurched with empathetic pain.

The sound of heavy footsteps outside the door broke the spell; Signe brushed her cheeks roughly and eased her leg off my lap.

Björn strode in, pausing when he felt the heaviness of the atmosphere. "Is everything... okay?"

"Yes," I smiled as brightly as I could. "Just discussing how I can help Signe stay off her foot tomorrow."

Björn lifted a single eyebrow, gazing between us with a dubious expression, but eventually he shrugged. "Okay, I think that's best. We should be fine without you tomorrow, Brenna. Perhaps you can also help Yrsa finish planting the vegetable garden?"

"Absolutely." I stood, making a show of stretching and yawning, before I crossed the room and settled onto my own bed-couch platform. "Goodnight, Björn. Goodnight Signe, Yrsa, and Astrid." The little one was already asleep in her nest of pillows beside Signe, but the others rumbled their goodnights. As I waited for sleep to take them so I could sneak out to my armor, I concentrated on how I could convince Signe to let me set her broken ankle.

twenty-three

BRENNA

THE DAY of Björn's departure for Ravndal had arrived, and he kept dallying, finding excuses to fiddle with things while Søren waited impatiently outside. The girls were also outside, waiting to see him off, and I'd remained to help him collect his supplies, but now I'd turned into family counselor.

"Björn, do you doubt my ability to defend your family?" I'd gotten well past the gentle encouragement and was in full-on sass mode. "Remember who you're speaking to," I hinted.

"No, I don't doubt you," he grumbled.

"So what is your issue?"

"I-" he sighed, his eyes tracking around the homestead as he avoided my gaze. "It's just that the last time I left, Signe fell. I wasn't here to help her. I can't help thinking that will happen again."

I rubbed the space between my brows, drawing on myself for more patience. "You do know the difference between that time and this time, don't you?"

He shook his head, cerulean eyes begging me to make it clear.

"The difference is I'm here. Even though you're leaving, the girls are not alone. I am here if they need help. So if you can trust that I am capable of taking care of them, then you can leave knowing that they will be fine while you are gone."

He appeared to have a static expression, but I knew better: I could see his jaw flexing under the neatly trimmed bulk of his beard. Björn's massive hands were picking up small things in the room, worrying them, then replacing them. It was almost comical, if I couldn't hear Søren cursing outside and didn't know the reason he was so concerned.

"Björn." I reached up to grasp each of his massive biceps with my hands, drawing his attention back to myself. "They will be fine. I won't let anything happen to them. Do you trust me?"

His nervous energy stopped, and Björn gazed deeply into my eyes, searching for something within them.

I gazed back at him as steadily as I was able, trying to convey security and trust, strength that he could count on.

Without warning, his massive palms rose to cup my cheeks, and Björn kissed me. It was rough, nothing suave or gentle with his approach. The stiff hairs of his beard tickled my face, prickling the skin below my nose even before his lips touched mine. My heart lurched into my throat, and before I could even kiss him back—before I was even sure I wanted to— he withdrew, gazing intently at me once more. "I trust you," he whispered, then left.

I staggered backward to the bench seat for just a moment, encouraging my head to catch up to my racing heart. What the hell just happened?

BJÖRN

I don't know why I did it. My concern for my sisters and their safety was real, and hardly lust-inducing.

But when I looked into her eyes and read the confidence and sincerity they held, it drew me to her. I had no words, just a single thought that occupied my mind.

I had to know what her lips felt like.

The impulse overcame every other thought in my head and I just acted on it without thought or reason.

Now, of course, as Søren and I trudged to Ravn-dal, a thousand things flew through my brain. Things I should have said, tasks I wasn't sure I'd completed before we left, a list of chores that needed to get done.

But the loudest one, the one that circled back again and again to the forefront of my mind: What did Brenna think?

Was she attracted to me at all? Or was I just a temporary source of food and shelter? Her expression afterward had been pure shock—she certainly didn't give me a clue about her feelings and I didn't stick around to find out.

Coward that I was, I left that kiss hanging in the air while I disappeared for a week.

Truthfully, it was fine. When I returned, if she acted as if it never happened, then I would too. Brenna didn't strike me as the type to lead a man on if she wasn't interested, so I would know how she felt when I returned.

I had far more important things to worry about for the next seven days. Namely: How to get an audience with the Jarl and broach the subject of our raiding party?

Søren was the brains of this operation. I was certain he had plans. However, I also knew I had far more at stake than he did, and we were planning to leverage my family and any goodwill that netted us to pull as many strings as we could. My parents' deaths, my sisters, Signe's condition; all of it could be enough to request an audience with the Jarl.

And then we'd just have to hope he'd be in an indulgent mood.

My mind drifted back to Brenna. Leif had promised to check in on the farm while we were gone. Thinking of the younger man, guilt again filled my heart; I knew he had a crush on Brenna. It was impossible to ignore the glow in his eyes around her. His entire demeanor had shifted, from grieving brother and wayward-minded poet to attentive lover, practically overnight. Eyes always darting in her direction, trying to anticipate her needs and offer her what she needed before she sought it herself, even if it was just a cup of water. Part of me worried he'd press the advantage of Søren and I being gone to make a pest of himself in our absence... and then I remembered there was no competition, implied or otherwise.

Of course, if Leif wanted to pursue her, he should.

And I shouldn't have kissed her. I knew how he felt before I did it. That was not the way brothers treated each other, and our relationship was more important to me than any woman could possibly be.

Søren, Leif, and I had a bond that no one could understand, or break. Resolving to keep that firmly in the forefront of my mind, I extended my stride to catch up to Søren a few feet ahead and engage him in conversation about our strategy for the Jarl.

This was where my head needed to be, and not on Brenna's lips.

No matter how soft they were, and despite the spark I felt between us in our shared breath.

It would never happen again.

twenty-four

BRENNA

SIGNE WAITED until Björn left to tell me what she wanted.

"Brenna?"

"Do you need something?" I was sweeping the packed-dirt floor of debris and tidying the home so Signe wouldn't feel obligated to do it. Yrsa had taken Astrid outside for a walk, and we were alone. Since I wasn't working in the field today, I still wore the soft woolen dress Signe had given me, and it brought a tiny smile to my lips every time I looked at it.

"I want to do it." The words rushed from Signe in a breath, as if she pushed them out before she could change her mind.

It took me a minute to catch up. "Do… what? Oh. Your foot?"

She nodded. "I think now is the best time, while Björn is away. It will be a few weeks before there is much work to do in the gardens. Yrsa can manage it for now. If Björn were here, I don't think he'd let you. But I want to try."

"You're probably right… but are you sure you want to do it without him here to support you? I won't lie to you: it will hurt a good deal. Especially given how swollen and damaged the area is, it won't be easy for me to manipulate everything back in place. I may not get it right on the first try and we might have to work it a few times."

Signe's eyes were wide, and she swallowed with difficulty before she replied. "I can brew some tea to help with the pain. We keep the herbs in the pantry."

"Signe, if you have tea to help with pain, why do you not drink it now?"

"I didn't see a point. If this is the pain I had to live with for the rest of my life, then I needed to get used to it. Besides, it makes me sleepy and I can't sleep while everyone else works."

My heart thumped painfully against my rib cage. This sweet, brave girl, enduring incredible pain because she needed to take care of her siblings. I had to help her.

"Okay. Let's get everything we need and set it this afternoon. We can have Yrsa take Astrid out of the house again… is there an errand you can send them on that will keep them out for a couple of hours? I need to concentrate, and Astrid won't understand what's going on. She may be frightened."

"Yes, I can send them to the river in the hills beyond the farm. There should be some early herbs and wild onions growing that we can have them gather."

"Perfect. I'll get everything I need together." My eyes drifted to the side with concern. "I wish we had someone here to help you through it, though."

Signe sighed, abruptly annoyed. "I'll be fine, I don't need my brother's hand for comfort."

"I know you don't, it's just... if it's really painful, I may need someone to help hold you still so I can finish." I didn't want to scare the girl, but I had to be honest. "We'll just have to do the best we can. I suppose if it becomes too much, you may pass out, and then it won't be a problem since you won't feel anything after that until you wake up."

I meant that to be comforting, but I realized as soon as I said it how it'd sound to Signe.

"Signe, I-"

"No, you're right, that would be better. I'll make the tea really strong," she added in a lower voice.

A knock at the door startled both of us. Signe's eyes turned meaningfully to the swords hung on the wall beside the door, and I took her hint. I pulled my Valkyrian blade from its peg, then opened the door carefully.

Outside, appearing so heartbreakingly beautiful I could have mistaken him for a dream, stood Leif. His hair was down today, parted down the middle and shining like gold in the morning light.

"Hello, Brenna. I promised Björn I'd check in while he was away. I didn't have much to do this morning, so I thought I'd see if there was anything I could help you with?"

Heat rose in my cheeks. "Leif, please come in. I'm not sure we have work to do, but you are welcome to visit."

I moved back to allow him to pass and caught the panicked expression on Signe's face as she hurried to arrange her skirts over her injured foot.

"Signe, it's good to see you," Leif smiled in her direction. "How are you feeling? How is your leg?"

The poor girl's face was beet red. "Oh, it's much better, thank you." Busying herself with the basket of wool beside her, Signe set about spinning it into thread and studiously avoided eye contact.

Leif glanced around the longhouse, rubbing his long-fingered artist's hands together, as if unsure of what to do next. He tucked hair behind one ear, then directed his attention to me.

"So... Björn and Søren will be gone for a week."

"Yes, that is what I understand. They were trying to get an audience with the Jarl, I believe." I cast my eyes meaningfully to Signe and pressed a finger to my lips to clue him in. None of Björn's family knew about the ship.

Leif nodded in understanding, changing the subject. "You've finished plowing and sowing the fields, and just in time. In town, they said we're due for a few days of rain this week. The crops will need it."

While I was curious how vikings actually predicted the weather—my money was on someone who made it their business to collect money for favorable weather reports—the topic wasn't exactly the most stimulating. I made a polite assenting noise and tried to come up with something else that was safe to talk about in front of Signe.

"Leif, I apologize, but I don't know very much about your family. I know you had an older brother. Do you have any other siblings?"

He seized the topic gratefully. "Yes, I have—had— three brothers, actually. Two now, and a sister. Arne is thirteen, close to Signe's age I believe, Gorm is eight, and Tove is two."

Signe flushed deeper at hearing her name mentioned and shifted in her seat as she continued spinning.

"Do you live with your family still?" I wanted to keep this conversation going—I knew nothing about Leif and was genuinely curious. I also wanted as much information as I could gather about Søren, and the first step to getting someone talking was asking about themself.

"Ahem," now Leif looked slightly uncomfortable. "Yes, I do. Only until I can earn my name and start a family," He added quickly. "Hopefully this summer will bring me that fortune."

At his age, most men he knew had already made moves in that direction, if not already settled. He, along with Björn and Søren, were definitely the outliers. Perhaps to him it was embarrassing, but to me... the customs that different cultures held about age had all become moot.

"It must be nice to have that time with your family," I encouraged. "I'm sure they appreciate your help at home."

"Yes," he agreed, relieved. "It is good to help my parents. But they understood when I said I would be here more this week, while Björn is gone."

"I appreciate that, but I'm not sure we have much for you to do. As you said, the fields are plowed and planted, Yrsa does an excellent job tending the animals, and between Signe and I we can manage the household duties."

"Surely there is something I can help you with? Even if it's just fetching water or cooking, I am happy to do it. Anything to provide comfort while Björn is away."

A thought popped into my head, and I glanced at Signe, whose eyes rose to mine in alarm. "Leif, how loyal are you to Søren and Björn?"

The younger man's clear blue eyes clouded with confusion. "We're like brothers... I'd do anything for them. Why?"

"If I were to ask you to help me with something, knowing Björn may not agree, would you do it?"

A flash of surprise crossed Leif's face. "I don't understand. Why would you want to do something Björn wouldn't agree with?"

"It will help him in the long run, but he may not

realize it yet. When he returns, he may be angry at first. But it's a good thing, although it will be difficult."

Signe's face had drained of blood, and she shook her head at me, pleading silently.

Leif glanced in her direction, weighing her reaction to my statement, then turned his gaze to me. "If you say it will be a good thing for Björn, I will help you. Now, will you tell me what this thing is that you need my help for?"

twenty-five

LEIF

WHEN BRENNA TOLD me what she intended to do, I was certainly surprised. I also understood why she said Björn wouldn't like it. He was fiercely protective of his sisters, and what she was planning was dangerous. It could go completely the wrong way, and Signe would lose her foot completely.

However, Brenna seemed to know what she was speaking about, and she was completely confident that Signe was about to lose her foot, anyway. If the result of inaction was the worst consequence that could arise from the action, then it made the most sense to at least try.

What she asked of me was challenging. Provide comfort, sure. Distract Signe while Brenna worked?

Absolutely. Hold her down if she started kicking? That one scared me more than I cared to admit.

I listened while Brenna described what she needed, then left with the agreement to return in a few hours. We definitely had extra cloth at home I could take, old fabric from clothes too worn to function any more. The other things she needed, well... I would do my best.

I enjoyed woodcarving as an art form—I was nearly finished with the figurehead for the ship—but making practical pieces for a function was not my strong suit. That was more Björn's strength.

But for Brenna, I would try.

By the time I returned to Björn's farmstead, a bundle under one arm, I could feel the adrenaline coursing through my body.

I'd never heard of such a thing as Brenna described. If she could actually heal Signe's leg, it would be nothing short of a miracle. Which wouldn't surprise me; Brenna was something other than an ordinary girl. It was clear enough for anyone to see. She was hauntingly beautiful, with skin that seemed to glow in the sunlight. She also knew things, spoke about things I'd never heard of. And the glimmer of soul in her eyes was entrancing... I felt as if I could see entire worlds in their clear pewter depths.

More than just my curiosity and trepidation about how Brenna would fix Signe's ankle, my concern about my role in this process was enough to send butterflies through my stomach. Signe was like a younger sister to me, and I hated to see her in pain. It would take everything I had to hold her in place while she suffered, even knowing the result would be that she could be healed.

Fervently, I whispered a prayer to Frigg that everything went better than Brenna feared, the tea worked so Signe felt no pain, and I could provide comfort by holding her hand and nothing more. When I reached the door, I drew in a deep breath, then knocked on the weathered grey wood.

"Come on in, Leif!" Brenna's muffled voice called from inside.

Well, here goes nothing.

BRENNA

Leif returned with a bundle of ragged pants, perfect for creating strips to help bind the ankle once I set it.

He'd also done an admirable job fashioning the splints I'd asked for. Padded on the inside with wads of soft wool, he'd hollowed two pieces of wood slightly, allowing for them to curve around her leg more comfortably. She'd need proper crutches after a few days—I was determined to keep her laying down as much as possible to make sure the adjustment took —so perhaps I could have him work on those once we got past this part.

Signe was quiet, likely terrified but keeping her fears to herself. She'd brewed her tea and was sipping it; the cup shook from her trembling fingers, causing the liquid to splash over the side at first. Frustrated with herself, she blew across the top to cool it and took a large gulp, then continued until she'd drained the cup.

I laid out my gathered materials on a chair at the long wooden table and set a pillow and a cushion on the tabletop.

Turning to Signe, I asked, "Are you ready?"

The tea appeared to have taken effect; she looked calmer, her eyelids drooping. When she stood, Leif rushed forward and scooped her up. Signe looped her arms around his neck and smiled up at him as he carried her to the table.

Yep, the drugs were definitely working.

Once she settled on the cushion, Leif glanced my way, unsure of what to do. His eyes were filled with concern for Signe, and he compulsively tucked the strands of golden hair behind his ear.

"Just have a seat next to her and hold her hand for now," I encouraged. "Hopefully it won't be too terrible and it'll be over quickly."

Relieved, Leif sat and grasped Signe's limp fingers, then spoke to her in a low voice. Her clear blue eyes were glassy, and she gazed at Leif's face as if he were some kind of vision she wasn't sure existed.

As gently as I was able, I eased Signe's slipper and stocking off. The bruising had spread even more; now close to half her foot was purple.

Concern rose in my throat, and I tried to swallow it down. "Signe, let me know if you feel anything."

I dragged my finger along her heel, across the sole of her foot, then lightly squeezed each toe. She responded to each touch, and I sighed in relief. For now, at least, she still had sensation in her whole foot.

There was still hope.

Pressing my fingers to different areas of her foot, then her ankle, I watched her carefully for reactions indicating pain. She winced from time to time, but nothing showing intense pain.

"Leif—give her the other thing, please."

His cornflower blue eyes flashed to my face with trepidation, then pulled the item from his pocket and handed it to Signe.

"Signe, I want you to put that between your teeth and bite on it. Sometimes when people are in a lot of pain, they clench their jaw; they can clench hard enough that it would damage their teeth. This will help."

Signe's glass-eyed gaze left Leif's face. She placed the stick in her mouth, and Leif clasped her hand, whispering to her with a tender smile on his lips.

His eyes turned to me, and I knew what he was saying without words: Let's get this over with.

twenty-six

BRENNA

DRAWING ON ALL OF MY CENTURIES'
experience, I probed more deeply at Signe's ankle.
She grunted but didn't move.

From what I felt, she had a slightly displaced fracture in the bottom part of her lower tibia, also known
as a pilon fracture. The area was incredibly swollen,
but if I could manipulate the piece in the correct place
and get her to stay off of it, it had a good chance of
healing. There didn't appear to be any ligaments
broken or out of place. The ankle was so much worse
than it needed to be because she refused to sit still.

I glanced up at Leif once more, nodded grimly,
and he met my eyes with encouragement before
turning to Signe with a huge grin. As he launched

into a story, I took a deep breath, felt for the displaced piece of bone, and squeeze it back toward Signe's tibia. The bloodcurdling scream that ripped from her lips tore at my heart, but it quickly devolved into sobs as I released the pressure. Leif pressed his forehead to hers and ignored Signe's powerful grasp on his hand. It couldn't have been comfortable; his fingers were turning purple. However, he continued whispering encouragement to her, and she held on.

There was a good deal of fluid in the way, but I was fairly certain I'd replaced the piece. Healing wasn't my strong suit. There were some among the Valkyrie who were gifted in the art, and I wasn't one of them. However, I called on my minuscule abilities now, drawing on the fortification I'd felt since receiving my armor. Heat warmed my chest, and as I concentrated, trickled through my arms, then down to my fingertips as I wrapped them around Signe's ankle. I could feel the anger of the swollen, abused flesh. The pain of the entire area radiated through my hands, now that I was openly communing with her spirit.

However, I felt the pumping of blood, the powerful flow of oxygen in and out. I concentrated further, and I could feel the rightness of the bones— the piece that had caused her so many troubles was back in the correct position. Focusing all of my energy on that bone fragment, I pushed what little healing ability I had into encouraging the bones to begin knitting together.

Sweat broke out across my forehead; it took a

great deal of power, power I didn't have, to heal a bone. The most I could do was infuse energy into the wound and encourage it to heal itself faster. If I could get it knitting together, wrap it up tight and keep it stabilized, and for Odin's sake, keep her from walking on it, we might be successful.

When I felt myself growing weak, I cut off the river of valkyrian energy and gazed down at Signe's ankle. It was perhaps too soon to tell, but the area already seemed less purple, slightly more red, than before.

Glancing up to check on my patient, I caught Leif gently stroking strands of hair away from Signe's sweaty brow. Her eyes were closed, her hand limp in his grasp.

For some reason, knowing I'd caused this tough girl enough pain to knock her out caused me more grief than I felt happiness knowing I'd helped her.

Leif glanced in my direction and caught my stricken expression. "It's okay. I don't think she succumbed to the pain. Most likely to the dream tea. She was peaceful when she fell asleep." His eyes were luminous with adoration, and he tipped his chin toward Signe's foot. *Let's finish this.*

I nodded, clenching my teeth and reaching for the materials I'd collected. First, I wrapped her foot and ankle as tightly as I dared with strips of fabric. I didn't want to make them so tight it was uncomfortable or cut off blood flow, but they could help reduce additional swelling and prevent the bones from moving around.

After that, I used additional strips to attach the splints Leif had brought me to either side, ensuring the entire area was bound and unable to move or twist.

Once I was satisfied with my handiwork, I had Leif help me move Signe to her bed and gently propped her foot up on pillows. I caught Leif's eye and tipped my head toward the door, and we left together so Signe could rest.

I felt drained, but happy. I'd been able to use my gifts, such as they were, to actually help someone who deserved it. And I was reasonably confident that it would heal. It might never be exactly as it was, but it could heal well enough she'd be able to walk without a crutch at the very least.

Without really discussing it, Leif and I walked quietly toward the barn. Yrsa and Astrid were still away fetching herbs, and aside from the occasional animal noise, the homestead was surprisingly quiet.

"That was..." Leif began, "incredible. I've never seen something like that. Where did you learn it? How did you know what to do?"

"Where I come from, people have dedicated life-times to studying the body. I picked up a few things."

"Incredible," he said again. "Do you think it'll heal?"

"I think there's a very good chance. I'll monitor it, and it's important that Signe doesn't walk on it until it's healed. She's such a stubborn thing, I'm not sure how I can convince her to stay off that foot."

"I'm happy to come over and help," he offered. "I

told my parents I'd promised to look after Björn's sisters. They already expect me to be here while he's gone."

"That would be very helpful, thank you."

"I'd do anything for you, Brenna. Just ask, and if it's in my power, I will do it. If it's not, I will find a way."

That wasn't the statement I was expecting; surprise warmed my cheeks. Pausing in our steps, I turned to him for clarification. "Leif, I-"

His deft artist's fingers cupped my cheeks with the lightest of touches, and with absolute adoration in his eyes, Leif moved in and pressed his lips to mine.

My first thought was the irony of having two men, men who considered themselves brothers, kiss me on the same day. *Leave it to me to become an instant source of problems between men who previously had none.*

However, then my thoughts returned to the moment. Leif's lips were angelically soft, his hands trembling against my skin. He remained for a moment, and I was absolutely frozen in place. Then, with a shivering breath, he leaned back and gazed into my eyes with intent. "I'm sorry if I surprised you, I just… needed to do that."

My heart was racing, and I waited a moment to gather my thoughts before I dared to speak. "You surprised me," I admitted. "Why did you kiss me, Leif?"

"I wanted you to know how I felt." His hands migrated from my cheeks to my shoulders. "I've never met a woman like you, Brenna. I've never been inclined to set up a homestead or start a family. Then, suddenly, you appear and it's all I can think about."

The guilt was intense; my stomach flopped sickeningly in my gut. "Leif, I'm not the kind of girl you build a home and family with." As attractive as I found him, I couldn't lead him on. He was a man who deserved a fresh-faced girl who adored him and would happily manage a homestead with a baby on one hip while he went off to raid. Not some bitter harpy who'd ruined more good boys like him than he could possibly imagine.

Leif was taken aback for a moment, then recovered. "That doesn't matter to me, Brenna. I want you, whatever you are. Just as you are."

His sincerity drove a dagger through my heart at the same time it drew a sarcastic chuckle from my lips. "You know nothing about me, Leif. You don't know what I am. How could you possibly want something you don't know or understand?"

"It doesn't matter," he shrugged. "I know how I feel. The rest is details that don't matter. Don't get me wrong, I want to know everything about you. But nothing you have to say could change the way I feel."

The dramatic declaration of love was so endearing, so innocent, and so misguided. The things I could tell this man, barely more than a boy, but I couldn't bring myself to say a word of the truth.

Instead, I told him, "You'd be better off forgetting those feelings, Leif. I'm no good for you. I'm no good for anyone." Sighing, I turned to go back toward the house. "You should go home, thank you for your help today, I know Signe felt much better with you there."

Doubt clouded Leif's eyes, but he schooled his striking features into a smile anyway. "It was my pleasure to help. I will be back tomorrow, Brenna. Just so you know, I don't agree with you—you're far too good for me, but I'm going to keep trying. Perhaps at some point we'll meet in the middle. Have you seen the other single men in this village? Time is on my side." With a cheeky wink, he turned and strode down the path toward home.

Oh, Leif. I wish I could tell you that time is most definitely not on your side.

twenty-seven

BRENNA

TRUE TO HIS PROMISE, Leif arrived at our doorstep shortly after sunrise, and only left when all the chores were done and we had eaten supper.

Thanks to his presence, Signe was a model patient. She accepted his help to move as she needed it, allowing him to carry her from her bed to the table, or closer to the fire. I checked her ankle daily, using my renewed energy to press more healing encouragement into the broken bones and stimulate the blood flow. Every night I snuck out after the others were asleep to don my armor and enjoy the weightlessness of flight, restoring the power I'd drained during the day.

And Signe was healing, quickly. Much more

quickly than she would have without magical intervention.

Leif made no more declarations of his intent to
make me his bride, but he seemed intent on showing
me exactly how valuable he could be as a mate. He
doted on Signe as if she were his own, telling her
jokes and bringing her little gifts.

If I reached for something, he was there to hand it
to me. If I carried something, he offered to take it or
help me with the load.

The attention was endearing, and very much
appreciated, given that Signe could not help. She did
minor tasks that didn't require her to move, but I
relied heavily on Leif's help to keep the household
running. He helped with a lovesick grin on his face,
beaming whenever I met his eye.

Guilt bubbled in my belly. I shouldn't accept his
help. Allowing him to be here, to give me his time
and attention, was only encouraging him. And I knew
I'd only break his sweet, innocent heart.

To make matters worse, I soon realized there was
another heart at stake in this equation.

Signe hardly seemed bothered about her foot, or
her work, when Leif was around. Instead, her focus
was entirely on him. She fussed with her hair in the
morning; her face lighting up when he arrived to
break his fast with us. Her eyes tracked him around
the longhouse, watching him possessively when he
stepped away to help me with something, then
beaming with pleasure when he returned to attend to
her needs. She started to need more and more of his

help, to fetch her something from the other room, or carry her around. When Leif left for the night, Signe sighed and gazed dreamily at the fire until she lay back and fell asleep.

This was a disaster in the making, and I did not know how to stop the train wreck I could see coming a mile off.

Leif was hopelessly crushing on me, and Signe on him. Even when he eventually got over me, he wouldn't be interested in thirteen-year-old Signe, despite her outward maturity. He saw her as a younger sister, his feelings toward her very familial. She was the little sister of his brother, and he was protective and caring, as a big brother should be.

And that was all.

But I could read the young woman's dreams on the girl's face. To her, Leif was a knight in shining armor—or a viking with the favor of the Jarl, since knights weren't even a thing yet in the 800's—who had come to her rescue at her darkest hour. He held her, and gave her affection, and he was hotter than any man in the viking ages had any right to be.

If I were Signe, I'd certainly have a crush on him, too.

But I wasn't, and unfortunately Leif's admiration was focused on my ancient, jaded ass.

Valkyries were legendary for our beauty; it was hardly surprising he was attracted to me. But I knew he wasn't the type to fall for a pretty face. Certainly, there were plenty of pretty faces around to choose from.

Leif was a far deeper, more intuitive soul. An old soul. He needed someone with the depth of character that most girls his age lacked.

A depth of character that Signe was far too young to understand.

And so I stewed in the storm that was brewing between Leif, myself, Signe, and inevitably Björn when he came back. He would either be furious at Leif for drawing the interest of his little sister, or furious at him for being oblivious to her interest and inevitably breaking her heart.

To be honest, there were a great number of things likely to draw Björn's ire when he returned tomorrow.

I suspected he would be angry when he found out I'd set Signe's foot. He'd never directly forbidden me from doing it, but it was risky and we'd waited until he left... decidedly sneaky.

Then there was the matter of Björn having kissed me... I still didn't know what that meant, or what he intended.

My stomach churned with misgivings. No matter how many things went well, there was bound to be something that exploded on all of this. I could feel it coming like the electricity of an approaching storm in the air.

To top it all off, I had yet to get to know Søren, or really even have a decent conversation with the man. I knew he was the leader of this little pack, and if I were to join them, I'd need his approval. How on earth I was supposed to win it, I had no idea.

After Leif left, I checked Signe's foot once more.

When I pulled away the wrappings, a significant portion of the purple bruising had faded to yellow and green. Her flesh was hot to the touch, but not red or shiny indicating any sort of infection or additional swelling. It just showed the blood was flowing well and healing the area at an astronomical rate.

I still didn't want to move it—the bones needed more time to knit together—but I needed to keep infusing my healing energies into the wound.

Wrapping my fingers around the area, I reached out with my senses to the fragmented bone. Sure enough, I could feel the concentration of energy that was focused around the break, and the tenuous connections that had been growing between the two pieces. It was working.

Pulling the energy from my core to my fingertips, I pressed as much as I could through my skin to hers, directing it to continue healing her injury.

Signe sat completely still; she trusted me implicitly now, having marveled at the improvement before her eyes.

When I breathed deeply and withdrew my hands, reaching to replace the wrappings, she asked, "What are you doing?"

"I'm wrapping your leg to keep it from moving," I answered mildly, focused on my task.

"No, I mean, when you place your hands on me and hum like that, what are you doing? Are you praying?"

I hadn't realized I was humming. My pulse quickened, and I rushed to answer her question as nonchalantly as I could. "Yes, I am praying to Frigg to help you heal."

"I didn't think Frigg was concerned with injuries."

"You're right, she's ordinarily not. But I figured it couldn't hurt."

"You do it every night." Her shrewd blue eyes observed my reaction. She hadn't taken the tea for pain today, and her senses were sharp.

"Yes, and your foot is healing very well. So I'd say it's working." I grinned at her as I finished affixing the splints. "I think if you stay at this rate, we might get you up and moving around soon. You still can't walk on it," I reminded her sternly, "but we might give you a little more freedom. I'm sure you're tired of Leif carrying you around."

Now it was Signe's turn to be coy. "Oh, I don't mind as much anymore. And if it's helping my foot to not be walking on it, then I can bear a bit longer."

I smiled indulgently. If I were Signe, I would definitely play up an injury in order to be carried around by a man like Leif.

"Well, Leif and I have a surprise for you tomorrow, and your brother will be back tomorrow as well!"

Signe made a non-committal noise and went back to her work. I smiled once more to myself and looked forward to the moment she fell asleep and I could sneak out to my armor.

BJÖRN

The week away had been too long. Try as I might, I couldn't stop my mind from circling back to Brenna.

Sometimes it was just images of her my mind had captured, pushing the plow or wiping an arm across her forehead. Sometimes my brain dredged up things she'd said, wondering if I'd perhaps responded the wrong way when she went quiet after I spoke.

Often, it was the moment I'd felt the insane need to kiss her, remembering every exquisite detail of that second, frozen in time, locked in my mind forever.

Followed by the thousand worries that had plagued me since.

I'd resolved to put it out of mind as soon as we left, and focus on the monstrous tasks at hand.

I'd failed miserably.

We'd succeeded in our mission, to a degree. Søren had secured a begrudging acceptance from the Jarl that, if our village had two ships, we might have two raiding parties this summer instead of one, and that he might lead one.

Of course, it seemed completely in vain because there were not two ships, so it was nothing for him to promise it.

But we knew, as they did not, that we had a ship ready to go.

Now, as we reached the end of our long two-day

hike back home, I was becoming increasingly nervous.

Nervous about how we'd get the craft to the water without the other oxen teams we'd planned on.

Nervous about how my sisters and my farmstead had fared in my absence.

And nervous about how Brenna would act when I returned. I told myself if she pretended we had not kissed, then I would pretend so as well.

I hoped I wasn't lying to myself about my ability to do that. I'd been so worked up about it this entire week, I was sincerely beginning to doubt I could.

I wasn't the type to doubt myself, but something about this woman kept drawing it out of me.

I still didn't know if that was a good thing or a bad thing.

Then there was the matter of Leif. If he was intent on pursuing Brenna, did I still wish to make a claim, if she seemed interested? Or would it cause strife between us that didn't need to exist?

Once again, my dominant emotion was guilt. Guilt that I was still thinking about Brenna long after I'd told myself to let her go because Leif obviously wanted her.

But if she didn't want him...

As much as I knew worrying didn't help, I couldn't stop myself from chewing over the same problems again and again during the trip.

It was a long journey, but we were almost home.

And then the truth would be revealed.

twenty-eight

BRENNA

ONCE AGAIN, Leif arrived first thing in the morning.

And this time, he brought another gift.

The crutches I had described to him, that I had requested he make for Signe. For homemade, they were a reasonably good approximation of a 'modern to the twenty-first century' crutch. The top was a cross-piece, wrapped in leather stuffed with soft wool. The crutches were each constructed of a single piece of wood, just the right length for Signe's body. He'd crafted a handle to each, down the correct length of the crutch for her hands to grasp, also wrapped in wool and pieces of soft suede.

Leif's eyes were positively glowing with excitement when I met him outside. "What do you think?"

"Leif, they're perfect. I think this will be exactly what she needs. I'll have to teach her to balance on them, but then she'll be able to move around and keep her foot off the ground so it can continue to heal."

"It's truly miraculous, what you've done," he offered seriously. "She was going to lose that foot; no one would argue that. Now she's looking at maybe being able to walk on it normally one day soon."

I swallowed down the emotion that rose in my throat. Damn armor had softened my heart. There were some advantages to being the cold-hearted, soulless bitch I'd become during my millennium without my Valkyrian armor. One being it was nearly impossible to make me cry.

Now, of course, I seemed to tear up every time the wind blew. "Thank you, Leif. I just did what I could to help someone deserving."

"So... what makes you think you are not also deserving?"

"What?"

"You told me you are no good for anyone, but as far as I can see, you are good, and you are deserving."

Heat flooded my cheeks. "It's not the same thing, Leif. You are deserving of more than I can give you."

"Once again, I disagree. Shouldn't I be the one who decides what I deserve?"

"Leif..."

"It's okay, we can talk about it another time. Just

think about it, Brenna. I'm still not giving up that you'll come to your senses. But for now, why don't we go show Signe what we've made her?"

I knew we were in trouble when I saw how Signe's eyes glowed as Leif presented her the gift. Even though he clearly stated the crutches were my idea, she had eyes only for Leif. At one point he even flushed with embarrassment under the intensity of her admiration, and abruptly excused himself.

Signe turned to me in confusion, and I moved in to help her navigate the crutches, demonstrating how to support her weight on the handles, not the piece under her arms, and use them in sync to swing her body and move with only one foot.

It took a few tries, but she started to get the hang of it.

"Very good, Signe! It'll take a bit to get used to it, and your hands will get tired, but this will help you get around much easier. Would you like to go outside and test them out with more space to move?"

"Let's do it," she grinned.

I guided her carefully through the doorway, and then she really let loose. Yrsa and Astrid, who'd been outside playing, ran over to join the fun and a game of chase took shape. Signe quickly realized her crutches gave her a powerful advantage compared to the gait she'd had before, and the girls squealed with delight and tore off in a different direction whenever she got close.

I'd never seen Yrsa this carefree, her serious little face replaced with sheer joy, cheeks ruddy with exertion. Signe was laughing, delighted with the freedom of movement, and Astrid was absolutely giddy with having two playmates.

I stood and watched this little scene play out, arms crossed over my chest and heart full.

It was at that moment Björn and Søren returned.

At first, the huge man's countenance was terrifying. I'd forgotten how big he was, and he glared at the three girls playing, then at me, and demanded in a harsh voice, "What is going on here?"

The girls immediately stopped, their laughter dying off as they stared with trepidation at their hulking beast of a brother.

Søren's clever, predatory eyes traveled from Signe's flushed face to the crutches under her arms, down to her heavily wrapped foot. His mouth didn't move, but he stared accusingly in my direction.

I swallowed, then jutted my chin. "I set Signe's broken ankle, and asked Leif to make her the crutches so she could get around while it heals."

Storm clouds broke out in Björn's eyes. "What do you mean, you set her ankle?" He asked in a low, dangerous tone, striding up to me menacingly and stopping inches from where I stood.

"I moved the broken piece of bone back into place, and have kept it wrapped and stabilized so it can heal." No need to add anything about the extra boost from Valkyrian magic.

"Signe!" Björn shouted, without his gaze ever leaving mine. I held his glare, and returned it with one of my own.

Signe crutched over, her body swinging smoothly in my peripheral vision.

"What did she do to your foot?"

Signe was not intimidated. "She fixed it, Björn. It's so much better, you wouldn't believe it. It barely hurts any more, and Brenna said in a few weeks-" She was cut off when Björn scooped her up under her arms, forcing her to drop her crutches as he swung her around.

His face transformed from barely contained fury to absolute joy in a split second. Signe laughed, at ease now that her brother was happy, and allow him to set her gently back on her good foot. Björn stabilized her while I grabbed the crutches she'd dropped and returned them to their owner. Signe grinned and crutched off to play with her sisters.

Björn's attention returned to me. "Brenna, I can't thank you enough. I..." he paused, apparently lost for words, then pulled me roughly to his body and kissed me. This time the whole of his hand cupped the back of my head, and my heart stuttered erratically. My knees went weak, my arms wound their way around his neck, and I kissed him back.

"Brenna?" Leif's confused voice sent my heart dropping like a stone to my stomach.

I pulled away from Björn, the guilt crashing like the coming tide over my chest. "Leif, I-"

"No, I get it," his hurt expression hardened, and he glared between Björn and I. "You're not good enough for *anyone*, but Björn you're apparently good enough for. Or did you mean no one else is good enough for *you*?"

With a look of pure loathing, Leif turned on his heel and tore off down the path back to the village.

Signe's eyes followed him, forlorn, and even Björn looked embarrassed.

Søren's clever gaze traveled among the remaining party, and sighed. "I think it's time we had a talk."

twenty-nine

SØREN

I'D SUSPECTED during our trip that Björn was hiding feelings for Brenna. I just didn't realize that Leif was falling head over heels for the girl while we were gone.

This certainly complicated things.

The one thing we absolutely couldn't do was to let a woman get between us now. We needed to be a solid team, a unit, and in order for my plan to work...

We needed to put an end to this quickly.

Björn sent the girls back inside to prepare our midday meal, and Brenna, Björn, and I walked up to the barn. It was the safest place to avoid being overheard.

We settled onto some crates in the loft, and my

eyes tracked between the two of them in absolute silence.

Björn's eyes were on his hands; he rubbed them palm-to-palm repeatedly, his fair hair partially concealing his face.

Brenna sat stiffly, arms crossed, and staring above our heads out into the larger portion of the barn where the ship waited. I wasn't sure if it was a trick of the light, or perhaps just that we hadn't seen her for a week. However, she was, impossibly, even more beautiful than I remembered. Shimmering, silvery-blonde hair, skin that seemed to gleam with vitality, and deep, soulful eyes the color of storm clouds. In a neat woolen dress instead of ragged work clothes, she couldn't be more different from the she-demon that interrupted our fight that first night.

I understood why both Leif and Björn wanted her. Even I was drawn to her in a way I couldn't explain. I'd found women attractive before, but not enough that I'd lost sight of my goals. I could still look away from her angelic face without too much struggle… but she tempted me.

"So…" I began, glancing between them both once more. "It seems we have some things to discuss."

Brenna's eyes dropped to my face, and she stared boldly back at me. "What exactly do you think there is to discuss?"

"Whatever is going on between you and Björn, and why it upset Leif."

"I don't see why that is any of your business."

"Something you need to understand is everything

212

that happens with Leif, or Björn, or their families, is my business. Anything that affects the harmony of our brotherhood is my business. And you have certainly upset that harmony in a very short time."

"Look, Leif told me he had feelings while you were gone, and I told him he should save his feelings for someone that deserved him. This one..." she gestured at Björn, "well I have no idea what's going on here."

"You don't believe you deserve Leif's affections?" I kept my tone light, but this statement made me extremely curious. She was hinting at a background we knew nothing about, and I certainly wanted to know more.

She sighed, rubbing a hand over her elegant brow. "Leif is a good man with a pure heart, and he deserves someone just as pure as he is. That is not me."

"What kind of purity do you think you're lacking?"

Brenna leveled a disbelieving glare at me, meeting my eyes with sarcasm. "Every kind."

"I don't know about lacking purity," Björn interrupted, "and I admit I had my doubts about you at the beginning. But since you've been here, you've shown nothing but hard work, integrity, and a generous heart. I put no value on purity as a moral if it does not encompass these things."

Björn's statement said more to me than he probably realized, and I paused to consider his words. That was high praise for Björn, who rarely offered an opinion on anything. I told him he needed to offer his sisters, particularly Signe, more praise and encouragement, so they didn't turn into female versions of Björn. He said he'd work on it.

But this praise for Brenna... it betrayed the depth of his feelings for her as clearly as Leif's declaration apparently had already.

I needed to stop it before it got any worse, and while I knew it was the right thing to do, I winced internally before I said the words.

"And what of Skarde?"

Björn's face turned sharply to me, his bright eyes questioning. "What of him?"

Brenna's storm cloud gaze had also shot to my face, and her eyes widened in horror.

"You remember how we met Brenna, don't you?" I pursued this conversation, internally damning myself to the underworld for what I was about to do.

"Yes, the woman almost killed me. But she spared my life, and you reminded me I had too much to do here to let her send me to Valhalla."

"Did you stop to wonder what happened after we left? Where Brenna went... who she went with? Perhaps that is what she's referring to when she comments about lacking purity."

Björn's gaze hardened, and his face turned slowly to Brenna. "I decided it was not my concern, and if she chose not to tell me, then I didn't need to know."

Brenna's wide eyes softened as she stared at Björn, clearly surprised and touched that he chose not to pass judgment on her.

My next words were bound to change that.

"Well, I can't say I went seeking the information so much as heard Skarde declaring it proudly in the village-"

"Søren—Please stop. I will tell him." Brenna's clear grey eyes darkened, and she glanced once at her feet before raising her chin proudly, refusing to be ashamed. "I slept with Skarde. I was stuck here without family, without hope, with nothing to my name except my sword. I needed shelter, and I don't regret my decision. There was certainly no one else out that night offering me a place to stay." Her eyes darted coldly to my face. "Perhaps, if you all were the honorable men you claim to be, you ought to have offered me shelter."

Her last comment sent a twitch to the corner of my mouth. I'd intended to shame her, anger Björn, and drive a wedge between them. Instead Brenna refused to be shamed, for which I found my respect for her growing.

However, my mission was successful with Björn. The dark red crept up the sides of his face, coloring his skin and revealing his emotions without him having to speak a single word.

"Skarde." The word was a soft, dangerous statement. A promise of pain and retribution.

And Brenna was still unrepentant. She didn't know.

It was time to throw a bit more fuel on this fire. "Yes, apparently Skarde has been bragging throughout the village that you were beaten by a small, nameless girl who came out of the night like a ghost. Also, that she happily pleasured him in a dozen different ways he'd never experienced, raved about his prowess in bed, and promised to return with every full moon because she loved his dick so much."

Brenna stifled a chortle; despite the seriousness of this issue to Björn—which she clearly recognized—the fact that she couldn't help a surprised laugh upon hearing what Skarde was bragging confirmed his version of events was not entirely accurate.

"I wouldn't say it went exactly that way," she offered slowly.

I didn't reply. I simply waited for Björn to respond, which I knew would happen once everything boiled to the top.

"You still don't get it, do you?" His gaze rose to Brenna's face, the full force of his fury now on display. "There was more than one reason we wanted to kill Skarde that night, that I still want to drain the life from him with my bare hands. He killed my parents, Brenna. We can't prove it, but we know it was him. Not only is he a worthless piece of shit excuse for a human being, he has no problem with killing people that are in his way, using others to get his way, and in summary he cares about nothing and no one but himself."

Brenna looked horrified. "Björn, I'm sorry, I didn't know-"

"Of course you didn't. You showed up here, stuck your nose in the middle of a fight you knew nothing about, and slept with the first man who offered you a bed." Rising to his feet, Björn towered over the smaller woman, who remained seated. "If you had appeared and simply asked for help, we would have gladly given it to you. Not everything has to be earned at the tip of a sword—we have more than enough space here to help a stranded woman.

"And despite how you attacked us that night without even knowing what the fight was about, I still opened my home to you. You've worked hard and earned your keep, I won't deny that. But this," he gestured angrily, "with the one man I truly hate. I can't."

Apparently at a loss for words, Björn descended from the loft and left Brenna staring after him in anguish. I remained, and I was torn: Björn was disgusted with Brenna, and Brenna would not have Leif, which solved our romantic entanglement. I was pleased that worked out so neatly.

However, there was also a small stab of guilt in my heart. While I'd done it for the good of the people I loved, I couldn't comfort myself completely with that knowledge as I watched the tears trickle down Brenna's perfect cheek.

I'd set out to hurt her, deliberately, and I accomplished my mission.

Just in time to realize I also felt something for this woman.

Life was certainly full of irony.

thirty

BRENNA

SOMEHOW, in the last couple of weeks, I'd pushed Skarde to the back of my mind. The men hadn't mentioned their conflict again, and I hoped it was one of those things that men fought about and then set aside as more pressing matters came up.

Now, however, I realized I was simply deluding myself. There was much more to this story than I knew, and I'd lived in blissful ignorance.

Until now.

Søren sat quietly, elbows on his knees, while observing me in the wake of the mess he'd made.

From the moment I met him, I knew he was the calculating one. I knew he was the one who pulled the strings. I told myself he was dangerous, to be careful with how I managed him.

I just didn't realize he was such a vindictive asshole.

Brushing the tears from my cheeks, I turned my anger on the man who'd stirred up this trouble. "Why did you do that?"

Søren gazed at me with a serious, impassive face. "He deserved to know the truth."

"He even said he didn't WANT to know; that it didn't matter, until you insisted on telling him. Why would you go out of your way to hurt someone you call your brother?"

"Denying the truth protects no one. It is better for him to be hurt now, knowing the truth, than to be more wounded later when the truth eventually comes out." His piercing green eyes dropped to his hands, and he added more softly, "The truth always comes out."

Perhaps he didn't expect me to ask. Or, perhaps, he didn't think I'd pick up on it. But now it was my turn. "What is the truth that hurt you?"

The shrewd man's piercing gaze rose to my face, scrutinizing me with an intensity that brought heat to my chest. He held my stare for several long, drawn-out moments, but I refused to back down.

As if I'd won the battle and earned an answer, Søren sighed and leaned back against the hay pile behind him. "I don't want to kill Skarde just because of Leif's brother, or Björn's parents. I have my own issues with him, my own reasons to believe he's an inscrutable jackass of a human being."

"And those are...?" I prompted. That was not nearly an adequate answer. I needed more.

"For one, Skarde has held down every man in this village, preventing any of us from receiving recognition from the Jarl, gifts, land, you name it. Skarde is the leader of our village's raiding party, so he is the one with the relationship with the Jarl. I don't know how they did things where you came from, but with nearly fifty men in the team, there should be plenty to go around. Instead, he heaps praises on one man a year, never the same one, and gives the rest of us no credit. Men like Leif's brother Troels, who last summer killed more warriors and collected more treasure than ten men. Skarde collected the treasure from him, presented the Jarl his share, and gave the recognition to his own brother."

"But how does he get away with that? Surely if there are fifty viking raiders, they should be able to take him down and replace him with someone who would better distribute the recognition?"

"Skarde uses promises, threats, even murder to keep everyone in line. Everyone only gets one year of glory, so in theory, eventually everyone gets a turn in front of the Jarl. Troels' death was a message to all of us: Try to go around me, and your wife will become a widow. Whenever someone grumbles, he is quick to squash it."

I chewed over that information for a moment.

"This is all terrible, but I still don't see how this is a personal reason for you to want to kill him."

Søren's eyes narrowed for a moment, then he sighed. "Skarde stole my wife."

"Stole your wife? How is that even possible?"

"When I was young—very young, barely older than Signe, I was in love with a girl. That girl is now Skarde's wife."

"Okay, I certainly understand why that would upset you, but how did he steal her?"

"We had a couple of years to wait before we could be married—I refused to marry before I had a home to give my bride—and an opportunity came up to earn a name and a spot with the Jarl. All the young men in the village competed for the honor of accompanying the chieftain to Ravndal, and it came down to myself and Skarde.

"I won't go into the details, but he cheated during our fight, and came out the winner. He received the honor, the audience with the Jarl, and eventually command of the raiding party. I told Dagny I wouldn't marry until I had the home I promised her, and she didn't want to wait. Skarde came sniffing around soon after, and it was done."

My heart ached for him. Someone he loved had betrayed Søren. Of course he was closed off to strangers. Clearly, she hadn't loved him if her head was so easily turned. "I'm sorry that happened to you. I understand the heartache you've suffered. But have you considered that perhaps you're better off?"

"How could you say that?" He spat. "Skarde has everything that should be mine, and I have nothing."

"Skarde has the wife you wanted, true. But if she so easily accepted him after she had promised herself to you, can you really argue that she loved you in the first place? And Skarde, holding onto his power by fear, is sure to see the end of it soon. I have seen more than one man taken down by his own hubris. It will come for him, eventually.

"It appears to me that Skarde has a wife who doesn't love him; he seeks comfort from other women, so clearly he is unhappy. He clings desperately to an empty power he is soon to lose. You have two friends that you consider brothers, and from what I can see, a future of possibility. So I ask you again, might you be better off than he is, despite appearances at the moment?"

Søren's bright eyes drifted to the side as he considered.

I waited patiently, feeling better for knowing more of the story. Finally, Søren returned his gaze to me, and the ghost of a smile curled his lips.

"Brenna, you have given me a gift. I certainly had not realized it before, but you are right. I feel an immense... relief now. Skarde still deserves to die for the other things, but I no longer need to mourn Dagny."

"Speaking of other things," I began, trying to be delicate, "Why does Björn believe Skarde killed his parents?"

"Björn's father, Ulfe, despised Skarde. He hated that the entire village was at his mercy. He was building a ship in the barn, much as we've done. It used to be a much bigger barn, nearly large enough to fit a full-sized ship. Just like Björn, Ulfe had shortened it in his plans to ensure it fit inside the barn. Skarde got wind that Ulfe was building it and confronted him. Ulfe didn't deny it. He refused to cower before Skarde.

"The next night, the barn mysteriously caught fire and both Ulfe and Björn's mother, Sif, died in the fire. Skarde got the entire village to help rebuild the barn, but only if it was significantly smaller. He claimed it was because the barn was too large before and was a fire hazard. In my mind, he wanted to make sure we couldn't build another ship here."

I could see how they drew that conclusion. It certainly seemed likely that Skarde, if he was truly as unscrupulous and sneaky as Søren believed, could have been behind it.

I scrubbed my hands over my face. "This is a lot to take in. So, now that your ship is finished, what is your plan? How do you intend to displace Skarde?"

Søren scratched at his jaw, barely disturbing his neatly trimmed beard. "I know nothing about you, Brenna. Something in me wants to trust you, but I don't know how I can. For all I know, Skarde sent you here to spy on us."

That one hurt. "Surely not. If you believe Skarde burnt down the barn, and that he would do it again if he knew there was a ship here, then for you to believe

I was some kind of spy for Skarde, you would have to expect the barn to be destroyed again already, or worse."

Søren's eyes twinkled, that hint of a grin playing on his lips again. "Fair enough, Brenna. I don't believe you're working for Skarde. But I also don't know why you're here."

My pulse picked up. "I told you, my chieftain was making me do unscrupulous jobs for him, and holding me hostage to his whims. I ran away, but in the storm I got turned around and crashed my boat. I swam to shore and ended up here."

"Where did you come ashore?"

My mind raced to answer—it was always best to give few details, keep things as vague as possible, and as simple as possible. "The shore in town."

"That must have been quite a swim, with that heavy sword you carry."

"I am a strong swimmer."

"And your village? Is it nearby?"

"Honestly, I don't even know where I am. I don't know how far I traveled, only that it was more than a day. What is the name of this village?"

Søren continued scratching his chin thoughtfully. "Our town doesn't really have a name. We just call it Porp. Is that name familiar to you?"

I searched my memory banks, but I didn't remember that village name from my last stint as a viking raider. "Nope, it doesn't."

"What was your village called?"

"Bekkr." I hoped it was as unfamiliar to him as his village was to me.

Søren just shrugged. "No, I've never heard of that one, either. Well, Brenna, whatever you went through in the past, I hope you're able to get the new life you were hoping for here. There is plenty to go around, for those who earn it." His last comment was pointed, and I glanced up at him curiously.

"Earn it how?"

He stood, brushing off his pants. "That's up to everyone to figure out for themselves. I ought to go home. Perhaps I'll see you tomorrow, if you're still here." With a nod, he descended the ladder from the loft and walked out of the barn without another word.

This conversation had certainly been a roller-coaster. First Søren outed me to Björn, as if deliber-ately trying to get rid of me. Then he filled me in on the history between the three men and Skarde, as well as some of his own personal history.

But just when I thought he was opening up to me, he reminded me I was a stranger he wouldn't trust any further than he could throw me.

Søren was a puzzle; I just didn't understand his motivation, or where his head was at. Did he like me or hate me? Did he trust me or not? I honestly had no idea. It seemed that just when I decided either way, he went the other direction.

Sighing, I stood and checked that my armor remained safely hidden before I descended the ladder.

Søren would have to remain a puzzle for now. I knew for certain Björn was upset, and right now, I needed to speak with him.

thirty-one

LEIF

THIS PAIN IN MY CHEST... I didn't have words for it. I fell so quickly, so hard for Brenna. It was like jumping off a cliff and landing on the solid rock.

I couldn't even make it make sense to myself. I barely knew the woman. She was beautiful, and kind, and clever, and had clearly experienced an entire world I knew nothing about. These were all admirable traits, but even together, they didn't explain the depth of my feelings for her.

Idly, I wondered if she was some kind of witch who'd cast a spell over me. It wasn't likely, but it was fun to consider as a way to ease the pain in my aching heart.

Björn. Like a brother to me. Of course Brenna was

attracted to him. With his sheer size, he could impress most women. But he was also more brooding, more masculine than me. Among my remaining brothers I felt like a man, but next to him I look like someone's kid brother.

It just wasn't fair. There was no way I could compete, not if that was what she liked. And of course it was. It was what all women liked. Big, burly, brooding men who grunted responses and came home with blood in their beards from fighting their enemies.

I was still embarrassingly unable to grow a full beard, so I kept what I grew clean-shaven. I was reasonably tall, taller than Søren, but even though I was muscular it wasn't the same kind of impressive size that either of the older men had. They liked to joke I could pass for a buff woman if I donned a dress, and while their teasing was all in good fun, I had to admit it hurt. Women like Brenna didn't want a pretty man; they wanted a strong, burly, masculine man.

And that wasn't me.

I cut through the patch of woods between my house and Björn's, whipping at the bright spring leaves that were still uncurling on the trees.

Fortunately, I hadn't declared that I loved her.

But I knew, in the depths of my heart, that I loved her. From the moment I'd laid eyes on her—really seen her—I'd felt something. I'd even been impressed with her courage when she got between us and finishing our business with Skarde. But it wasn't until I saw her in the bright sunlight, practically glowing, that my heart lurched in a way I didn't quite understand.

And now I could never have her.

Or... could I?

Was I counting myself out of the race before it even started?

Brenna had appeared as surprised by Björn's kiss as I had been. Perhaps I needed to be more aggressive, show her I meant what I said, that I wanted her.

That I would fight for her.

My heart raced, pulse pounding in my ears.

Yes, Björn was bigger than me, more masculine perhaps.

But I had skills he didn't. And maybe those skills, and a little aggressiveness could make all the difference.

I wasn't giving up on Brenna yet. The ache in my chest eased as I stepped quickly through the woods, plans surfacing in my mind to show Brenna that I was a far better fit for her than Björn.

BJÖRN

Brenna and Søren stayed in the barn for a fair amount of time. I assumed continuing to talk. Since I had no interest in explaining my foul mood to Signe, I climbed to the hills instead of returning to the longhouse. Nestled between our field and the sheer rock face was a small outcropping of boulders, and it was here I liked to stretch out when I needed to clear my mind and find peace.

I'd told myself that what Brenna did before she turned up at our door didn't matter. I sincerely didn't want to know; I was fairly certain the knowledge would bring me less peace and more trouble.

Sure enough, that woman was trouble.

Of all the men in our village, Skarde was the one I absolutely hated. And Brenna's pointed criticism was correct: None of us had offered her a place to stay. Granted, she had come out of nowhere and fought against us—she could hardly expect us to turn around and invite her into our homes, even knowing she did not know Skarde's history.

However, it was equally unfair for me to be so angry, knowing I'd left her no alternative.

I knew that. Logically, I knew it was unfair.

But gods, it hurt. I had barely the time to recognize the softening I felt, deep within my heart, for Brenna, before Søren delivered the news that she'd spent her night with Skarde before coming here.

Wait a minute. Why had Søren decided now was the time to tell me this piece of information? We'd been on a trip for a week, just him and I, and he hadn't seen fit to mention it then. He clearly knew before we left, we hadn't spoken to anyone since we returned.

He sat on the knowledge and waited for this moment to tell me.

Of course.

Because it wasn't important for me to know until he realized how I felt about Brenna. And once he knew, he wanted me to be angry at her, perhaps disgusted, and so he dropped that tidbit and sat back and waited for me to blow up.

Which, of course, I did exactly what he expected.

Damn him. I was not a stupid man, but I often felt that way when dealing with Søren's cleverness. It felt as if he was constantly playing a game. Sometimes I was playing with him, on his team, and sometimes I was merely a tool.

I thought about marching down to the barn and calling him out for manipulating me, but in the end, it was information I needed to know. Whether I agreed with how he withheld it until he could get the result he wanted, it didn't really matter. The most important fact was that I knew Brenna had spent the night with Skarde, and now I had to decide what to do with that knowledge.

I considered my feelings for Brenna without Skarde. I'd been excited to see her as we returned. And first seeing her, then realizing how she'd helped Signe, watching all three of my sisters playing joyfully, my heart had nearly burst with admiration I needed to show her.

That admiration came in the form of the kiss. It was as unplanned as the first, but far less confusing. I knew what I felt in that moment: I was happy to see

Brenna; I felt a surge of warm feelings for her, and I wanted to kiss her.

I wouldn't say I loved her; not yet. It was far too soon and there were far too many unanswered questions about her past.

The real question was: once I added knowing that she had given her body, even just for one night, to Skarde, did that change how I felt about her?

I knew Brenna had a history she hadn't told us. One look in her eyes was enough to know she had been through more hard times than we could imagine. It wasn't difficult to imagine she had had a husband, or a lover, or both, in the past. I could hardly expect that she would be untouched, and I certainly didn't resent her for it.

However, was Skarde different from other men? If I didn't mind, didn't expect her to be untouched, could I make the argument that Skarde was somehow worse, somehow left her dirtier than any other man?

As much as I recoiled against the idea, the image of Skarde's hands on her flesh, I couldn't imagine her somehow sullied from the contact.

Despite contact with him, there was nothing that made her less of the woman I knew her to be. A strong, fierce, kind, and, yes, beautiful woman.

And so I knew in that moment that even if she spent a hundred nights with Skarde, it wouldn't make her less in my eyes.

I laid on my rock, watching the clouds roll by through the perfect blue sky, and let the anger melt from my body.

I glanced back toward the homestead when I heard the barn door creak open and closed; Søren left, not glancing my way at all. He headed straight back to the path that led into town.

Not long after, I heard the barn door again, and I knew it was Brenna. I wasn't ready to have that conversation, so I remained on my rock and let her continue into the house.

However, it hadn't occurred to me she would want to seek me out to talk. When I heard the approaching footsteps, it honestly startled me. I caught up quickly, realizing who it must be. When I knew she was only a few steps away, I sat up and turned to face her.

"Hi," she offered in a solemn voice. "Björn, can we talk?"

"Come on up," I gestured, offering my hand to help her climb the small mountain on which I'd perched.

She scrabbled up easily with one tug and claimed a spot beside me.

"Björn, I'm sorry about your parents. I assumed it was an accident. I didn't realize you believed they were murdered. That's just... horrible. Horrible and sad and wasteful."

"Thank you."

She tipped up her chin and faced me with a note of pride. "I'm not here to apologize for staying with Skarde. He was kind to me, and whether he is a good person is not for me to judge based on experiences that aren't my own. I believe that you all have your

235

reasons for disliking him. I understand that—I had my reasons for doing what I did as well. My life is my own, and I don't make apologies for how I choose to live it. Not any more."

I was powerfully curious about her life before she came to us, but now was not the time to ask. Even with that enticing hint at the end.

"I don't want an apology from you, Brenna. I don't blame you for the choices you made, given what you knew, and I don't hold any resentment toward you for them."

Her eyes widened slightly in surprise, but other than that, she didn't react.

"I confess it shocked me to hear that way, given… everything else. But I shouldn't have been surprised. I knew you didn't have many options, or many friends, before you came to us."

Brenna's hands were together, clasped gently in her lap. I reached out and pulled one free, pressing it between my massive paws.

"But I hope you know now, you have friends here. Myself, and Signe, Yrsa, of course Astrid. But also Leif and Søren. We can be your family here, if you'll let us."

Emotions warred on Brenna's face. Her chin trembled, eyes softening, then hardening before softening again as they turned glassy with moisture. My heart thudded, aching in response to her obvious pain.

"Björn, I can't tell you how much it means to me, for you to say that. I don't have a history of making and keeping friends, I'm actually terrible at it. I don't let myself get close to people, it only gives them room to hurt me.

"But I couldn't help getting attached here. I don't regret my choices, but I was so worried you could not look past them and it would make me wish I could undo it all."

Now I couldn't help myself. Using the one hand I was already holding, I pulled Brenna close and enfolded her in my arms. She leaned in awkwardly at first, before I squeezed her tightly enough to lift her onto my lap in a more comfortable position for us both.

Wrapping her arms around my body, Brenna pressed her face to my chest and whispered, "thank you."

I set my cheek on the top of her head, my arms loosely around her shoulders, and replied, "No, Brenna, thank you."

And I meant it. I was grateful she was in our lives now. I didn't know what magic brought her to us, or for what purpose, but as far as I could tell, it was very good indeed.

With Brenna pressed against me, I stared peace-fully off into the distance. The clouds rolled lazily toward the fjord, where sunlight shimmered on the crisp blue waters and sea birds cried out for lunch from the fishermen in the village, returning with their catch.

And I felt home.

thirty-two

BRENNA

I DIDN'T KNOW what to expect when Leif showed up the next day. He'd been so hurt when he saw Björn kiss me that he left without allowing me to explain anything.

Things had certainly improved with Björn in the wake of Søren's news, but he hadn't kissed me again. We went through a rather quiet afternoon, with few chores to complete thanks to Leif's help throughout the week. Signe figured out how to navigate the house on her crutches swiftly, and now my concern was that she would get reckless and fall into the fire.

I couldn't chasten her, though. It was such an incredible difference, to see her formerly serious face, the one that had looked far too old for her thirteen years, suddenly transform into that of a carefree girl appropriate to her age. Björn watched her as if he couldn't believe his eyes, and even Yrsa, though she still spoke little, grinned happily as she completed her chores. Astrid, of course, noticed the change, but wasn't really old enough to understand the weight that had lifted from Signe's shoulders. She only knew that Signe could chase her now, and seemed happier, which also made Astrid happy.

So our evening passed pleasantly enough. I once again tended to Signe's foot. Björn watched me carefully, wanting to see how much the ankle had improved and positively exclaiming when he realized how far along her healing was. I could have sworn there were tears in his eyes, but he turned away before I could be certain. I finished my special brand of healing, then wrapped her up and set her free. Once everyone was asleep, I got my freedom in the form of soaring through the night sky, whole and at peace with my tiny world and everyone in it.

I woke in such a good mood, feeling positive about the future. I actually found myself humming the melody of some inane pop song I'd heard on the radio a thousand times before Odin ripped me out of the future and sent me back here. And the memory didn't upset me any more, which was a pleasant surprise.

Then reality came crashing back down, as one exquisite, lovesick, viking man.

He knocked on the door just after dawn, as he had while Björn was gone. Perhaps Björn thought it was a stranger he needed to protect us from; I wasn't sure. But he rushed to answer the knock, filling the doorway with his massive body, and yanked the door open with a scowl.

My heart was already racing; I knew who it was, and I had no idea how this would go.

"Leif, hello, how-" Björn adapted quickly, his tone softening to greet his friend.

"Where's Brenna?" Leif's tone was cold, and he pushed past Björn to charge into the longhouse. When his bright azure eyes met mine, the resolve on his face hardened. He marched directly to me, then cupped the back of my head with his hand and pulled me toward him.

I didn't know what I expected, but it was not for Leif to storm in and kiss me.

Once again, his lips were incredibly soft, and the aggressive way he'd approached and kissed me made my knees weaken despite my surprise.

But this felt wrong; this wasn't Leif, and knowing the audience we had I could only imagine how bad this situation would to become.

As gently as I could, I pressed my palms on Leif's chest and pushed him away. Heart pounding, my eyes darted to Signe, who'd frozen in the act of swinging her way over to say hello.

"Signe, I-" she didn't wait for me to speak. Unleashing a heart-wrenching sob, Signe crutched her way out of the door that Björn still held open.

"Great," I sighed, throwing my hands up and

casting my eyes skyward. "Leif, why would you do that?"

While Leif had seemed pleased with himself before, his expression now turned unsure. "I thought you kissed Björn because you liked that he was more manly. I thought if I was more aggressive with you…"

"Leif, I didn't kiss Björn, he kissed me and I held on at the risk of falling. I don't like him better than you," at this Leif's eyes lit up, "or the other way around. What is going on here? Is this some kind of competition now?"

At the second part of my statement, Leif's hopeful expression had fallen.

"I just thought… perhaps… you needed me to do a better job of showing you what I wanted."

"No, Leif, I don't. I know what you want. But I am not a woman who will ever settle a home or have children. I need you to understand that is not something I can give to you. It is not about being more masculine, or more aggressive, or more… like him," I gestured to Björn, who seemed just as confused as Leif. "I can't *have* children, do you understand? All I am good at, all I am good for, is battle and fighting and occasionally fixing up the wounded. I have nothing else to offer." Sighing, I wiped my hands over my face from the bridge of my nose outward to my brows, pressing to force the tension away. "Now, there is a little girl whose heart is broken that I need to go speak with. If you'll excuse me."

I pushed past Leif and ignored Björn on my way through the door. Outside, leaning against the far side of the animal pen and sobbing into the horse's neck, was Signe.

Walking up to her, I let my steps be slow and obvious so she'd know I was coming if she wanted to straighten and pretend she was fine.

Apparently, this time, she didn't. Signe continued crying, even knowing I was there.

"Signe... I'm sorry." I tried to infuse as much of the pain I felt on her behalf into my voice as I could. "I wish he hadn't done that."

"I thought you wanted Björn," she glared at me with accusing, tear-swollen eyes. "I thought you wanted to stay here with us. I thought you cared about us."

"Signe, I do care about you. Deeply. I didn't know Leif was going to do that, and I certainly didn't want him to."

"Then what are you apologizing for?" She sniffled, wiping her nose on the sleeve of her woolen dress.

"I'm sorry that what he did hurt you. I have to tell you—as a man, he is completely oblivious to the way you feel about him. He didn't know it would hurt you."

"So, I should tell him?" The spark of hope in her eyes stuck a dagger in my heart.

Ugh, this was going to be the hard part. "Signe... Leif isn't going to return your affection. I know that for a girl your age, you are incredibly mature. You've shouldered the responsibilities of a woman since your mother died, and you've done an incredible job.

"But Leif sees Björn as his brother, and you, Yrsa,

and Astrid, as his sisters. Whether you are deserving of being admired by him for all that you've done, for all that you are, it doesn't matter. He won't love you the way you're hoping. I could have tried to tell you more gently, but I believe you are a strong enough woman to handle the truth, and so I told you the truth. But I know that doesn't mean it hurts less. And for that, I'm so very sorry."

Signe held onto the fence, her chin trembling as she considered what I said. Then, with a loud sob, she threw her arms around my shoulders and cast her weight on my body, knocking her crutches to the ground.

Signe's face tucked into my neck as I stroked her golden hair, and I held her quietly while she cried out the painful tears of her first crush.

thirty-three

BRENNA

WHEN SIGNE and I returned to the house, Leif had gone, and we could mercifully have a peaceful breakfast. Only the occasional sniffle from Signe or giggle from Astrid interrupted the quiet.

Björn and I went out to check the fields after our meal. It had rained twice since we planted, but we needed to make sure the soil was moist enough for the seeds to germinate and sprout. We focused on the work for a while, no mention of the earlier events, and while the underlying tension was still there, the shallow simplicity of the task was comfortable.

When we finished with the oats, we ended up on Björn's little outcropping of rocks. Björn sat with one knee up, the other dangling off the rock. His golden blonde hair was neatly braided on the top today, beard a little wilder than I was used to. Even though his posture said 'relaxed', his energy didn't match it. I could practically hear his thoughts. The desire to bring up what had happened earlier with Leif was thick in the surrounding air. And yet he hesitated.

"Go ahead," I invited.

Björn sighed. "What you said to Leif, about not being able to have children or settle a home… did you mean that?"

I nodded. "I can't have children. I have no place being any man's wife, and I honestly don't believe I was built for it. I'm too restless… this is a wonderful home, but I can't see myself staying here for the rest of my life. And I should, I *know* I should. This should be everything I want out of life, but it's just not."

"What do you want from life?" Björn's deep voice was smooth, untroubled. Merely curious.

"I was born to fight, Björn. It's what I am good at, it's when I feel most alive. A home already built, a farmstead already settled? That holds no adventure for me. Where I come from," a lump formed in my throat, and I swallowed it down, "Where I came from my sacred duty was to protect my friends and family, my people, my home. I dedicated my life to it. And then my home was destroyed, my people slaughtered, and those of us who were spared forced to serve… the chieftain. He didn't risk letting us fight, in case we turned against him. So he forced us to serve him in different ways. Not like that," I rushed to add, as he straightened with fury at the implication, "but not what I was born to do. And so I escaped, and I've hidden here, pretending to be a farmer. But it's not who I am."

Björn was silent for several moments, considering my words. His deep ocean blue eyes were heavy, his expression serious, when he finally spoke.

"I always imagined myself marrying, fathering children, and raising them on a farm much like this one. I thought I'd find the right woman and make a home, heading out in the summer to make my name and returning to her in the fall.

"It didn't happen how I imagined. I never found a girl I wanted to marry when I thought I should, and the challenges to making a name for myself have been many.

"Then my parents died, and suddenly I had a home, and a family, and all the pressure without the partner I'd imagined. Signe became a mother to her little sisters, and I leaned on her heavily to manage the household. I did not know how to do it—I confess I never paid attention to the work my mother did. I just assumed I'd have a wife to do those things. Fortunately I had Signe, or everything would have completely fallen apart.

"Having you here, even before I truly knew or trusted you, was a relief I didn't expect. To know there was a fully grown woman to manage things, ease the burden on my little sister who shouldn't have had to be so responsible at such an age, help with all of this," he gestured to the fields behind us, "it has taken so much weight off of my shoulders. I know it is not where you want to be, and I understand now that you don't want to stay, but I'm grateful you're here now. I can never thank you enough for fixing Signe's ankle, and the changes your presence has made for all three of them. I hope you understand how much you've done for all of us. For me. And whether it's something you want, we consider you family."

The stinging sensation of tears bit at the back of my eyes as I blushed under the weight of his gratitude. I'd turned up here just hoping to work and secure a bed to sleep in and food to keep me alive. Affecting this kind of change in someone else's life was not my specialty, nor my intent.

And yet, the change the four of them had wrought on me was intense. I'd never imagined myself caring for children, and yet that's exactly what I'd done since I came here. Sure, Signe managed a lot of the more motherly duties like bathing Astrid and mending clothes—she was far more maternal than I could ever be.

But hadn't I comforted her in the wake of her first heartbreak? Hadn't I made silly faces to drag a begrudging smile from Yrsa? Or sung little songs for Astrid so she could dance around the longhouse giggling?

The realization that, despite never wanting a family, I'd somehow adopted one, flooded my chest with emotion.

"Björn, I... thank you for welcoming me into your

home. Into your family. I..." words were really difficult at this moment, but Björn seemed to understand.

He wrapped a massive arm around my shoulder,
pulling me into the warmth of his body, and said, "I
don't know where your path leads you, Brenna, but
you're welcome to stay with us as long as you like.
Anything I can do for you, you are welcome to it."

The offer was endearing, but the idea brewing in
my mind was certainly outside of what he imagined. I
needed to bide my time a bit longer, prove that Signe
could manage on her own, before I put my plan into
action.

Björn and I sat restfully, comfortably, on his rock,
both entertaining our own visions of what the future
held.

thirty-four

SØREN

THE DAY of the first raid was quickly approaching, and we still had no plan for getting our ship to the shore. Björn's farm was a two-hour walk from the village harbor. We built the ship on a wheeled base, but the sheer size of the construction was far heavier than the single team of oxen we had access to could pull. I had no animals, and Leif's parents only had a single horse. I suspected that the men who'd promised, then backed out of letting us use their oxen, were afraid of retribution from Skarde. They didn't know what we needed them for, but not much happened without Skarde knowing about it. He was the type of bastard who would interfere just to be a dick without even knowing what he disrupted.

Despite the spring planting being completed, everyone I asked couldn't spare their oxen for a half day. My skin was boiling with rage after the tenth 'sorry' I received to my request. When Björn's barn had burned down, we had villagers coming out of the forest with carts laden with timber and offers of as much access to beasts of burden as we needed.

Now, suspiciously, all of those same people had no help to spare. Frustrated, I hiked up to Björn's farmstead to discuss our problem. Maybe if he approached them instead of me, the villagers would be more apt to help. The indignation gnawed at my gut, but I didn't have the luxury of being affronted. People didn't like me; I'd always rubbed them the wrong way, and my current status as an unwed man with no family and no real property to my name at the ripe old age of twenty-five made them distrustful. But they did like Björn, and we had to use what we could to accomplish our goals.

Leif shouldn't be too far behind me; I'd stopped by his family's home to tell him to meet us when he finished his work.

Even though it was a bright summer day outside, not one of Björn's household was out of doors when I arrived. Confused, I approached the house and knocked.

I scarcely recognized the man who answered the door. Björn's expression was positively jubilant, his eyes sparkling; a far cry from the withdrawn, serious man he'd been since his parents died.

"Søren! Excellent timing, you've got to see this!"

He ushered me inside, and I scanned the longhouse for the source of his excitement.

At first I didn't get it; there was no gigantic surprise to behold. Astrid was dancing around as usual, Yrsa holding one of Signe's hands and Brenna the other as they walked toward us.

Then I realized the surprise: Signe was walking, without the aide of crutches. A closer look at her ankle told me it was heavily fortified with pieces of wood strapped tightly to her leg, and she walked delicately on it, unable to flex the foot. However, she was beaming with joy as she walked, clearly without the pain she'd experienced scarcely two weeks before when we left for Ravndal.

"Can you believe it?" Björn exclaimed, clapping a heavy hand on my shoulder. "Brenna is truly a miracle worker."

"I think, if we're careful, she'll be able to walk on it without support in a day or two. Mind you, not a lot to start, but she'll be able to get around, as long as she wears the brace." Brenna glowed with joy, her clear grey eyes shining as she grinned in our direction.

"It's a miracle, truly," I agreed quietly. There was absolutely no way Signe's foot could have healed so quickly on its own. This woman was clearly a witch or possessed some powers we didn't understand. Björn, as excited as he was for his sister, was oblivious to the threat here.

Brenna's radiant gaze traveled between Signe and Björn. But when her eyes landed on my face, her smile fell. I stared back at her, certain my thoughts translated accurately to my expression.

I know you're hiding something, and I will get to the bottom of it.

BRENNA

Søren... it always came down to Søren. The way he watched me, hawk-like, predatory, left no doubt that he still didn't trust me.

Even during our joy for Signe's rapid recovery, Søren was like a storm cloud on the horizon, heading my way with the heavy inevitability of a summer thunderstorm.

As much as I wanted to avoid it, I knew this was one I needed to face head-on.

When things had settled down, I got Søren's attention and tipped my head toward the door. He nodded, and we both slipped out without announcing our departure to the happy family inside.

Søren had a powerful energy about him; it was impossible to ignore, and I imagined he made plenty of humans uncomfortable without them even understanding why.

I was drawn to the energy he exuded. It was like shivers that ran over my skin, causing nearly the same tingling sensation I felt around the Asgardians when they got too close. He was clearly human, but... there was something special about him.

And I suspected that is how he knew, even if he didn't understand it himself, that I wasn't exactly what I'd declared myself to be. He clearly had a sense about people, an innate internal compass that told him more than his eyes and ears alone could learn.

We walked in silence along the fields, which were just brightening with tiny green shoots. My heart thumped unevenly as I debated what to say, how much to tell him. I needed to tell him something, that much was clear. But was there a partial truth I could give him without revealing everything?

Living in this simpler time was so much more difficult. In the twenty-first century, if things got awkward or people suspected, I could just disappear to a new state, a new country, a new continent, and start over. I'd become so accustomed to avoiding entanglements I could pick up and go without a second thought.

Here there was no such thing. I was stuck with the people I'd found—at least for now—and I had to make it work.

Somehow, I had to get Søren to trust me.

I stole a glance in his direction to gauge his level of distraction.

At just under six feet, Søren wasn't tall for a man. Scarcely a few inches taller than me, in fact. Beneath the simple grey-blue shirt and brown woolen pants he was thick with muscle, far more functional and less showy than Leif's body. His dark blonde hair was still meticulously braided into a thick tail that reached his mid-back and tied with a strip of dark brown leather. The bottom part of his skull, just below his ears, was freshly shaved, as was the meticulous line he maintained of his precise, sandy-blonde beard. Søren was all sharpness, from the severe cut of his hair to the hard planes of his face and striking kelly green eyes.

My eyes dropped to his hands, which were fisted tightly.

I needed to say something; he was frustrated with waiting.

"Søren, I thought we should talk," I started with more confidence than I felt. "I feel as if I've gotten to know Björn, and Leif somewhat, but I know so little about you."

Søren's sharp jaw flexed beneath the sandy hairs of his beard. "I'm more interested in you, Brenna. You say you've gotten to know Björn and Leif, but would they say the same thing about you?"

"I don't know what you mean."

"Oh, I think you do." He stopped walking and turned to face me. "We know nothing about you. You've told us a weak story about how you came to be on our shore, but there's a lot about you that doesn't add up. I don't know you, and if I don't know you, I can't trust you to be around the people I care about."

"What do you want from me, Søren? I don't have a great story to tell you about where I come from. It's not a pleasant story to tell, it doesn't make me happy to share it."

Søren's bright eyes flashed. "I don't want a pleasant story, Brenna. I want the truth. I want to look into your eyes and not feel you're hiding things from me. Until we reach that point, I will continue to mistrust you, and that mutual mistrust will affect everyone around us. I told you about Skarde; I told you about Troels and Dagne. You know all of our painful stories, and yet you tell us nothing about yourself. Still. Leif and Björn have softened to you despite your secrets, but I promise you I will not."

Søren moved in closer, his face mere inches from mine, and glared down at me with dark promise pouring from his countenance. "I can feel the secrets on you, smell them, and they cling to you like a dark cloud. I have few people I trust, because I have powerful instincts about people and I listen to them. I feel the goodness within you, but it's buried deeply beneath secrets so dark it confuses me. So either you tell us the truth, and trust us as we have trusted you, or leave now. I don't want Leif, or Björn and the girls, to get any more attached to someone who will leave them wondering if the person they know was a stranger after all.

"Leif will be here soon. I suggest you take the time to decide if you will run again, or if you will finally tell us the truth."

He held my gaze with his piercing, predatory eyes for one long moment, then turned on his heel and marched back toward the house. I stood, frozen in place for a long moment, then slowly trudged up to Björn's boulder to think.

My first thought was that Søren had to be the offspring of some Asgardian. There was no way auras could be so visceral for a regular human being. If he was being straight with me—which I wholeheartedly believed he was—I had to conclude he was, at the very least, descended from an immortal. I needed to learn more about his family, his parents, and unearth more of his history.

More pressing, however, was his frightening ulti-matum: Tell them the truth, or leave. Now, I had a little silver to my name, and one decent dress. Björn would probably give me some food and supplies at the very least, and now that I knew Ravndal was a few days' hike away I could head there and hope to start over. Maybe bide my time and just fly at night to travel more quickly. Find some menial job, survive, learn, and maybe, eventually, get a place in front of the Jarl.

But that plan sucked. I'd certainly miss out on the opportunity to join the raids this summer—there was no telling how long it would take for me to find another chance to join a crew. And I'd have my armor with me. Not a lot of places to hide a package such as that on the road, or in a larger, more crowded village. It was a dangerous idea to start over.

And here I had the perfect opportunity. Three men who need a fourth on their team, preferably more, and more importantly, who had all shown me kindness. Good men. Men who cared for their families and each other.

All I had to do to stay was tell them everything. Trust them with as much sincerity as they'd shown me.

It was one thing to trust someone enough to sleep under their roof. It was entirely a different one to reveal that you're an immortal creature, one of the legends they weren't sure existed, and that even more importantly, you were among them because you were being punished. Of course I didn't want to reveal myself as a valkyrie to humans: you never know how they would react. It was terrifying when I'd told Helgi I would never age, trusting him with that single, irrefutable fact. That he'd loved me enough not to care was a once in a lifetime occurrence for me. I hadn't met a single person since Helgi that I was willing to trust to that degree again. True, I had also been reticent to open up my heart again, as frail a thing as it'd been in the broken person I was without my armor.

But something told me Søren wouldn't be as surprised as the others; he suspected something out of the ordinary. And Björn, and Leif, did they love me enough to accept me as I truly was?

I didn't kid myself that they loved me the way Helgi had; not yet, at least. I'd scarcely known them three weeks. But if it was enough to earn Søren's trust, and they already felt affection for me, then perhaps it would work.

In the distance, back at the homestead, I watched

three tiny figures emerge from the longhouse and head into the barn. In the stretching afternoon sunlight, Björn, Leif, and Søren were as distinct to me as if they stood directly before me. I knew them; I knew their shapes, the way they moved, the countenance they each bore.

While my eyes tracked their progress, Søren's head turned and his penetrating gaze met my eyes as if to say, this is your chance.

My heart thudded against my ribcage: there was no choice. I needed these men, and they needed me.

It was time to tell them the truth…

And I knew exactly how I'd do it.

thirty-five

BRENNA

FIRST, I collected my Valkyrian blade from the longhouse. Sword in hand, I marched up the barn and ignored the men who paused in their discussion of the boat when I entered. Instead of joining them, I climbed to the loft and retrieved my hidden bag of armor.

"Brenna?" Björn's voice called, confused.

"Just... give me a minute, okay? I need to talk to you all. I'll be right down." As quickly as I was able, I slipped on all the pieces of my armor, aside from the breastplate and collar. Replacing my woolen dress, I carried the much lighter bag, along with my sword, back down the ladder.

Søren's sharp gaze tracked my movements carefully, as if he was prepared for me to do absolutely anything, given that I'd turned up with my sword in hand. Leif just smiled warmly with his perfect mouth, and Björn lifted an eyebrow. "You... wanted to talk to us?"

Here goes nothing. "Yes. I have appreciated your kindness, and your trust, and your honesty with me. And I know that I have been less than forthcoming with you all. I've told you precious little about my history, and I-"

"Brenna, if you aren't ready to tell us everything, it's alright," Björn interrupted, glancing meaningfully at the other two. "We understand if-"

"Let the woman speak, Björn." Søren's voice, while not as deep as the much larger man's, rang with authority. Björn glanced at him sharply, but didn't say another word.

Sighing, I began again. "I know you have questions about where I come from and how I ended up here, and I've given you vague answers. I'm going to tell you the truth, but I need you to understand now that it will sound... impossible. Just know that in the end, when I've finished, I will prove it to you. I only ask that you listen carefully to what I say and... try to believe me."

My eyes tracked from Björn's deep ocean blue gaze, to Leif's bright azure, and finally to Søren's suspicious leaf green stare. He nodded slightly, encouraging me to continue.

I opened my mouth and immediately choked on my desiccated throat. After a brief coughing fit, I swallowed some moisture to soothe the tickle and tried again.

"I told you I was from a village where I'd essentially been enslaved by the chieftain to do his bidding, and that I escaped hoping to start over.

"This is the basic truth of my story, but the reality is much larger, and more complicated, than that sounds. Just... once again, please try to hear me out before you stop listening. I promise I will prove my story is true." I drew in a deep breath and just forced myself to spit it out.

"The truth is that I am a valkyrie. Yes, those valkyries, who select the Victorious Fallen from among the dead, and send them to Valhalla." I waited for some kind of reaction, but they all simply stared at me.

Taking this as a good sign, I continued. "But the truth is far more complicated than that. The story you know of the valkyries is a falsehood. We came from the tenth realm of Odin's domain... or what used to be the tenth realm. Odin decided he wanted the valkyries for himself, to serve him on Asgard. Our sacred, sworn duty was to protect Valkyr and all the people on it. Odin was far more powerful than us and destroyed our home in his quest to enslave every last valkyrie.

"He brought us to Asgard to be his servants, but he soon realized valkyries were terrible housemaids." The memory brought a wry smile to my lips. "Eventually we struck a bargain: we'd stop attempting to kill him and instead perform the service of selecting the warriors to fill the halls of Valhalla, if he returned our armor and swords and allowed us to live in Valhalla as well.

"When Odin captured us, he took away our swords and armor. What he didn't realize was that they were no simple weapons. Through the ancient magic of Valkyr, we imbued these items with our very life force, and in return, we lived forever to serve Valkyr. We won't die unless these nearly indestructible items get destroyed. Our swords became our hearts, so that we might never strike down a person who was pure of heart. They can read the intent of a person, telling us if the person is worthy of living on. If their intent was good or evil. If they have goodness in their heart or only darkness.

"We imbue our armor with our spirit, you might say our soul. In addition to its myriad of gifts, the armor protects us, heals us, helps us retain our own connection to other living things. When Odin took these items away, he literally took away our hearts, our souls. We were dark, empty beings devoid of love or hope. It was a terrible time for us, and the return of them restored us. We were willing to do Odin's bidding in order to be whole again."

I paused, not really sure how to explain the next part.

"Okay... but that doesn't really explain how you got here?" Leif encouraged gently. "If you were happy doing Odin's bidding, why are you here now?"

"I didn't say I was happy doing Odin's bidding. I said we—the valkyries as a whole—were willing to do it in order to become whole again. But it wore on me. What you don't understand, what no one on Midgard understands, is that Valhalla is a terrible place. Yes, it's beautiful, and yes, there is a glorious battle every day and there is feasting every night.

"But do you realize what is not there? Your families. Everyone you've ever loved. If they are not among the chosen, the Victorious Fallen, they go on to another plane of existence. The chosen are stuck in a purgatory, forced to repeat the same thing day in and day out, for eternity, until Ragnarok. They enjoy it at first, they drink and they fight and they celebrate their power, their strength, their glory.

"And then, quietly at night, they begin to realize we have tricked them. They are not surrounded by their loved ones, and they have games and feasts yet are starving for something that actually matters to them. They weep, every one. Every insurmountable warrior you've ever known who has died gloriously on the battlefield; imagine him weeping into his pillow at night, wishing the valkyries had never chosen him to go to Valhalla. They begged us to send them back, to make them cease to exist at all, to send them wherever their families went.

"We were powerless to fulfill those requests. Once chosen for Valhalla, you remain there until Ragnarok. And the weight, the pressure of that role, crushed me. The crying kept me awake at night, tore at my mind, until eventually I told Odin I could no longer do it. I refused to send one more poor, misled viking warrior to Valhalla knowing he'd end up crying into his pillow at night.

"As you can imagine, Odin didn't take that well. Since he couldn't compel me to do his bidding, he punished me. Knowing that taking away both my sword and my armor would turn me into a being who didn't care at all, Odin stripped me of my armor but allowed me to keep my sword."

I held up my weapon and presented it handle first so they might examine it.

"It is a Valkyrian blade; I promise you have never seen its equal. It will not dull, it will not rust, it will not fade or tarnish. Go ahead, you can hold it."

Søren was the first to grab the pommel and examine it closer. His face betrayed no emotion, but his green eyes glowed as they took in the detailed carving on the blade and the exquisite handle and cross guard.

"Deprived of my armor, Odin banished me to Midgard. Unable to move on, unable to be complete or whole or even truly happy without my spirit, and stuck to live through every age of man and occasionally do Odin's bidding."

Søren had passed my blade to Björn, and Leif was still listening with rapt attention. "So, that's how you ended up here?"

I rubbed a palm over my forehead. "Yes, basically. Odin banished me here to suffer." It seemed as if this was plenty of truth to tell him for now. I wasn't sure the fact that I'd already lived through these ages of man, and then had time rewound like a watch and ended up here for a second time, was really important to share at this point.

"It's a very intriguing story," Søren began slowly, "and also completely insane. What kind of idiots do you take us for?" The hard edge to his tone did not surprise me, even though my heart sunk just a little to hear it.

"Søren… you said you have instincts about people. Are those instincts telling you I'm lying, or is that only your human brain warring against how you feel?"

He frowned, then shook his head as if to clear it. "It doesn't matter what I feel. What I know is that the things you say are impossible. I asked you to tell us the truth as a show of trust, and this is what you tell us. Fairy stories. Gods and valkyries and magic. I should have known better." The disgust on his face hurt, but I wasn't surprised.

"Did you forget I promised to prove it? If I were to prove myself, I expect you to keep my secret. I require your word, on your honor, that you will not tell another soul."

Søren sniffed. "What, a fancy sword? It is nice, I admit it. I haven't ever seen anything as fine as that blade. That doesn't mean it's magical."

He was starting to piss me off. "Look, you wanted my truth, and I told you. I will show you something even you can't deny, but I demand your promise not to reveal me to anyone else. Give me your word, or take me at mine. Trust goes both ways."

Björn's eyes were serious as he handed my sword

to Leif. "I give you my word, Brenna, I will not betray your trust."

Leif nodded. "Yes, me too, you have my word."

All three of us turned to look at Søren, who stared at me for an interminable moment. Finally, he said, "If you show me something incredible, irrefutable proof that these stories you've relayed are true, I promise not to reveal your secrets to anyone else."

My eyes rolled to the back of my skull, but I accepted that was probably the best I'd get from him.

Reaching into the sack at my feet, I retrieved the breastplate of my armor. When I pulled it out, Björn's eyes grew as big as saucers, and Leif gasped audibly. Søren raised a brow, but didn't say a word.

"Is that the armor Odin took from you? How did you get it?"

"Loki brought it to me," I confessed, almost afraid to admit that out loud in case Odin was watching. "The third night I was here, he appeared and I stashed it in the barn. Björn, you remember how the day we plowed the oat field I suddenly had so much more strength, more resilience? This is why. I wore my armor for a while, slipped out while you were all asleep. I've done it every night since. It's also what has helped me heal Signe's ankle. I was never one of the Valkyrian healers, but I have a small amount of energy I can direct, share, to help someone heal themselves. That's why she's improved so rapidly."

Björn and Leif both stepped closer to examine the breastplate, their reflections distorted in the gleaming metal.

"It's very pretty, but I'd hardly consider that irrefutable proof, Brenna." Søren's tone was deeply sarcastic. "If this is the best you've got, I suggest you pack up your things and head off now."

"Listen, I've had enough of your shit," I snapped, wheeling on Søren with a surge of anger. "Just stay here." I carried the breastplate to the other side of the ship, where they wouldn't see me whip off my dress and attach the metal piece over my bare breasts. Once it was in place, I braced for my wings to emerge, then drew in a deep breath and stepped into view.

thirty-six

SØREN

I DIDN'T KNOW what to expect of Brenna's big 'reveal', but I certainly didn't expect her to emerge with giant bird's wings. Or in shiny metallic undergarments that revealed an uncomfortable amount of her flawless skin.

I understood that this was her armor, and that it covered the important parts.

But it certainly left a lot of parts exposed. I couldn't stop my eyes from raking over every inch of skin that a man rarely saw on anyone but his wife. Bare knees, the curve of her waist below the breastplate, a fair amount of flesh above that same piece, and even the tender skin of her upper thighs.

Sweat broke out on my upper lip, and I swallowed

uncomfortably. It took every ounce of willpower I had, but I dragged my eyes away from the juncture of her legs and forced myself to focus on the massive wings, which I knew were the biggest part of this secret.

They were beautiful, brown like a hawk's wings but flecked with metallic hints of gold that reflected the muted sunlight in the barn. As we watched, lost for words, Brenna stretched her wings out and revealed their true expanse. The feathers closest to her back reached nearly to her ankles, the outer tips even longer. Standing in front of the ship, I realized her wingspan was nearly half the length of a boat meant to carry ten men.

"Brenna," Leif's voice was barely more than a whisper, the worship in his voice evident. "You are *magnificent*." If he'd been intrigued by her before, now she had absolutely bewitched him.

Björn hadn't moved a muscle since Brenna came back around the ship. He continued to stare, eyes wide, as if he were afraid he'd blink and she'd disappear.

Brenna's eyes tracked from Leif, to whom she smiled softly, then to Björn, and finally she met my gaze. The clear grey of her storm cloud eyes was like solid crystal, bottomless and faceted with light. In fact, she seemed to shine subtly in the afternoon sunshine that flooded the barn through the windows, as if she made her own magical glow.

"Do you believe me now, Søren?" Her voice carried the authority of command, a single note of hurt threaded subtly throughout. My doubt bothered her, even if she didn't want to admit it.

I didn't doubt her any more. "I believe you, Brenna. Thank you for telling us the truth, and sharing this secret with us. I will not betray you to anyone."

Björn and Leif rushed to affirm their promises of keeping her secrets.

Brenna explained more details about how her magical armor worked as Leif peppered her with questions. I hung back, mainly working on trying to calm my overt physical reaction to the sudden exposure of so much feminine skin.

She was beautiful; there was no doubt about it. And the power she exuded, the absolute truth and ferocity of her very being when she was, as she called it, 'whole', was enough to make my knees weak and mouth water.

But that instinct that drove me, that guided me, told me this was it: the piece I was looking for. I didn't know how yet, but Brenna was the key to our success.

Now I just had to figure out how she fit.

LEIF

I knew there was something special, almost ethereal, about Brenna the first day I laid eyes on her in the sunlight. Now, seeing her in her full glory, it was like having the clouds removed and seeing the power of the sun for the first time. I nearly dropped to my knees and bowed before her when she spread those magnificent wings and revealed her true majesty.

Eventually, she ducked back behind the ship and removed the breastplate that made her wings appear, donning her dress and removing the rest of her armor. It made her slightly less intimidating, to see her in a simple woolen gown, but I would forever hold the image close to my heart: Brenna in gleaming armor, wings spread and sword in hand, powerful and terrifying and heartbreakingly beautiful.

It didn't matter that she couldn't have children or settle a home—I wanted none of it. I wanted—I *needed* —to be with Brenna. I would follow her to the ends of world and beyond, to the halls of Valhalla despite all the terrible things she'd told us about the place, just to be near her.

For all of my life there wasn't a single girl who had drawn my interest, and I finally understood why: my destiny was to be with such a creature as men had never seen except in their dreams.

Björn was burdened with a ready-made family and home, but one look at his face told me he felt the same as I did. His eyes danced with conflicting emotions; desire and absolute devotion warred with duty and guilt. I pitied him, but was secretly pleased I had no such problems.

I was one-hundred percent free to offer myself to Brenna and accept her exactly as she was. No requirements, no complications, no limitations.

Søren's attitude had shifted. He was no longer disbelieving; he couldn't refute what Brenna had shown us so clearly.

However, he still hung back, thinking as his eyes gazed, unseeing, in her direction. Søren lived so much of his life within his own head, it was difficult for me to read his expression and understand what he was thinking. Björn knew him a little better, but not much. Søren was an enigma to both of us sometimes, and we simply trusted that he would tell us the information we needed to know.

And for the most part, he did. Sometimes he held on to details he didn't think we needed, or bits he revealed at a later time for reasons that often eluded me. However, he was always right.

So I wasn't surprised that he had withdrawn, thinking, even now.

I just hoped he wasn't suddenly thinking he was interested in Brenna as well.

I didn't want to fight Björn for her, and I definitely didn't want to face the same ordeal with Søren.

But whatever it took, I knew in the end she would choose me.

No matter what I had to do to make that happen.

thirty-seven

BJÖRN

BRENNA RETURNED to the house to help with chores, and Søren, Leif, and I remained in the barn to discuss how we'd get our ship to the shore and convince a fourth man to join us.

We took our seats in the loft as usual, but the conversation rapidly turned to Brenna's surprising revelation.

Leif glanced between Søren and me, making an airy declaration of his intent. "She seems to be under the mistaken impression that I require children and a homestead to be happy, and I'm certain that once I explain I need neither of those things, we'll have things sorted between us soon enough."

Søren said nothing, watching Leif with a patiently curious expression.

Heat rose in my chest. "I certainly would not require children of her, and she's clearly far beyond being a farm wife. Plus, now that Signe is on the mend, she can take over the homestead duties well enough. She also seems to love being with the girls. I don't think that's an issue for her. I think Brenna would prefer a home that already has a family, rather than no family at all. She was simply saying she could not give a man a family; I already have one."

Color raced to Leif's face, his tone becoming sharp. "You're making quite a few assumptions on her behalf, but have you actually asked Brenna what *she* wants?"

"I think what she wants was pretty clear with the way she kissed me," I snorted.

Leif rose to his feet. "Lest you forget, she kissed me too!"

I glared at the smaller man from my seat, then rose to my full height to gaze down at him. "Is that what happened? I seem to remember you kissing her, and she pushed you away. At least that's how it looked to me."

Indignation colored his tone. "And what happened between you? Oh, that's right, *you* kissed *her*. So it seems to me we're on the same level, you and I."

"Enough." Søren's voice was sharp, but low. "We are not here to battle over Brenna's affections. Right now our concern is getting our ship to the shore, and finding a fourth man to join our team, so we can raid. Don't lose sight of our goal: Displacing Skarde as the leader of our village raiding party is our primary, our *only*, concern. Whatever happens with Brenna is a distant second in my mind. As it should be in yours. We need to stop bickering among ourselves and remember that we are a team, if we are ever to get this plan off the ground.

"Now, I have a plan; an idea, perhaps. But in order for it to be successful, the both of you would need to give up your designs on Brenna for now. At least for this season."

Horror dropped like a stone in my stomach. If I gave up my designs on Brenna, she might leave, or choose Leif, or any other viking. She could have whomever she wanted; I needed to lock in my advantage while I had it.

Leif and I started arguing our disagreement with this suggestion immediately, and Søren cut us off. "Enough! What is most important here: removing Skarde and making a name for ourselves, finally having a proper opportunity, or bedding a woman you barely know? You need to make a choice, and make it now. We can't continue fighting amongst ourselves if we hope to have success as a team."

"So how does Brenna play into your plan?" Leif's sharp jaw worked, but he said nothing else, waiting for Søren to clue us in.

The older man glanced between us both, then looked meaningfully at the seats we'd abandoned. Søren hadn't stood. He remained on his crate and waited for us to resume our positions. Once we did, he told us his plan.

As he laid out all the details, I could see the logic, the brilliance behind it, even though I didn't like it. But he was right: in order for it to work, we all had to give up hopes of her becoming our wife. There would be no room for it in our circle. If we were to make it, we had to function as a team, a unit; a single family. There was no way bitter feelings or competition could divide us over a woman.

Even a woman such as Brenna.

And so we agreed on all of it, under one condition:

That Søren be the one to explain his plan to Brenna.

SØREN

I claimed a few minutes alone with Brenna. Now, knowing her truth, the feeling between us was much improved. The dark cloud of secrets no longer surrounded her; her energy was lighter, relieved, to have her secrets out in the open.

There remained a small dusting of unsettled thoughts, but nothing that made me question whether or not I could trust her. Every person had a few things they kept to themselves, and Brenna was clearly no exception. I could hardly blame her for it.

It was impossible, once more walking alone with her, to forget the shocking amount of her flesh I'd seen. The image flashed in my head again, unbidden, and I felt myself harden despite my best intention of treating her as a warrior instead of an object of lust.

The truth was, there was no woman I could recall desiring as much as I now desired Brenna. She stood before us, skin bared and wings spread, powerful and glorious and enticingly luscious, and my desire flared into an inferno in my gut that I hadn't quite put out yet.

Once more, I ripped my mind from that image and focused on the matter at hand.

"Brenna, I asked you for the truth, and you gave it to me. Thank you."

She nodded in acknowledgment, but said nothing. Her clear grey eyes remained on the steady slope ahead of us, silvery braid tossed over one shoulder.

"I have a question for you: is it possible for you to help us bring our ship down to the shore?"

She shrugged, nonchalant. "I don't think it'd be a problem, particularly if we hooked it up to Björn's oxen. I can help pull and steer, slow it if necessary. We'd have to do it in the black of night, so I wouldn't be seen."

I ran a hand over my chin, scratching at my beard as I thought it over. "I think that would work. If someone is out, you could duck inside and we'd just be the idiots moving something far too big with only two oxen. Would you be willing to do that for us?" It seemed to me, knowing the truth, the best approach when dealing with a celestial being was to ask politely.

"Yes, I will help you."

"Thank you. Brenna, I have another proposition for you. Leif, Björn, and I discussed it and we agreed: assuming Signe feels she can manage the household, we'd like you to join our raiding party."

Her eyes swept quickly to meet mine, surprised. "Truly?"

"Yes. You said you are a warrior. We've seen you in action. Your sword and armor certainly speak to the truth of it. You'd be an invaluable asset in battle, and we need a fourth member that we can trust. I will extend that trust to you. Given your history, I can't imagine your plan is to hide out here, pushing a plow, and keeping your head down for however many years. You want to earn gold, and you want to leave. Am I correct?"

Her eyes darted to the ground, arms crossing over her chest. "I don't have solid plans," she hedged. "I can't stay in one place for too long; my appearance never changes and eventually people notice. So yes, I need gold, and I will eventually need to leave."

My heart sunk slightly, but at least she confirmed my suspicions.

Brenna stared into the distance for a moment as we walked in silence, then stopped and turned to me abruptly as if she'd suddenly made a decision.

"Søren, I know this is your plan, your team, your

ship. But I'm going to tell you something I didn't share in the barn. It wasn't important to my story, and I didn't want to distract everyone from the most important parts of what I had to say.

"However, I know you need more than just my word to work on, and since the request I'm going to make of you is a big one, I'm going to tell you why you should grant it."

Brenna's clear grey eyes held my gaze, penetrating, heavy with the gravity of what she was about to tell me. She wanted me to know she was serious.

"I have done this before; all of it."

"I don't understand, done what? Joined a raiding party?"

"No. I said Odin sent me here to punish me, and that part is true. But this isn't the first time he's done it. I've lived over a thousand years on Midgard, Søren. I've seen the world go through wars and famines and plagues and technology you couldn't even fathom. I hid from Odin because I didn't want to do his bidding anymore, and he eventually found me. He spun back time, as if the life—lives—I lived never happened, and dropped me here to start again, all over. I don't know exactly where we are, but I suspect the village I was in last time is somewhere northeast of here. Do you understand what I'm saying? I've done all of this before, and I know what needs to be done, where we need to raid, to get more treasure than even the Jarl can imagine."

There was no hint of duplicity in her eyes; they were as clear and steady as they'd been when she first revealed her wings. She was right; if she'd simply told me she knew where to go, I might have questioned her. But if she really had seen the future...

"I know you've shown me some incredible truths today, but I'm not sure I can wrap my head around traveling to the future on top of everything else. Can you take me? Show me?"

Brenna's eyes rolled, and she released a frustrated sigh. "No, I didn't travel to the future. I lived through centuries on this planet, and then Odin whisked me to Asgard and turned back time on Midgard, then sent me back. I have no control over it. It's all Odin's little plaything. But here is my point: I know where to go to gain treasures your Jarl will take notice of. We will force him to recognize us as the superior team, over Skarde, once we turn up with so many riches. We wouldn't be haphazardly raiding along the shores of Europa. We can make targeted strikes to places I know hide incredible wealth. I know because I've been there, I've seen it. Do you understand?"

I tried to absorb the implications of her words. "So with your knowledge, we could easily outstrip Skarde's performance, even with our smaller crew and ship?"

"Easily."

"Excellent. So what is your request, in exchange for this valuable information?"

Brenna's gaze didn't waiver. "I want you to let me captain the ship and lead the team."

thirty-eight

BRENNA

I KNEW I was taking a tremendous risk; Søren was the leader of the trio. It had been apparent to me since I'd fought Björn into the mud that first night.

But if we were going to work together, they needed to trust me completely. Which meant Søren needed to give up control and trust me, so the others would follow. Otherwise, he'd continue to second-guess me, hold meetings with the other two without me, and decide whether I needed to know something instead of allowing me to make that decision.

That wouldn't work for me.

Søren's jaw flexed repeatedly as he clenched his teeth, staring at me without a single blink of those predatory green eyes.

I knew the decision he was weighing: tell me no, and risk me refusing to help them at all, or completely give up control of the plan he had crafted, the team he had built, and trust me, a virtual stranger, to do a better job than he could do himself. I knew Søren's instincts were good, but I wasn't operating on instinct —I actually knew where we'd find the treasures we sought. I could see his pride, his belief in himself, warring with the idea of relinquishing control to me.

I held his gaze for a long, silent moment while he considered, refusing to drop my gaze or back down.

His bright green eyes narrowed, and Søren crossed his arms over his chest. "I propose a test."

"A test?" I released a disbelieving laugh. "That sounds to me as if you're wanting a free sample of my knowledge, without offering me anything in return."

"Not exactly. Our village has a tradition: Before we depart on the summer raids, we hold a competition to see which will be the lead ship. Until now we've never had a second ship, so Skarde's ship has automatically been declared the winner. We hold the event for ceremony only. A sort of festival, really.

"We need to get our ship to the harbor tonight in order to compete in the games tomorrow. If we win, we will be lead ship, which means we can force Skarde to give up some of his crew, flesh out our team, and have a much better chance of success. Otherwise he holds their allegiance and we will have just the four of us."

"I've already agreed to help you with the ship."

"Yes, that's not the test I'm proposing. I think you

should lead the team for the trial tomorrow. If you win and beat Skarde, you will be the captain for the summer raids. If you fail, we are stuck with our four-person team, and you will take orders from me. I will tell you only what I want you to know, and you will give me all the information I need to lead our team to honor and recognition by the Jarl."

This was an interesting proposition. While there was an implied challenge, an assumption that I would fail, I also knew I had participated in, and led, more raids in my many lifetimes than Søren ever would in his single, brief life. It had been awhile, but I still knew the ins and outs of a viking *drakkar*—it would be like riding a bike, certainly.

I leveled my gaze at Søren. "I need your word that no one on this team will try to sabotage me, since I will depend on all of your performance to be successful."

Now it was Søren's turn to laugh. "It is in all of our best interests to win this; believe me, Björn, Leif, and I want nothing more than to beat Skarde in this trial, and every raid thereafter. We need the extra men to row and weigh down the ship in order to cross deeper water. It would be extremely foolish of us to throw this competition just to keep you from becoming the captain."

I thought for another moment, but it was certainly the best offer I would receive. Reaching toward Søren, I offered him my hand. "I accept your offer. If I win this challenge against Skarde, I am lead for the team. If I lose, you remain the lead and I will still contribute my knowledge to ensure we secure the spot before the Jarl."

Søren accepted my handshake, and we shared a conspiratorial grin that verged on challenging.

When we turned and began the walk toward the homestead, I asked, "Are you going to tell me what this competition comprises?"

He just shook his head, still grinning. "No, I don't think that's important. If you are as experienced a viking as you say, it shouldn't be a problem for you."

Okay, there was definitely a challenge implied in that statement. With nothing more to go on, I decided to dredge up all the memories I had of viking warfare and get ready to move the ship in preparation for tomorrow.

thirty-nine

BRENNA

I WONDERED how they intended to get the ship out of the barn; certainly, it wouldn't fit through the tiny doorway we used. Björn had to duck to pass through that door.

I should have known Søren had a plan. Leif and Søren left for supper and to allow us to get the girls settled. Once the night had fallen and we told Signe we'd be out for a while in case she woke while we were gone, we headed out to the barn. Björn opened the shutters to let in the moonlight, and I climbed the ladder.

Ducking up to the dark loft to change swiftly into my armor, I was out of sight when Leif and Søren entered the barn. Just for the hell of it, I took a leap from the loft and let my powerful wings slow my descent to the floor. The wind they kicked up blew dirt and bits of hay over the men, and they cringed in surprise.

I landed, smirking, and tucked my wings back. Truthfully, the barn was a rather tight space with the boat filling the entire first floor, but I couldn't help showing off just a little.

Leif recovered first, and he beamed at me with absolute adoration. "Just full of surprises, aren't you, Brenna?"

"Maybe," I grinned in response.

"I have a surprise for you. It required a quick change, but I hope you'll approve." Stepping forward, Leif handed me a cloth-wrapped bundle. "Open it!"

Slightly nervous, I unwrapped the gift and gazed at it in confusion. "Leif, is this…?"

"Yes, it's you. We needed a figurehead for the ship, and I wanted to do something other than a dragon. I took you as inspiration, and what was originally meant to be flowing hair and fabric became your wings."

The carved and polished figurehead was incredible work, particularly given the tools Leif had at his disposal. It was the head and torso of a woman, neatly tapered at the waist to fit the prow of the ship, with delicately carved features and detailed hair that flowed behind her. At some point, the hair took on the curves and angles of wings, with individual feathers cut into the wood.

"Leif, thank you. I don't know what to say, I've... never been made into a figurehead before."

"I wanted something beautiful and powerful to represent us, and I couldn't think of another creature that represented that better than you." His cheeks were flushed crimson, visible even in the relative darkness. "You should attach it. It's the last piece."

I considered flying up to do it, but there really wasn't room to get a good takeoff, and it was a little unnecessary. Instead, I clambered up the side of the cart they'd built the ship on, and with minimal effort forced the pegged bottom of the figurehead into the hole carved to hold it. It fit perfectly.

Once I was back on the dirt floor of the barn, I turned to Björn. "So, I agreed to help get this beast down to the water, but no one has mentioned yet how we're getting it out of the barn?"

Björn, a hulking figure in the relative darkness, grinned. Moonlight played on his pearly teeth. "Oh, we have a solution for that, Little Bird."

That pulled me up short. "Little Bird?"

"Yes, that is what I'm going to call you now. Fitting, don't you think?"

Indignation bubbled in my chest. "No, I do *not* think. In case you haven't noticed, I'm neither little, nor a bird. I'm a *valkyrie*. Do you need me to pull out my sword and remind you?"

"Well, to me, you are little. And you have wings, like a bird has wings. So, to me you are a Little Bird."

"I absolutely refuse to answer to that." I glared at him as impressively as I was able, in the darkness with him nearly a foot taller than me. My wings shuddered as I attempted to fold them tighter, and the sound of the feathers rubbing together was audible.

"Ah, it seems I've ruffled your feathers, Little Bird. My apologies, it's not an insult."

The indignity of this human talking to me like a child, this man who couldn't even fathom the number of years older than him I actually was, set my blood boiling. "You will not call me Little Bird."

"Oh, and how will you stop me?"

Inspiration struck. "A wager. If I win the challenge tomorrow, you may never call me Little Bird again."

"Agreed. And if you lose, the name stays."

"Fine."

"Fine."

"So," I huffed, "how are we getting the boat out? Or are we all just going to stand around the entire night, coming up with stupid names for people that don't make sense?"

Søren and Leif were barely visible in the darkness, having crossed to the side of the barn where the door led back to the house.

"Like this," Søren called, and pushed at the wall near the ground. Leif pushed from the other side, and the wall moved.

Somehow, they'd built a hinge into the wall, attached to the frame. Björn rushed forward with a pole—I didn't see where he got it from—and propped Søren's side of the wall up. He repeated the process with Leif's side, and now we had a clear path to pull the ship through the front of the barn.

It was easier to see now, with the wall open and moonlight pouring in. "So, do you approve of our design?" Søren grinned, evidently pleased with himself.

"It is very clever," I admitted. Far more clever of engineering design than a viking should have produced. Typically, their structures depended on the support of timbers all around the house. This was an open-frame construction that wouldn't be introduced for centuries. Suspicion warred with admiration in my heart. How could Søren have dreamed this up? It seemed impossible, and I couldn't help suspecting interference from Asgardians.

And if they were interfering, it was bound to be bad news for me.

While I'd been thinking, Björn had gone to fetch the oxen. Now he hooked their yolk up to the wooden cart that cradled the ship and set them to work to pull it out of the barn.

But though he called and cracked the whip more than once, the ship didn't budge.

This was definitely my cue.

Björn fetched me a rope, and I secured it to the front of the cart and around my waist. On the count of three, Björn once again whipped the oxen forward, and I took to the air, pulling with all the strength of my magical wings.

After a slow, painful creak, the ship moved. It had settled into the ground under the weight, but once the wheels began rolling, it went more smoothly. The oxen could now manage the pace, and I untied myself and focused on helping to steer.

It was a slow, torturous process. We had to descend quite a way, and at times it took all of my strength to stop the cart from rolling over the animals. Other times the weight was enough that the ship didn't want to follow the curve of the path and I had to push from either side, carefully guiding it down the hill to the waters of the fjord.

Finally, we reached the shore, and eased to a stop on the gravel beside the larger, more traditional *drakkar*.

"So, how do you intend to get it into the water?"

Søren wiped an arm across his sweaty brow. We'd all been working hard, but the men didn't have the benefit of magical, soul-powered restorative armor. "We have to turn it and back it into the water. It needs to get deep enough that the ship floats off the cart and we can just cast it off."

After that journey, the oxen were hardly interested in this circle and back-up maneuver Søren had planned. It took a lot more whip than coaxing, but we eventually got it into place and began slowly easing the wooden cart into the fjord.

When the oxen were nearly up to their bellies in chilly water, the ship started rocking. A few more steps back and I took to the air, pushing with all of my strength to ease the ship from the wooden cart. Once it was completely free of the cart, it bobbed sickeningly a few times, then settled into the water as if it were home.

Søren, Leif, and Björn all cheered, and I added my voice to their joyful noise. "Okay, now what?"

"Now, we go for a sail." Søren grinned.

forty

BRENNA

THE MEN HAD LOADED the mast, sails, and oars into the ship before our descent, and now we set them in position. Our sail was a plain off-white canvas, and Leif attached it quickly to the crossbars on the mast before we pushed off.

"Where are we going, exactly?" I grunted as I pulled my oar. They designed the ship for men, not valkyries, and my wings were pressed uncomfortably to the wooden floor of the boat.

"We're just paddling around the outcropping of rock over there," Søren tipped his chin. "I don't want anyone to know about our ship until we're down here in the morning. You know, in case anymore *accidents* happen."

I understood all too well. We lived out of town, and the festivities didn't start until later in the day. If people saw a second ship early in the morning, there was no telling what could happen.

The waters were calm, and it didn't take us long to navigate around the corner Søren indicated. It hid a tiny cove, with a pebbled beach barely large enough to justify the name. We steered the ship up onto the rocks, and Søren secured it by tying the prow to a nearby boulder.

After climbing the narrow path to the top of the cliff, we started the trudge back up to Björn's farm. Before too long, Leif, then Søren, peeled off toward their homes, and it was just Björn and me.

I had donned my woolen dress and carried my breastplate in a bag over my shoulder, with the rest of my armor concealed beneath my clothes. It made the most sense to avoid being seen with my giant wings if we could avoid it. I'd been tempted to offer Björn a ride—it would certainly have been faster—but something told me that would be a far more intimate act than I was willing to share with him at the moment.

Björn seemed to be lost in thought. He'd never been loquacious, but he usually had something to say, occasionally. We walked for over a half hour without a single word, not even a careless taunt about the nickname he gave me.

"Björn, is everything okay?" I had to ask. It was driving me mad. I'd dropped a lot of information on the guys today, and I wasn't sure they had really processed it all.

He didn't answer my question. Instead, he asked me one of his own. "Brenna, do you plan to leave?"

Ugh, this conversation again. "I can't stay forever," I said as gently as I could. "I don't age, and people eventually notice. Especially in a village this small. It will just cause problems until there's nothing I can do but run away. It's not like I relish the idea of moving every few years."

To be honest, I had a bone-deep weariness from the moving that still existed from my first spin on Midgard—a weariness that even my armor couldn't fix. Like a scar that had healed over, but was never quite the same. "I just don't see how I have another choice."

Björn was quiet for another long stretch, and then he muttered, "I understand. How long do you think you can stay?"

"It depends on a few things," I answered honestly. "Ideally, I'd be able to accumulate some wealth, make a name for myself, earn the favor of the Jarl, and receive a few gifts. That takes time, seasons, years. But if an opportunity comes up for something better, I may have to take it."

"What kind of opportunity?" The question was sharp, to the point.

"Well, if I can earn enough to secure passage to… well, you've never heard of it, but there's a place called Iceland. A few vikings have already visited this place, presumably by accident. But more will make treks there on purpose. It's a beautiful place. If I can get passage on a ship to Iceland, I may take that opportunity. It's out of the way, empty, and I could build a home and stay there for some time with no one knowing something was different about me. If I can secure enough wealth to buy what I need to live on." I shrugged. "So there are a few considerations."

He fell silent once more, and we finally approached the end of the road where his homestead waited, bathed in the light of the waning moon. He waited while I slipped out of my remaining armor and hid it in the loft, emerging from the barn with just my sword once more.

Before we reached the door to the longhouse, Björn paused. "Brenna, I... well, just know when you decide to leave, you don't have to go alone. Okay?" He turned and opened the door so I couldn't ask any more questions, then gestured me inside. I cast him a cautious smile in the low light of the burned-down fire, then settled onto my cushioned bench and considered everything that had been said throughout the day.

It was late, and I was tired. But I stayed up far longer than I intended, mulling over the past and preparing for the future.

forty-one

BRENNA

BY THE TIME Björn and I reached the trail to the secret cove, Søren and Leif were already waiting, and most of the village appeared to be on the shore of the nearby harbor.

I imagined Søren planned for some kind of dramatic reaction from the crowd when we came around the corner, and to some degree, he got it. I heard someone shout excitedly, and then a sea of indistinguishable faces turned in our direction. Some jeers, but even more cheers rose from the crowd. As we approached, I could pick out Skarde among the group: his reddish blonde hair was braided, his beard trimmed, and he looked altogether neat and presentable for a viking. A dramatic brick-red cape, pinned over his shoulder, stood out among the assembly—there was not a single person with a garment of the same color.

Of course, my crew had also taken care to clean up. Signe had tended to both Björn's and my hair, weaving intricate braids that created a delicate crown for me and left the lower part of my hair hanging loose, and creating a pattern of smaller braids on the sides of Björn's head with one larger one that went down the middle, the bottom of his hair also loose. He'd donned a clean, off-white tunic, belted over dark brown trousers, with a chocolate cape pinned over his right shoulder. I simply wore the same woolen dress Signe had given me, accessorized with my leather belt and sword. The hair was my one accessory, and Signe's work had certainly made the silvery color sing with the way she wove the plaits.

Leif's hair was down and shone like gold as it drifted in the breeze. He wore a neat, pale-blue tunic that complimented his impossibly bright eyes, and brown trousers with a brown cape. I attempted to avoid staring at him too thirstily... the man was just impossibly pretty.

Søren wore a cleaner version of what he wore every day, just a light brown tunic belted over brown trousers, but added a cape over his sword arm as well. His sandy hair and beard were tidy as usual, head freshly shaved below his ears and hair neatly tucked into a single braid.

When we reached the shore, the displeasure on

Skarde's expression was easy to read. He marched over, and Søren hopped off the ship to meet him.

"What is this?" He gestured to our ship. "A boat for dwarves?"

Laughter erupted around us, and Søren's fingers flexed, but he maintained his calm. "We have brought a ship to compete in the traditional games before the summer raids. Even though they have been ceremonial for the last many years, it seemed like the right time to bring them back to life. A genuine test of viking skill and honor!"

The crowd burst into cheers, and Skarde looked as if he wanted to argue, but thought better of it. "Of course! It will be nice to have some competition, for once. You will take the role of captain?"

"No, I will not," Søren grinned. "Our captain today will be Brenna." He gestured in my direction and smiled like the Cheshire Cat as Skarde turned my way.

The scene played out in slow motion, as if it were from a movie I'd seen in what felt like another lifetime. Skarde, surprised by the name, lifted an eyebrow as his head turned, painfully slowly, in my direction. The shock when he recognized me was like a ripple across his features, beginning with the drop of his jaw, spreading to widen his eyes and lift his brows.

I walked toward him, hand on my sword. I could feel a hundred pairs of eyes tracking my every move, but I did my best to ignore them and keep my focus on my target. "Hello, Skarde, it's nice to see you again. From what I hear, you have a vastly different recollection of the night we met than I do."

The laughter crescendoed, and I paused to allow everyone the enjoyment of hearing the full story. "But let me address your version. As for me pleasuring you in a dozen different ways, I know you have difficulty counting, but I'd hardly call a single position change a dozen. To my recollection, you passed out far too soon to give any woman pleasure, particularly a woman such as me—not something I would rave about. There is no way I'd be interested in returning for that every full moon." I smiled sweetly up at him as the color in his cheeks darkened. More quietly, I added, "Next time, perhaps you ought to just appreciate the gift you received instead of trying to pretend it was so much more. Then you might not be humiliated in front of the entire village."

Skarde's hands were fisted, knuckles white with straining against his desire to strike me. I knew without looking that Björn and Leif had joined us and now stood directly behind me. Skarde's eyes rose to something over my head, and he seemed to think better of unleashing the anger he had been building.

"Well," he replied with a forced jovial tone, "I think we ought to get on with the competition, no?" The cheer rose like a wave from the surrounding villagers. Skarde threw a beefy arm over my shoulders, and steered me further up the beach as the crowd made a path through for us.

In a wide, empty circle of rocks on the beach sat

something that made my heart lurch, then begin racing full steam.

If I'd known, I'd never have agreed to this challenge. It was so cruel I would almost think Odin had planned it himself.

"What exactly is this challenge?" I hissed at Søren.

Skarde grinned as if he'd just been given a gift. "Oh, your friends didn't tell you? The challenge is for the captains to drink copious amounts of beer, then guide their blindfolded teams out to the other side of the fjord and back. First one that makes it back is the winner." His lips curled into a lascivious grin, and he added in a lower voice, "I'm sure the entire town is looking forward to how you behave with a few beers under your belt, Brenna. I certainly remember well."

I sighed, allowing my eyes to drift back to the twin barrels on simple wooden tables, each with its own mug, that waited for us.

"Whenever you're ready, *captain*."

forty-two

BRENNA

POUNDING BEERS WASN'T DIFFICULT; I had lifetimes of experience pouring alcohol down my throat.

The difference was that, this time, I didn't actually want to.

I wasn't trying to forget anything or drown my misery. It didn't taste good; I didn't revel in the fuzziness that slowly obscured the edges of my thought. I just kept filling my mug and pouring the lukewarm brew down my throat to reach the bottom as quickly as possible.

Skarde and I each had our own mini barrel to finish. I gathered that the sooner I finished, the better; we could load up and set sail as soon as the barrel was empty. And we had plenty of advantages: for one, I was not nearly as affected by the alcohol as I would have been without my armor. It wasn't here, clearing the toxicity from my system now; but it had fortified me enough from the hours last night that my body processed the booze faster and more efficiently than a normal human.

Second, we had a smaller team and a smaller ship. It wouldn't take us as long to load onto our boat and launch out into the water as it would Skarde and his several dozen warriors.

But Skarde had the advantage of all those men rowing together, with experience under their belt. They would have a great deal of power out of the gate.

He also knew exactly where this route went, while I'd have to puzzle it out, fuzzy-brained, on the fly. I tried not to think about how the ship, rocking in the waves, would feel.

Plus, the man was enormous. He was clearly at an advantage when it came to fitting all of this booze in his gut. I comforted myself with the thought that I'd be able to throw it all up as soon as we got on the water and purge my system of the alcohol I no longer wanted.

With each cup we poured, the crowd grew rowdier. Skarde's men huddled around him, jeering at me, congratulating him on his epic manliness.

Behind me stood my three teammates. They clapped with each finished cup and called an encouraging, "You can do it, Brenna!" But it was a drop in the ocean compared to the noise of Skarde's support. A headache was growing in my temple, and I knew this event would cause an epic hangover tomorrow. Maybe I'd sleep in my armor, try to stave it off.

As I finished my last cup, my eyes drifted to the shore to gauge our route. The crowd had cleared a path to allow us to the ships, but what concerned me now was the sky.

It had been a bright, robins-egg blue when we arrived, and in the course of our little drinking contest thick, slate-grey clouds had crept in. Dark patches, nearly black, flashed with lightning over the water. The wind off the fjord picked up, the waves growing rough in the distance and crashing onto the rocky shore.

Draining the last drop of my beer, I held the cup upside down, then dropped it on the rocks and wiped my face with the back of my hand. In a fit of showmanship, I kicked the table over, revealing that my barrel was also empty, before I lurched toward the shore.

My guys let out a shout of triumph—Skarde was still drinking—and Leif and Björn took off running toward our ship. Søren stayed behind to walk with me. Not steadying me, just staying near in case I needed it.

I lurched a few steps but kept my feet beneath me as I made my way unsteadily to the ship. With so much liquid in my gut, I already felt like I was at sea. I clambered up into the boat and as soon as we pushed away from the shore, the sloshing in my gut grew worse. It was coming up, and soon. I just hoped I could get far enough out that the people in town couldn't see it when I poured all that beer back into the water.

A loud cheer told me that Skarde had finished his barrel, and his team was on their way. We needed to get moving.

As soon as we turned the ship around, my guys tied their blindfolds on and waited for my command. The sail was already down, wind puffing out the fabric and dragging us gently forward.

I realized too late we should have practiced commands beforehand, but there was nothing for it now.

"Okay, unless I say otherwise, I want you to row on a five-count. Oars to front is one; in the water two, pull for three and four, and lift on five, returning to front for one again. I'll start you out. Keep count in your mind so you can continue without cues. One!"

The guys pushed forward and down on their oars, lifting the tips out of the water.

"Two!"

They lifted the handles, dipping the oars into the water.

"Three! Four!"

They pulled back on the oars, pushing the boat forward.

"Five!"

They pushed down again, lifting the oars from the water.

"One! Two! Three! Four! Five!"

We repeated the count together a few times until they were moving smoothly in sync.

I glanced at the rapidly shrinking village and decided it was safe for me to lean over the edge and empty my sloshing stomach.

The relief was immediate, and my mind was instantly clearer. While I would have preferred to lie down for a nap, I bucked up for the challenge.

Fortunately for us, the wind was blowing in the exact direction we needed, helping to barrel us along in the right direction. I knew it would be problematic on the way back, but we'd face that challenge when we reached it. For now, we were skipping along the water, only battered a little by the waves and encroaching storm. Skarde was far enough behind us now that he wasn't too great of a concern. The sailing was smooth.

I called out occasional commands to keep my rowers in sync, but for the most part, they did well. My mouth was sour with the taste of old beer vomit, but I had nothing besides seawater to wash it out with, so I just did my best to ignore it. The winds of the storm were stronger here, whipping ferociously at my hair and tugging on my dress. I could see Skarde's sail was also full, the striped fabric straining against the force of the wind. His crew of over fifty men were all working hard, their oars like the dozens of legs of a centipede all crawling forward together.

I took the time to plan when we had to turn around. There was a large rock we apparently had to steer around—I was fairly certain I could see it now, waves crashing against the tall, skinny formation of dark grey stone. We'd be able to use the wind to steer around it, but unless a miracle happened and the wind shifted, I'd have to drop the sail and we'd be relying on oar-power to get us back.

Of which Skarde had significantly more than I did.

I explained my plan to my crew as we neared the stone goal post, and when I turned to gauge our distance from the target, something odd caught my eye.

A flash of lighting seemed to strike the very rock we were meant to sail around, revealing a shadow that looked like the outline of a man...

Heat drained from my face, and dread settled in my gut like a heavy stone.

Surely not. What was he doing here?

As we prepared to take the hard corner, my eyes remained glued to the top of the rock; Sure enough, Thor stood on the top, clutching Mjöllnir, his long blond hair whipping in the storm winds.

Anxiety clutched my chest, but I remembered my team was blindfolded and needed me to guide them. I pulled at the sail, turning it to capture the wind and instructing my team to maneuver our way around the rock.

Abruptly, the wind shifted direction, and suddenly it was filling our sails and pushing us back toward the village.

My heart swelled; *thank you Thor!*

I got my team back in sync, and we were rowing our merry way across the water. The wind began to let up, but I didn't think too much about it. It was still blowing in the right direction and we had a good pace going, thanks to the lighter craft and strength of my oarsmen.

I glanced back to spot Skarde, and my heart dropped to my belly: Skarde had nearly caught us. His oarsmen were hard at work, but most noticeably, his sails were taut, billowing with wind.

"Guys, we need to row faster. Skarde is catching up. Let's increase the pace on my count - one, two, three, four, five!" I shouted frantically, and the ship lurched forward with renewed energy from my team.

But I already knew it was too late. Skarde's ship had overtaken us, and the man himself leered in my direction as they passed.

No doubt he attributed his success to his incredible leadership, but I knew the truth. As the ship passed, I could see the source of his impressive speed all too well. Thor—appearing to run on solid clouds— chased Skarde's ship. His cheeks puffed out, blowing to fill Skarde's sails and push him home. Lightning crackled around him, striking the water and flaring outward. Our ship rocked in the aftermath of waves as they continued, and our sails fell limp once they'd passed completely.

"How could you? It's not fair!" I shouted into the wind at Thor's back, furious and miserable and utterly hopeless.

I'd never had an issue with Thor. Despite all the Odin drama, he had never so much as lifted an eyebrow in my direction. So why was he suddenly helping my enemy? Had Odin put him up to it? Was there more at play in this village than I knew?

My team continued rowing at full speed, although we'd already lost. We could hear the cheers when Skarde's skip landed, and they'd completely disembarked by the time we reached the shore. Of course, Thor was nowhere to be seen, the storm clouds rapidly dissipating and revealing glorious blue skies once more.

Naturally, I had to allow Skarde's unearned celebration of his own prowess—it wasn't as if I could point out that Thor had helped him. Even if they believed it, no one would understand that Thor hadn't been helping Skarde succeed, so much as preventing me from winning.

The alcohol in my system dragged me down. Combined with the depressing reminder I was always going to be playing a game against beings far more powerful than myself, I felt my spirits sink to a place I hadn't experienced since before I received my armor.

I knew, logically, this was a minor loss. We would still go on raids, and I still knew where to find the real treasure, and I could still earn enough to get me on my way to Iceland.

That didn't help the disappointment filling my chest.

forty-three

BRENNA

WE TOOK part in the rest of the festival, good-naturedly congratulating Skarde on his victory. Søren introduced me to the chieftain, Åse, who was sincere in his compliments about my ability to both drink and captain a ship. There was something there, a moment when I thought he was going to say something else, but then it had passed.

We hung about, enjoying in the celebration, until the afternoon shadows grew long and we could make an excuse about the long walk back to Björn's farm.

But when we could finally slip away and head up the path toward home, the atmosphere took a decided turn toward the dark.

My head was pounding, and I was in no mood to

explain why I was so utterly hopeless, but I felt like they deserved an explanation.

"Guys," I paused on the path, and the three men stopped with me. "I feel as if you should know what happened. I need to bring it up because it may continue to be a problem for us."

Leif was quick to reassure me. "Brenna, it's okay. It was a long shot to begin with. Skarde had so many more men to row. We didn't honestly expect to win it."

At that revelation, my eyes flashed to Søren, who stared back at me, his face impassive, unrepentant.

So he set me up to fail. *Figures.*

"Even so, we were very far ahead, and then Skarde gained on us, rapidly. Because Thor helped him."

"Thor?"

"Are you sure?"

"You can't be serious."

"Yes, I know Thor when I see him, okay?" I leveled a glare in Søren's direction at the insinuation that I was mistaken, or making it up. Did he forget who I was? "He was perched on that rock we sailed around, and at first I thought he was there to help me, turn the wind and push us back to the shore. But then when Skarde turned, Thor focused the storm on Skarde's sails and ours fell flat. He pushed him ahead of us."

"Why would he do that?" Leif was genuinely curious.

"I don't honestly know, but it can't bode well for

us. If Odin has Thor helping him to thwart me, it's possible every time I set foot on a ship he could stir up trouble for us. If there's more going on in this village, that could also be a problem for us. You've mentioned before how Skarde seems to constantly, impossibly, succeed in the face of stronger or cleverer men. Who's to say that he's not receiving help?

"I hope that Skarde is receiving help, and not that all of Asgard is against me. If that's the case, we can work with it. As long as we aren't in direct conflict with Skarde, we don't have to worry about interference. If it's all of them trying to punish me... well, there's no limit to how they could make things difficult for us."

"I can't believe that Thor would come down from Asgard just to help Skarde win this contest. How would it benefit him? Why would he care?" Søren challenged me again.

"Well, that's what we have to figure out, Søren. If it's about helping Skarde be successful, there may be a bigger game at play than we realize. If it's about punishing me, it may be more problematic than we thought."

Søren rubbed at his bearded chin for a moment, thinking. Finally, he said, "We'll figure it out," and started walking uphill again. I shrugged at the other two, and we continued along the path.

Leif turned at his spot, Søren soon after, and once again it was just Björn and I climbing toward his farm.

"Brenna... just so you know, I believe you. About

Thor. I heard you shout at him, and there's no way you'd have said that to Skarde."

"Thank you," I replied, my voice low.

"And I think it was unfair of Søren to have you take that challenge when you didn't know what it would be. I heard you get sick on the boat, too," he confessed. "How is your stomach?"

"My stomach is fine. It's my head that's pounding. I should probably drink more water and eat something. I'd kill for a tylenol." I muttered the last bit to myself, not expecting him to hear me.

Björn glanced at me curiously. "What is tilynole?"

The dark chuckle escaped my chest in a huff of breath. "Just a kind of... magic we had, where I came from. It made headaches disappear, like that!" I snapped my fingers.

"You had that magic where you were a valkyrie? Before Odin?"

I hesitated, then nodded. It was the easiest explanation. "Yes."

"What was your home like?"

We spent the rest of the journey discussing Valkyr, and while the memories brought a smile to my lips, it ached deeply within my heart to remember that my home was no more. To think of the memories that would be indelibly tied to places that didn't exist. And people who no longer lived.

Sadness for my losses merged with the depression brought on by alcohol and the afternoon's defeat, and I felt heavy under the combined force of it all.

As we approached the homestead, we realized the

entire side of the barn was still propped open. Björn and I glanced at each other and redirected our feet toward the barn without speaking a word. He lifted the mat of boards that created the wall, and I removed the massive posts from first one side, then the other. Once the wall was replaced, I stepped toward the door to the barn and told Björn to go on without me. When he tried to insist he would wait for me, I had to explain.

"I'm going inside to put on my armor and fly for a while, Björn. It'll help me recover, deal with the sadness in my heart better. I'm only a half a person when I'm not wearing it. Eventually it catches up to me."

Stubbornly, Björn shook his head. "You know, I've watched you Brenna. I've thought about this a good deal, and I know you are attached to your armor. I'm sure it holds a great deal of importance to you.

"But I don't believe you are half a person without it. I believe you might not be *exceptionally* strong of heart, or spirit, without it. Perhaps there's something there. But when you first came to us, you weren't heartless, nor were you soulless. Yes, you were sad. You still cared about Signe's injury, trying to determine how you could help her. You still played with Astrid and were still gentle with Yrsa."

He stepped closer, the bright moonlight bleaching his golden hair to silver and glittering in his dark blue eyes. My heart throbbed in my chest; I knew that look.

Björn's voice dropped, his tone becoming deeper,

gruffer with emotion. "Despite besting me in a sword match, and listening to me claim I wanted you to send me to Valhalla, you held back. Was that a heartless, soulless person who did that? No, I don't think so. Brenna, whether you believe it, you are a good person, a kind person, a *whole* person, without your magical armor. I see it, and so can anyone with half a brain." Large, warm palms rose to claim my cheeks, and this time when Björn kissed me it was so gentle, so sweet, that I sighed and leaned back against the door behind me.

Encouraged, he pressed forward, and my hands reached up to pull me closer to him.

The hairs of his beard tickled my nose and chin, but I didn't mind. This man—this man had seen me at my absolute lowest of lows, and didn't consider that to be a broken person. He saw beauty in me, good-ness in me, even when I was without my armor. That alone was enough to make me cling to his body for comfort. I needed someone to see me that way. Not just the side of me I showed them; Björn had seen me crying into the laundry tub in absolute despair. If he believed I was still a worthy person in that moment, then perhaps there was something more, something I wasn't seeing.

My lips parted, and I welcomed his tongue to explore my mouth with a lick of his lower lip. The invitation eagerly accepted, Björn pressed me harder against the door, his hands dropping from my face to trace down my neck. One continued down to cup my breast while the other reached behind me, braced against the wood. My body warmed under his touch, heating with the desire to get closer, feel his skin under my fingertips.

The loud whinny of the horse sent us jumping apart and glancing toward the house guiltily. I didn't see anyone coming, but bless that horse for bringing me to my senses.

"Björn, thank you for saying those things. I still feel like I need to don my armor and go for a flight. Perhaps you're right, and it's some kind of crutch that I should outgrow. But for now, I trust it."

Still breathing heavily in the wake of our kissing, Björn released a long, slow breath and nodded. "Go, then. Do what you need to do." He ran both hands over his braided crown of hair and turned toward the longhouse.

"Björn?" My heart was throbbing a mile a minute.

"Yes?"

"Would you like to wait for me?"

forty-four

BRENNA

THIS TIME, I let him watch me don my armor.

Well, most of it.

I slid the fauld on under my skirt, then hiked the fabric up to buckle on my cuisse and greaves. Björn reclined in the pile of hay, watching the moonlight play off the mirror-like shine of my armor. He was almost hidden in the darkness, a shadow among shadows. But the light reflected in his eyes as he watched my risque armor show.

Finally, I pulled off the dress to attach my tassets to the fauld, exposing my breasts to the cool night air and Björn's gaze. I heard his intake of breath and smiled to myself as I continued my work. My nipples pebbled instantly in the chill, goosebumps rising all over my upper body. My lower body was warm and comfortable, thanks to my armor, and so would the rest of me be in a minute.

Once the gardbrace was attached to the breast-plate, I slid the entire piece over my head and reached behind my arms to buckle it into place. As soon as the last buckle set, there was a powerful rush of wind from my wings appearing. It was almost as if they flew in from space and attached themselves to my back on a whim, diving in and stopping abruptly.

This time Björn definitely gasped, and it drew a chuckle from my lips as I buckled on my vambrace. The warmth, the wholeness, immediately began filling me. Already my sense of humor was returning.

"I wondered... how that happened," he explained, sounding almost sheepish from the shadows.

"I understand. It seems like there has to be more to it than that, but they literally just appear out of thin air. Like I said, it's magic." I grinned in his direction, and could just make out the gleam of his answering grin in the darkness.

"So, you'll wait here, then?" It felt strange, hopping from the loft to exit through the door like a normal person and just leave him here, knowing I was off flying around.

There was a grunt and some shuffling, and Björn appeared from the shadows. "Actually, I was wondering if I could go out and watch you?"

"Watch what? I'm just going to go fly around, stretch my wings."

"I know. It's just so… incredible. Do you mind?"

I shrugged. "Sure. I could just sit here and chitchat, but honestly having the wings off all day makes them restless, so they need to get out and flap around a bit. That's the only reason I do it."

"The only reason?" Björn's quizzical expression was audible in his tone, if barely visible in the darkness.

"Okay, it's also fun," I conceded. "Shall we?"

Björn turned toward the ladder. Before I could think twice about it, I offered, "would you like a lift?"

"A lift?" Of course, the phrasing didn't translate well from English.

"A ride… I could hold on to you and we could fly down… instead of the ladder." My cheeks were hot; thank Frigg it was so dark in here, he couldn't see me blushing.

"Oh… okay." He shuffled in my direction, and I raised my arm to his shoulder.

"Put your arm around my waist and hold on." As gently as I was able, I lifted off with my wings and glided us to the floor.

Björn gripped my body tightly, pressing his hip to mine and squeezing along the length of my body. His rapidly beating heart betrayed his emotions; he acted nonchalant, but I could feel the trepidation in him.

However, we landed safely on the ground a few seconds later, no worse for the wear. His grip on me eased, and then he stepped to the side awkwardly.

"So… what now?"

"Well… now I go outside and fly around, and you watch, I guess?" This was his plan, after all.

"Right. Let's go." He gestured me through the door. I tucked my wings tightly and ducked to prevent them smacking on the doorframe. It took awhile to remember how big they were, but I was getting the hang of it.

"I guess… I'll see you in a bit?" I still wasn't exactly sure about this. It felt awkward to me, him just standing on the ground watching me enjoy myself in the sky.

Björn nodded, his eyes gleaming in the moonlight; a hulking shadow with shining, excited eyes. "Go on."

Turning, I took a few steps away from him and launched off, the gust of air from my wings kicking up dirt and bits of straw, sending a swirling cloud around my audience. I waited until I was high enough he couldn't see my expression in the dark sky, then turned and glanced at him. I could still see his face clearly, bathed in moonlight and tilted upward.

He was smiling.

At first I just kind of flapped around, wondering if he was expecting me to do something interesting. Then I realized that what he wanted to watch was me enjoying myself, so I tried to stop overthinking and just do what felt good.

I soared through the air like superman, driving across the sky with my hands forward. Then I performed several loop-de-loops, barrel rolls, and spins. When I glanced back at Björn on the ground, his smile had grown wide, stretching across his face. I'd never seen him smile so big—he was the happiest I'd ever seen him, watching me being myself. He looked so much like Helgi this way.

The reminder of Helgi stabbed my heart, and I coasted on the light breeze as I considered. It took me awhile to see it; yes Björn was a large man, as Helgi had been. There were certain physical characteristics that were very similar. But at first, Björn's personality had been so closed off, I didn't think the two had anything in common at all. Helgi had always been so warm, so sweet and thoughtful and comforting. He didn't press, but he seemed to know exactly when my weakest moments were, and stepped in to bolster me up.

And now here was Björn, doing exactly the same style of bolstering support. Arguing that I was stronger than I believed. Reveling in my strength, but supporting me in my weakness.

It was as if Björn was Helgi reincarnated, or perhaps Helgi had been Björn reincarnated, given that he wouldn't be born for a few hundred years from now.

My heart was telling me something, and it was time to listen.

With a surge, I drove my body straight upward, then allowed myself to slow, stop for a heart-wrenching pause, then tip backward and dive back toward the ground.

I landed gently, just a few feet from Björn. My skin was humming with joy and excitement and a deep, aching longing that had been building ever since Björn wrung that dress out for me, what felt like ages ago.

I stepped up to him, watching his features grow somber as he read the tension in the air, and pulled his head toward mine.

forty-five

BJÖRN

I DIDN'T KNOW what to expect, but the expression on Brenna's face when she landed, floating from the heavens like some kind of ethereal creature, set my pulse racing. There was a steadiness to her clear grey eyes, a surety that hadn't been there when she took off.

While I didn't believe she was half a person without her armor, I could see the change it brought over her. The self-doubt, the confusion and fear, seemed to melt from her like hot candle wax when she took to the skies.

Standing before me was a powerful creature who knew exactly what she wanted.

And for some reason, that was me.

Brenna reached up and tugged on the back of my neck, pulling my face down to hers, and kissing me with a searing passion our previous kisses hadn't held. My arms instantly snaked around her body, my fingertips brushing the feathers at her back as her tongue explored my mouth. I pressed against her lips, arching her armor-clad body into mine. My erection pressed uncomfortably against the metal undergarments she wore, and the flares and curves of silver, while beautiful to look at, clearly were not meant to allow anyone close to her.

She giggled against my lips, understanding my distress as I tried to caress her skin and kept running in to metal. "Come on," she slipped her fingers between mine and tugged me toward the barn.

Once we made it inside, Brenna stood in the streams of moonlight pouring through the open shutters and turned her back to me, lifting the bulk of her long, silvery hair. "Can you help me with the buckles?" Stretching a wing back carefully, she revealed the latches that held her breastplate in place.

I unlatched the buckle on each side, then she turned to face me. When she spread the hinged metal, her wings popped out of existence in a soft whisper of feathers. "Will you help me pull it off?"

I swallowed, trying to moisten my suddenly dry mouth, then reached forward to tug on the piece of armor. Brenna lifted her arms, allowing me to pull the entire metal breastplate from her body.

Clearly, there was magic in this armor. Where her skin had been warm to the touch before, her flesh abruptly pebbled in the cool night air as if she hadn't felt it until the metal was gone.

"Now this part," she let her hair swing behind her back and gestured to the pieces that were strapped over her feet and shins. A flirtatious, playful gleam shone in her eyes, but not a single hint of shame.

She was beautiful and powerful, and if she wanted me on my knees for her, I was happy to oblige.

Kneeling, I lifted one of her feet to rest on my leg, and set to work unbuckling her magical armor. First, I uncovered one delicate foot, then the silky skin of her calf. I kneaded her flesh between my fingers, drawing out the experience as I slowly undressed her heavenly body.

After I finished with her lower legs, she showed me where the buckles were hidden for the pieces covering her thighs. My heart beat faster, but I took my time here too.

Brenna gazed down on me in the darkness, her skin faintly luminous in the cool light of the moon. Once I freed the first thigh-piece, I couldn't stop myself from leaning forward to press my lips to the soft, milky-pale skin. My rough, calloused hands bit into the tender flesh as I squeezed, and Brenna moaned lightly in response. Her eyes fluttered closed, and her leg trembled slightly.

Good, so she is of the same mind as I am.

I set to work on her other leg, freeing it from its metallic cage and attending to her naked skin with kisses.

All that remained now was the piece on her arm, and, of course, her shiny silver underwear.

While I waited, Brenna gazed down at me with hooded eyes, removing the arm piece and the large, ornate sidepiece that clipped onto her bottoms.

Then she stopped and glanced around as if searching for something.

Apparently locating what she desired, Brenna crossed to the dark corner of the barn and returned with several clean, folded pieces of canvas. She laid them out neatly, as a stack in the middle of the floor, then returned to grab my hand and tug me toward them.

My heart was absolutely racing now, a nervous sweat trickling down the back of my neck. What kind of pleasure did an immortal being take?

With a gentle tug, she untied my belt, then detached my cape from my shirt, flinging both items aside. A small smile played on her lips, but she didn't speak. Instead, she pulled up on my shirt, and I stopped to let her remove it completely.

Finally, she told me to sit on the makeshift bed. When I was settled, she stood over me, bare in the moonlight except for the metallic covering on the one part of her body I was now desperate to explore.

As if she understood exactly what I was thinking, Brenna reached to her hip and unclasped the last remaining barrier between her body and the cool night air. The piece slipped down past her thighs and gave me a clear view of the treasure that awaited me at the juncture of her thighs. When she stepped forward I thought she intended to allow me a taste, but she pushed my shoulders back to the floor and tugged at the string holding my pants up. My erection was already straining at the fabric, and the small grin on her lips widened as she glanced at it, then lifted her moonlit eyes to meet mine.

I found myself inexplicably nervous under her knowing gaze, and I felt compelled to say something. I tried to ignore the heat of my skin where she gently brushed her fingertips while she removed my clothing. "How can I give you pleasure?" It was more of a desperate gasp than the manly offer I intended.

"Hmm, tonight, I will take the pleasure I want. Perhaps another time I will show you how to pleasure me. But for now…" she threw a leg over my hips, fingers digging into my chest, and leaned down to whisper in my ear. "Tonight, I will ride you like a bear, *Björn.*"

forty-six

BRENNA

I COULDN'T RESIST MAKING the play on his namesake, given that Björn meant 'bear' in ancient Norse. And the man was a bear: Big, burly chest, corded with muscle and covered in a fine coat of downy-soft hair that tapered on his belly until it expanded again near his hips. His body was large and thick between my thighs, skin hot and already slick with sweat in sheer anticipation. The heat of his skin was tantalizing between my legs, and I resisted the urge to rub myself against his belly.

Leaning back, I gazed at him for a long, pregnant moment. The moonlight washed out his coloring. His golden hair and beard could have been Helgi's reddish tone. The deep blue of his eyes was dark in contrast with the brightness of his hair, and his lower lip pinched between his teeth. His expression betrayed his confusion: Björn was a man who wanted to take charge, but also wanted to please. I'd just told him that what would please me would be my taking control, and so now he fought against his instincts to give me what I wanted. Desire coursed through my body, pooling in my belly and making me slick with anticipation.

His massive hands slid along my legs, starting on my calves, sliding along the bend of my knees, then following my thighs back toward my hips, where they rested just above his groin. The light scratching sensation of his rough palms on my delicate skin left goosebumps in their wake. A shudder rippled through me, my nipples tingling and hardening in anticipation. It had been so long since I'd had someone touch me this way, just drinking in the sensation of each other's fingertips on skin.

Björn's fingers squeezed the flesh of my hips, but he still resisted the urge to steer and simply watched me, waiting for my cue.

Finally, I leaned forward and pulled his pinched lip free with my teeth, then dove into his mouth with my tongue. His tongue rose to meet mine, and his neck strained to return my sudden pressure with enthusiasm. While his hands remained on my hips, his fingers clenched, pulling my body tighter against him as him his body flexed beneath me.

My nipples brushed his chest, tingling at the light

contact, and the clench in my core was all the encouragement I needed to get on with it.

I let one hand slip along his side, dragging my fingers lightly against his skin and noting the twitch response. When my hand passed over my body, I pulled away from his mouth, preventing him from following me with my other hand on his chest. Groping behind me, I delicately stroked the fiery skin of his erection, and the strangled groan he released in response made me grin.

With no desire to tease Björn, nor myself, any more, I lifted my hips and stroked his head against the slick flesh between my legs, angling it to my entrance. The mere sensation of his hardness pressing on my soft, slippery skin sent shudders through my belly, my eyes half closing as a moan escaped my lips.

I kept a firm grip on his shaft and Björn, half-crazed with desire, tried to muscle my body down faster with his hands on my hips, as I slid onto him at my own pace. He couldn't rush me; I wanted to feel every inch as he filled me, appreciate each fresh sensation as he went deeper.

"Woman, you're going to kill me," he growled, chin thrown back and hips bucking.

"Easy, my bear," I teased. "We'll get to the fury soon enough. Right now is the calm before the storm."

As if remembering that his mission was to give me what I wanted, Björn relaxed his grip and eased the tension in his hips. He drew in a deep, shuddering breath, then waited for me to take my pleasure.

When my flesh hit the skin of his groin, I placed a few gentle kisses on his chest as I adapted to the feeling of his girth.

Then I sat up. The change put pressure in all the right places, all but guaranteeing, as I moved, that I would come, and hard.

First I started slowly, and Björn adapted quickly, pushing and pulling at my hips as he tried to match my rhythm with his body.

I pulled his hands from my hips and placed them on my breasts. It was a quality distraction for him as he squeezed and flicked my nipples, a pleasurable addition to my experience, and a removal of his interference in my work.

My pace picked up, my flesh sliding and grinding against Björn's, my heart pounding. I got the angle just right, and I felt the first tingles of my oncoming orgasm. Sweat trickled down my neck, sticking the mop of my hair to my skin, but there was no time to stop and adjust. Now I was on a roll. I had to keep going.

Björn groaned his appreciation, his face scrunched up as he concentrated on holding out. The noises of our sexcapades seemed to echo in the empty barn: my panting, his groans, and the wet, squishy noises where our bodies met.

It's so close... my body took on a direction of its own and I gave into it, following the instinct as it chased down the impending climax. Björn's hands dropped from my breasts and gripped my thighs, knowing better than trying to steer this time and just holding on.

When I finally came, I shouted my release in a pained, almost heart-wrenching cry. My hips twitched against Björn a few more times, and I collapsed against his chest, gasping. Truly, it was a release, with a depth I wasn't expecting that made me suddenly, surprisingly, teary. My heart banged against my ribs, and I felt the pounding of Björn's heart beneath his sweat-slick skin.

Björn's fingers stroked my head, and when he spoke, his voice rumbled in the barrel of his chest beneath my ear. "Have you had your pleasure, Little Bird?"

I grinned despite myself. "Yes, but I told you not to-"

With a shockingly fast move, Björn flipped me onto my back without disconnecting our bodies. My legs wrapped around his waist instinctively, and when he thrust deep into me again, the furnace of my desire blazed to life.

"Good," he growled, "because now it's my turn. You rode me like I was your bear, but now I will show you how the *bear* rides."

There was a mischievous glint in his eye, and I was momentarily concerned that this would be one of those rides during which I'd need to hold on with both hands and legs. But it turned out Björn had a few surprises up his sleeve.

He was a much more patient lover than I expected; he worked in long, slow strokes, easing out and sliding back into me with a delicious flick of his hips that turned *me* into the frenzied one. I pulled on his shoulders, trying to pepper him with kisses, using my legs for leverage to try to speed up his pace.

But Björn wouldn't be rushed. Each thrust was patient and deep, and despite the lack of rapid friction, I felt myself rising to orgasm again.

"I see you, Little Bird," he purred in a gravelly voice, drawing my eyes to his steady gaze. "You want to rush, but trust me—it will be all the sweeter if we take our time."

I nodded, then continued to hold his gaze while I focused on the slow, steady build I felt in my core. The way our bodies slid together, fitting, disconnecting, only to rejoin and fit again.

It was not easy for him; his skin was so hot I watched wisps of steam rise from him in the chilly night air. Sweat poured from his body, mingling with my own and puddling in the hollow between my breasts.

I felt him throb within me; he was close.

And knowing that was all it took to send me over the edge. This time, my orgasm wasn't a screaming, slapping affair. It was a wave that began with the curling of my toes and sent shudders up my body until it erupted in my belly like a volcano.

My entire body clenched, clamping down on Björn's dick inside me and triggering his orgasm. I felt him pulse once, twice, three times against my tightened walls, and he groaned his release before collapsing on top of me. My legs remained locked around his hips for a few minutes until I could draw in a deep, shuddering breath. Then I relaxed my muscles, easing myself back onto the nest of canvas, and stroke his sweaty brow.

Björn. Bear. The name suited him. He was large, intimidating, strong, patient, and yet surprisingly gentle in the right circumstances.

I smiled to myself, knowing the ache in my hips would ease by morning, but he might need a little more time to recover.

If he got to call me Little Bird and I couldn't do anything about it, then he deserved a nickname of his own.

He was my Björn. *My Bear*.

forty-seven

BRENNA

AFTER WE'D COOLED off and dressed, Björn and I returned to the longhouse and shared one tender, lingering kiss before we stepped inside. The girls were already asleep, and Björn crossed to his own sleeping bench while I stretched out on mine.

But despite the busy, exhausting day, sleep wouldn't come. My mind spun with doubts. Was getting involved with Björn a bad idea? I still hadn't sorted out the Leif situation. Part of my heart pulled to him too; his artist's soul, the way he seemed to read me, understand me, the way no one else could. His admiration was like a wellspring of good for my heart.

Guilt bubbled in my chest; he would be upset if he

knew I'd slept with Björn. Crushed, even. It wasn't as if we'd talked about it, but I knew Björn wasn't the type who just wanted a roll in the hay. Tonight meant something to him. It would mean something to Leif, too.

Did it mean something to me? My mind flip-flopped faster than pancakes on a diner griddle. Björn meant something to me, and tonight, the emotion I'd felt when we were together... I couldn't call it fucking, despite my desperate desire to do so. He thwarted me at every attempt to make it purely sex. His gentle touches, steady hands, serious gaze; no, it was all more emotional than I wanted to admit, and I felt it when the tears prickled at my eyes as I came.

There was something there, something between us.

But lest we forget, there was also Søren. He was distant, and calculating, and difficult to read. He was also intelligent, powerful, and smoulderingly intense. The way he could read people as if he looked into their souls, as if he could read my soul when he gazed into my eyes with his predatory stare. Even now, still damp with sweat from making love with Björn, the thought of sex with Søren sent a ripple of desire through my belly. The intensity he would infuse in every touch, the way his absolute control would make my knees weak before him... it was so hot to imagine. I wasn't sure I liked Søren, but I admired him, and I desired him. Perhaps it was a dangerous combination, but I wasn't one to deny the truth.

Complicated relationships aside, did I really

believe it was in my best interests to stay here? Perhaps, if I'd insisted on ingratiating myself with Skarde, I might have had a chance. My lips turned down as I thought about what 'ingratiating myself' with Skarde might have entailed. He hadn't been horrible to me, in fact far more gracious than I expected, but everything I'd heard about him since made me question that assessment.

For a moment I wondered if Søren and the others might have exaggerated how horrible Skarde was... for all I knew, Søren could have lied about what Skarde reportedly said about me.

I swept that dark thought from my mind as soon as it popped up. Søren was calculating, but he was no liar. Nor were Björn or Leif, and they were certainly not calculating. All three of them were honorable, I was certain of it. So I trusted their word that Skarde was as terrible as they described.

Although, if Skarde was receiving help from the Asgardians, I needed to find out what exactly was going on there. Was Thor helping him just to thwart my success? Or was there a bigger machine at play in this small viking village? The gods loved to play with their subjects, almost as much as the Greeks claimed their gods had toyed with their lives. It wouldn't surprise me if Odin had dumped me here for a purpose.

Well, that settled it. If Odin put me here to serve some nefarious plan, then I needed to leave. There was no way I could escape, make my own way, if I let him continue to manipulate me.

So I needed to determine why Odin placed me in this village, and if there was more involvement here than just Odin toying with my life.

And if I didn't like what I uncovered, I would leave.

My heart pinched when I thought about how that would affect Björn, Leif, and Søren. And Signe, Yrsa, and Astrid, who had begun to treat me as an older sister; even, at times, a surrogate mother...

But there was nothing for it. They would all grow old and die eventually anyway, and there was nothing I could do to stop it.

So I just needed to remember my priorities were to set myself up for a good life for my future.

Everything else was just a distraction.

forty-eight

BJÖRN

SOMETHING WAS WRONG.

When we rose the next morning, I wasn't certain how to behave with Brenna. I wanted to take her in my arms and kiss her warmly, but I held back, knowing it was probably too soon to act that way in front of my sisters. There would be plenty of time to explain to them; for now, it could be a secret we treasured between just the two of us.

But Brenna wouldn't even hold my eye. I caught her gaze briefly, and her normally clear grey eyes were clouded, troubled. The change in her demeanor weighed on my mind throughout breakfast.

As soon as I was able, I got Brenna alone outside and pulled her to my chest, resting my cheek on her head.

Living among us, Brenna had taken on the scents of my home. The distinctive fragrance of lavender in the soap my mother taught Signe how to make, among others, clung to her in a comforting cloud. Even so, there was a note that was all Brenna; something elusive and warm, like sunshine. I inhaled deeply, savoring the tantalizing fragrance, and waited for Brenna to relax into me.

She remained stiff, awkward and uncomfortable, as if she didn't want to be there. My heart lurched in response, suddenly questioning if I'd been mistaken.

"Brenna, is everything… okay?"

"Yes." Her response was flat, and she didn't move to wrap her arms around my waist or even to pull away. She just… stood there.

So I pulled back to search her face. It was closed off, any trace of emotion hidden behind an impassive mask.

"Clearly it's not," I hinted. "What's bothering you?"

She stared at my forehead unseeingly, as if she were looking through me.

"Brenna, look at me." I used my 'I mean business' voice I reserved for when the girls weren't listening.

As her eyes dropped to mine and focused, I saw the change in her demeanor. All of her hard edges softened, the wall she'd built through the night crumbling. "I have to leave," she sighed.

"What? Why do you have to leave?"

"Because the Asgardians are involved in this village. If they have their fingers in everything that takes place here, there's no way I'll ever get ahead. I might even make it impossible for you, and Søren, and Leif, to get ahead. Odin is determined to punish me, and I don't want to take you all down with me. I don't even know why Thor was involved yesterday, but it spells nothing good for us." She leaned away from me, crossing her arms over her chest, creating a barrier where before there was none.

"So now you just give up? And what, leave? Where will you go?"

"It doesn't matter. I'll find a new village, earn a place, and carry on. It's not as if I have a choice," she added bitterly. "Eventually I always have to move on."

"Maybe eventually, but no one is forcing you to leave now. We haven't even begun the summer raids, and you're a part of our crew. How are we supposed to show up that worthless piece of shit Skarde without you?"

"I don't think you can do it *with* me, don't you see what I'm saying? If Odin, and Thor—and who knows which other gods—are involved, he will *always* win, and whoever is with me will *always* lose. You're better off without me."

"That is not necessarily true. You're making an assumption, with bits of information that you don't even know what they mean yet. Why are you sabotaging this before we even see if it works?" I realized, too late, that there was more than one application of my question; our raiding ship, but also whatever had grown between the two of us. I wasn't certain which one I was arguing for more.

"I can't let myself get attached to people here, if I'm just going to have to leave," she snapped. "I already care about all of you too much; if I have to leave anyway, it's better for me to leave now before I get in any deeper."

"Ah, so that's what this is about." My heart sunk as I finally understood. "You're running away."

"No, I'm not running away. I'm trying to do what will be best for everyone," her tone became indignant, eyes flashing.

I gave her a hard stare and shook my head slowly. "No, you are running. A minor challenge from some gods—which we don't even know what it means—and you scurry away? No, that's not the issue. You're running because you're getting too attached to us. Maybe all of us, maybe just a few of us." My eyes tracked to the longhouse, and Brenna turned to follow my gaze.

I knew she cared about my sisters, and I knew she cared—at least a little—for Søren, Leif, and me.

And clearly, that scared her.

When her eyes returned to mine, I saw it—the fear. For all she'd been through, for all she'd lost, she was terrified to open herself again to that pain. "Brenna, you don't have to be afraid of us. We won't hurt you. We will be here for you. Just don't give up on us yet."

"Don't you understand? It's not about you. At least, not that way. I'm afraid that Odin would hurt you... one of you, just to punish me. He doesn't care about people. To him, we're all toys, playthings, that he can make do his bidding. His sense of honor, of justice, only serves his self-interest. He would have no qualms against hurting you solely for his own amusement. I don't want to be the reason something awful happens, just because I was here and you were kind to me." Her voice hitched at the end with emotion, and I almost lost it.

Placing my hands on her shoulders, I met her gaze with as much confidence as I could bring to my expression. "Nothing is going to happen to us, beyond what was always meant to happen. Besides, don't you think it's our choice to decide if we want to take that risk? Don't I get a say on whether I want you to stay in my life?"

"You didn't have a say on when I entered it," she sniffed.

"Didn't I?" I scratched my beard and raised my eyes to gaze over her shoulder, as if thinking deeply. "As I recall, you turned up and I could have turned you away that first day."

"You wanted me to leave. Signe made you let me stay."

At that, I actually chuckled. "Oh, and you think Signe is the boss of me, hm? You don't think I could have laid down the law if I wanted?"

She looked surprised, as if she honestly hadn't considered that. "I just assumed-"

"That Signe wanted you here and I didn't, I know. Well, I certainly wasn't keen on the idea at the beginning. But Signe was right—we needed someone here, and there were no better options in the village. It was the smart move to try you out and see if you would work, rather than trying to hire some unscrupulous man to look after my sisters. Now, of course, Signe is perfectly capable of running the house again. Thanks to you."

A hint of a smile curled the corner of her lips. "So you liked me from the beginning?"

I cleared my throat, abruptly uncomfortable. "I wouldn't say I liked you right away. More like, I didn't hate you at the beginning and grew to appreciate you more as we got to know each other better."

"I see." Such a simple phrase, but when she said it, I heard the emotion behind it. She saw through my bluster as if I were made of water, and I did not fool her. "Well, I still think it would be better for everyone if I left and tried my luck again somewhere else."

A voice I knew very well barked from nearby, "Why on earth would you think that?"

I grinned. Søren had impeccable timing. He marched in our direction from the longhouse, Leif a half-step behind him. Søren's face was serious, his refusal to betray his emotions like armor he wore, just as real as Brenna's metal pieces. To me, it was plain as day to read him; he was surprised and upset that Brenna wanted to leave.

"Brenna believes that Thor's appearance yesterday, helping Skarde, means she's putting us in danger and we'd be better off without her."

Even Leif was indignant, pushing his hair behind his ears and appealing to her with sincerity. "Of course we wouldn't be. And you don't know why Thor was there—we do not know if that had anything to do with you at all. For all we know, he's been helping Skarde for far longer than when you landed on our shore."

"That's what I told her." I shrugged, glad I now had backup in this argument.

"Don't you think it's quite a coincidence that I get deposited in this village by Odin, and Thor just happens to show here weeks later? How often do you think the Asgardians appear on Midgard? I promise it's not that much."

The loud, obnoxious caw of a crow shrieked from the fence to my left, and Brenna jumped in response, her eyes wide with trepidation as she took in the black bird.

"Oh no…"

At just that moment, I heard the crunch of approaching footsteps on the gravel path behind me.

Everyone's eyes turned in unison, and we gazed upon the sprightly older man who approached with a dark grin on his lips.

forty-nine

BRENNA

I SHOULD HAVE KNOWN. Odin's appearance here was as inevitable as the sun rising and setting, the moon's cycles, and the change of seasons.

He'd dressed to fit in, disguised as a strong older viking: sporting a rich purple tunic and matching cape, belted over dark brown trousers. His flowing steel-grey hair was woven in detailed plaits, complete with intricate metal beads to force anyone to conclude that he was someone of importance, even among average men.

Of course, he'd disguised his true face, choosing instead to appear with two twinkling sky-blue eyes instead of the patch-covered empty socket he actually possessed.

Hughin cawed resentfully at us once more—tattle-tale—and flew to land on his master's shoulder.

The men arranged themselves around me, Björn at my back and Søren and Leif at my sides. Odin glanced curiously at our positions and his amusement at my expense deepened.

"Brenna!" He greeted as if we were friends. "It's so nice to see you. It looks like you've been busy since you arrived. I'm impressed."

His compliment felt slimy. If Odin was impressed, I must have done something wrong.

"I'd say it was nice to see you too, Odin, but it's not. What do you want?" The sharp intake of breath from the guys told me they hadn't really wrapped their head around the fact that the old man before them was the god himself until I addressed him by name.

"Well, I have a bit of a problem with which I need your help. You see, I had a wager going with Frigg, and some more people got involved, and well, now the stakes are rather high."

"I fail to see how this is my problem." My arms folded over my chest and I glared at him.

"You will! Patience, please. So Frigg and I had a disagreement about what happened—you know, the first time all of this happened," he waved his hand through the air vaguely, and my stomach lurched.

I hadn't told the other two guys he rewound time to drop me here, and Odin just casually mentioned it like no big deal.

"And Frigg believed it was another of your Jarl's

teams that had shown up Porp this year. She insisted, in fact, that Skarde did so poorly he wasn't even called before the Jarl at the end of the summer at all.

"So, I suggested a wager: I win if Skarde is called before the Jarl, and Frigg wins if he is not."

My pulse started racing... it was all beginning to make sense.

"You dropped me here on purpose, to help Skarde, didn't you?" The accusation was thick in my tone, and the men shifted quietly, but said nothing.

"Of course I did. I couldn't have him dying because of these three," he gestured at my friends. "And I figured once you'd found a safe space to land, you'd stay there. I counted on you making yourself invaluable to the first person you came across, and you did. But then you left." He shrugged. "And somehow ended up here, with these men."

"You asked Thor to interfere in the race." It wasn't a question. I already knew the answer.

"Yes. If you beat him, Skarde wouldn't appear before the Jarl and, once again, I'd lose. So I called on Thor to help me. Frigg insisted I couldn't directly interfere, but she never said I couldn't ask someone else to interfere on my behalf."

"I still don't get why you're here. Skarde is all but guaranteed to succeed again. By all reports, he's the Jarl's golden boy and sure to get the best assignments."

"Well..." Odin scratched at his thick, wiry grey beard. "The fact is, I've remembered that Frigg is right. The ship from Toft will receive an assignment

from the Jarl that he doesn't believe holds much treasure, but it's actually an incredible trove."

"Good for them." I continued to glare at Odin
with one eyebrow raised.

"I want you to help Skarde."

"You have got to be kidding me."

"Not kidding. I need to win this bet, and that
requires Skarde to do well. If you compete against
him with what you know from your last go-round,
I'm fairly confident that will make things far more
difficult for him. But if you help him, he's all but
assured to win."

"I still don't see why I should care if you win your
wager."

Odin made a disappointed noise, tut-tutting his
tongue against his teeth. "Brenna, you know the rules.
You're here to help me, and in return, I leave you
mostly alone. I promise you I could make things far
more... inconvenient for you if I wanted to."

"I've scarcely been here for two weeks, I'd hardly
call that leaving me alone."

"Brenna... I'm disappointed. After our last chat, I
thought you understood. But, perhaps I can offer
some enticement... would you like to get your armor
back?"

Björn coughed behind me, and I elbowed him
swiftly in the ribs to shut him up. "I'm listening." The
longer he was ignorant that I already had my armor,
the better for me.

"Skarde will be here soon... we'll just say someone
gave him the brilliant idea to make friends and bring

you onto his team. I want you to help him, join his team, be his muse, make sure he does really well. If Skarde ends up before your Jarl at the end of the season, we will have a discussion about your armor."

"Not good enough—I will not join Skarde's team… but I will make sure he is in front of the Jarl at the end of the season. And when I do, my armor is mine."

Odin scratched at his beard again, considering. "I accept."

I stepped forward and offered my hand, which he shook before winking.

"Come on, Hughin, let's go home. Heimdahl!"

With a crack of thunder, a shimmering rainbow descended and enveloped the old man, and moments later, he was gone.

BRENNA

IN THE WAKE of Odin's abrupt departure, Björn, Søren, and Leif all stared at the spot where the rainbow had swallowed him, as if they expected him to reappear. After an awkwardly long time they seemed to snap out of it, and I felt three pairs of eyes on me, burning with questions.

Sighing, I waved my hand through the air in a vague approximation of circle. "Go on."

"Was that really-"

"Did that just-"

"Why would he-"

"Stop!" I shouted. "Let me specify—one at a time, ask away."

"Was that really Odin?" Leif apparently was a

little shaken by the Asgardian's abrupt appearance and disappearance.

"Yes, that was the old bastard himself. Congratulations, consider yourselves blessed." I made an approximation of the cross, then realized they wouldn't get the joke.

"And the Bifrost—that's what that was, right? I didn't think it would look like that." That got analytical fast.

"Well, I don't know what to tell you, that's how it looks."

"Strange. I thought it was a bridge."

I sighed, already weary of this line of questioning. "It's a bridge between worlds... it's more of a figurative bridge. If Odin needed to actually walk to Asgard in that old man's body of his, it'd take him ages. Obviously there is magic involved."

"So why did he come here?" Björn sounded genuinely confused.

"Seriously? You heard him."

"He wants you to help Skarde—to do exactly the opposite of what we're trying to do."

"Right."

"And in exchange, he'll give you your armor, which you already have."

"Sort of."

Søren interjected. "She said it differently. Did you notice?" His shrewd eyes met my gaze, a ghost of a smile on his stern face. "You said 'my armor is mine' not 'you will give me my armor.'"

I grinned in return. "Yes, exactly. So he can't

complain when he discovers that I already have my armor—it becomes moot."

"Moot… What does that mean?"

"Nevermind. The point is, the agreement is that I keep my armor if I help Skarde appear before the Jarl for recognition at the end of the season."

"I don't see how you're going to do that while we beat him."

"Simple: I'm going to invite him to join *our* team."

At this, all three of them guffawed. "Skarde will never join our ship."

"Not at first, no. But I will leave the offer open. And when he comes crawling back, after realizing that we are far outstripping him, I'll renew the offer. With the addition that he will continue to captain his own ship and declare us lead ship. Porp will bring in far more gold and treasures than that other village, we will guide Skarde to a few choice spots to raid, and when the Jarl summons us, Skarde will be with us. That is the offer I will make him, when the time is right."

Søren's sharp green eyes clouded as he considered, then turned to me, positively luminous. "That might work," he agreed. His lips curled into a genuine smile, by far the biggest I'd seen in the three weeks I'd known him. "You're cleverer than I gave you credit for, Brenna."

"Thanks, I'll take that compliment." A dash of heat rose to my cheeks in response, but I returned his grin.

Leif glanced between Søren and I, still holding

each other's gaze. His open expression dipped into a small frown, but he said nothing.

"So, what now?" Björn asked.

"Now, I think the three of you ought to make yourselves scarce while I have this conversation with Skarde," I hinted. "There's no need for you to antagonize the man. He's already coming all the way here to request my help."

"Oh no, I want to stay here and witness this," Björn's thick arms crossed his muscled chest, and he widened his stance as if he intended to grow roots in the spot.

"She's right," Søren interjected. "Let's wait in the barn. Come on," he tilted his head toward the structure and stepped off, expecting the others to follow.

With a sigh, Björn left, and Leif remained behind, still watching me with a slightly confused expression.

"Leif... is everything okay?"

"I dunno, Brenna. Is everything okay?"

My eyes drifted from the longhouse, to the path that led to the village, then toward the barn and the backs of two retreating men.

Slowly, I returned my gaze to Leif and smiled reassuringly. "Yes, I think everything is going to be okay, Leif. Go on, I'll follow up when Skarde leaves and give you guys all the details. Promise."

Sighing, Leif turned and followed the others. I was just on my way to splash water on my face and freshen up when Skarde's figure appeared on the path from town.

He was white as a ghost, his entire expression best described as 'confused', and he kept looking around as if fearful someone would jump out and yell 'boo!' at him.

His pale blue eyes landed on me, and the relief in his gaze told me Odin hadn't revealed that I wasn't a normal human.

Thank Frigg for small favors.

Skarde's reddish-blonde hair was braided completely down his back today, nothing fancy but still groomed. He wore a simple tunic and pants, with a heavy leather belt to hold it up. He marched up to me, the surprising blend of confusion and relief on his face striking me as humorous.

I decided to play dumb.

"Hello, Skarde, what brings you here today?"

He hesitated, pausing a few feet away, before speaking. "I'm not completely sure, if I'm being honest," he confessed. "I… you're going to think it's crazy. But I promised the crow-"

"Crow? You promised a crow you'd come visit me?" My left eyebrow lifted, and I let my lip curl in a teasing smile.

"It wasn't a normal crow," he snapped in response to my derision. "It was a *talking* crow. And the crow said-"

"Oh, so it was a *talking* crow." I crossed my arms over my chest and my smile deepened. "That makes more sense. Go on."

"Woman, you know what a talking crow means," Skarde stepped forward and hissed under his breath, as if afraid of being overheard. "It was Odin in disguise!"

"Oh, so you just had a chat with Odin himself! Well, that is incredible. But why are you whispering? Surely you want to tell everyone."

"Will you-" he began shouting, but then lowered his voice. "Will you please just let me tell you what the crow said?"

I nodded and gestured for him to proceed without speaking again.

"The crow—Odin—told me that in order to succeed this summer, I need to recruit your help. So I'm here to ask you to join my ship."

"I'm sorry, I already have a ship," I shrugged. "You're welcome to join mine."

"What? No, you *lost*." He seemed genuinely shocked I declined his offer.

"Perhaps I did. Perhaps the contest wasn't fair. Either way, I have no interest in helping you succeed. What's in it for me?"

Now it was Skarde's turn to raise an eyebrow, as if I impressed him. "I will mention you to the Jarl when he calls me forward at the end of summer."

"Nope, not good enough. When my crew is the most successful this summer, the Jarl will call *all* of us forward because we are a team. So you offer me nothing I don't already have."

"You assume you will outperform me? Hah, you dream, woman."

"I dunno, Skarde, you're the one here asking for

my help, so it seems you need something I already have."

His eyes narrowed, color rising in his cheeks above the line of his beard. "I don't need anything from you. The crow said you were important! I don't want your help."

"Oh, so it's the crow who needs me? Okay, introduce me to your feathered friend and I will see what he offers."

"Grrreaaahh!" Skarde's arms flew into the air in frustration, but he didn't try to swing them in my direction.

Smart man.

"You're welcome to join my team if your crow tells you the only way to be successful is to work with me. I will not be working under you, Skarde. Sorry."

"You're being stupid. Anyone can see that tiny toy boat you call a ship won't survive a single trip across the open water, let alone a summer's worth."

"Well, that's where we disagree. I guess we'll see what happens this summer."

Skarde scratched at his auburn beard, thinking. "What if we do another trial?"

"Why would I agree to that, when you've already won?"

"You just claimed the contest wasn't fair. So what if we repeat it?"

"And how would you propose to make it more fair?"

"We could… have the chieftain set us a task, something to collect, instead of just a race. Whichever ship makes it back with the most treasure in the allotted time wins."

I thought it over. Even if Thor helped them move faster with his wind, he couldn't help them collect more treasure. With a smaller crew, we were at a disadvantage for helpers, but we had more room on the ship for the haul, and we were a lighter craft. We could take longer to collect the treasure and travel faster to make up for the difference.

"Agreed. Tomorrow, we'll meet at the harbor and collect whatever treasure the chieftain designates. No beer chugging. If you win, I join your crew. If I win, you're on your own."

"Deal." Skarde held out his hand. I accepted the shake. "I'll inform the chieftain. Noon tomorrow."

Without another word, he turned and marched back down the path.

fifty-one

BRENNA

THE NEXT DAY, it appeared as if the entire village had gotten wind of our little rematch and came out to watch the spectacle. Skarde was acting much more self-assured than he'd been yesterday. I comforted myself with the memory of him rambling about a talking crow. *If only they could have seen him yesterday, his adoring fans wouldn't be quite so... adoring.*

It didn't matter. When I informed the guys of the deal I made with Skarde, they were dubious at first. But I explained all of our advantages, and eventually they were on board.

Today, I wore my armor under my clothes, and donned one of Leif's tunics and pants instead of a dress. It was far more practical, and while a little large for my frame, a much better fit than Björn or Søren's would have been. My breastplate was in the sack, of course. I couldn't walk into town with my valkyrie wings—but it was nearby if I needed it. Something, some instinct, told me I might. Even if I didn't end up adding the breastplate, wearing the rest of my armor fortified me, strengthened my body and my confidence.

With my sword in hand, I was positively cheerful facing down our opponent today. I wouldn't be downing excessive amounts of beer, and I was absolutely certain I was up for whatever challenge lay before us.

"Sheep!" Åse, the chieftain, declared. "A flock of sheep I need to collect waits on the far side of the fjord. Both ships will depart, and whichever ship returns with the most of my flock wins."

At this, Skarde guffawed out loud. That bastard, he set this up. We had a significantly smaller ship. When I was imagining something like treasure, there was no way there could be a hoard large enough to fill their hull. Skarde only had roughly two dozen men standing beside him, half of what he had on the first challenge. Suddenly he had a massive amount of room for cargo, and I was in a much smaller ship. I was depending on our ability to be more agile, more clever.

But a flock of sheep? I glanced at Björn, Søren, and Leif with concern. I hadn't planned on livestock. Søren's jaw flexed, but he simply nodded in response and waited.

He was letting me play the role of captain again, honoring the arrangement with Skarde.

"Very well," I agreed, thinking fast. "I assume we're all using the same number of crew as we had last time as well?"

Åse rubbed his chin, looking over the assembled teams. "Yes, you should have to use your full crew. Skarde, where are the rest of your men?"

Skarde's grin dropped, but he called for the rest of his crew, who clearly hadn't intended on playing today. When his glare turned my way, I smiled sweetly back at Skarde and waved. "May the best viking win!"

Skarde just grunted and marched off toward his ship. Now, at least, he couldn't take advantage of his much larger ship being only half manned. He still had the advantage of some space on us, but not much. His men were crowded within their ship, every bench full, when we prepared to set off. Someone blew a horn, and we pushed out into the water.

Once again, it was a bright day, with no threat of storm clouds this time. We worked well together as a team; the guys rowing in sync while I trimmed the sail to catch the wind. Even with Skarde's extra manpower, we were neck and neck as we approached the shore.

Where, true to the chieftain's word, waited a flock of sheep. These weren't as fluffy as I imagined, since they'd just been shorn of their wool. All the better for us. Our hull was deep and we could just pack them in.

By the time we pulled up on the sand, we already had a plan in place. Björn, Søren, and Leif hopped out, forming a daisy chain to pass the animals to me on the ship. Skarde sent out his raiders and sure enough, they each snatched one sheep and ran back to the ship, mobbing the side in their hurry to dump their animal and fetch another.

We had a smaller team, but we were certainly more efficient. As soon as Leif handed me a sheep, I turned to drop it to the floor—by the time I turned back to him there was already another waiting for me. Bless the shepherd, who thoughtfully massed the animals so closely for us.

I spared a glance at the opposition: they were in total chaos. Several would try to corner the same animal at once, sometimes fighting over it, and then having to wait and make their way through the bottleneck to drop it on the ship. Their low-hulled boat, meanwhile, was looking rather full of sheep, including many that had claimed spots on the benches. I was curious how many Skarde thought he could reasonably take and still have room for his team.

By the time our ship was full to the gills with bleating farm animals, Skarde and his team were struggling to push theirs out into the water. Half of his men were standing, having nowhere to sit, and the ship sat so low in the water it looked as if a tiny wave would take them out.

We were more careful, and I was grateful for the high hulls of our ship. Yes, it was smaller, but even loaded up with livestock, we had no fears the water would overtake us. Skarde was a good way ahead by the time we were clear of the shore. I didn't get why he was in such a rush, since there was no time limit for this contest. Perhaps it was simply because they were in danger of capsizing?

It seemed my powers of prediction were getting stronger, because Skarde's ship began rocking dangerously from left to right, the hulls inches from being swamped. Skarde, realizing his peril, began shouting angrily, pointing at several men on his ship. I couldn't hear what he said, but when a fight broke out, I got the gist of it:

He was telling them to get out of the boat and they were refusing the order.

We were still at least a half-mile from the village, and he wanted fully dressed men to just jump into the freezing fjord and swim? What kind of psychopath was he?

I kept an eye on the drama, but my fears were soon confirmed: Skarde threw four of his own men off his boat, and set the others rowing furiously to pull ahead as we gained on them.

The men in the water, now realizing we were their best option, began swimming toward us. They were freezing, and panicked, and if we let this get away from us, they would swamp our boat trying to get aboard.

And we'd all go down into the waters of the icy fjord.

fifty-two

BRENNA

I HAD TO THINK FAST. Despite our heavy load, we were still too high on the sides for them to climb easily in without tipping the ship and our cargo. We had one length of rope we could use to help pull them in, but how to do it safely?

I quickly told the guys my plan, and we allowed the ship to coast toward the stranded vikings. When they neared, I shouted to them. "Listen! We will get you all out of the water, but I need you to be patient and not swamp our ship in your hurry to get dry. Do you understand?"

They grunted their affirmation, and I tossed the rope to the first one. Björn and Søren were the heaviest, so they moved to the opposite side of the ship to provide counterbalance, and Leif and I hauled on the rope to help the soaking warrior to climb aboard. He took up a position midship, grabbing the tail of the rope to help us haul up the next man.

Once we had all four aboard, we now had extra weight without extra oars for them to help us get moving. Thanks to continuous replenishment from my armor, I took a spot on an oar and let Søren captain us back to shore.

The trip was slow. We now sat precariously low in the water and the waves had picked up. But we had all of our sheep, and we had four additional, enormous, viking warriors aboard. It seemed as if Skarde had just picked the four heaviest men on his team to kick off with no consideration of their strength in rowing or skill at swimming.

Idiot.

When we finally scraped onto the rocky beach, the roar of the crowd brought a small grin to my lips. They watched us rescue the men Skarde threw overboard, and were not as admiring of his ruthlessness, suddenly.

Åse came forward and eyed me curiously, but said nothing. He counted the sheep in our boat, his eyes drifting repeatedly to the soaking vikings who now refused to rejoin Skarde's team.

"Here are the numbers: Skarde brought over seventy-three of my sheep." The crowd cheered. "Brenna brought over sixty-six sheep." The crowd grew quiet, even though Skarde and a few of his cronies cheered.

"However..." Åse took a long pause, as if considering. "I would say that every man, woman, and child in my village is a member of my flock, and worth at least twice the value of a sheep. Since Brenna returned with four more men than she started with, I would say her number is seventy-four. Therefore, I declare Brenna the winner!"

There were some jeers—mainly from Skarde's crew—but the vast majority of the villagers were pleased with this decision. It seemed it was actually possible for a viking to be too ruthless.

Skarde looked absolutely murderous, but as Åse stared calmly back at him, he seemed to think better of his ill intent and instead shoved his way through the crowd.

It was like the viking version of 'try me bitch' and I almost lost it. Even in the mid-800's A.D., men were fucking dramatic.

Åse approached me with a benevolent expression. "I cannot grant you status as lead ship, since Skarde already won that privilege. However, if you continue to show this kind of... fortitude, it will be my pleasure to introduce you to the Jarl at the end of the season. I have a feeling we can expect to see more surprises from you, Brenna. Make sure your ship is ready for the first raid next week." With a nod and a twinkling brown eye, the older man strode away, chatting with another villager.

"Brenna!" Björn's booming voice drew my attention away from the village chieftain. I turned to see him approaching with the four dripping men we'd rescued from the depths of the fjord. "This is Halfdan, Njal, Sten, and Erik. They have requested to join our crew."

Now that we were on solid ground, I could appreciate just how big these men were. Falling somewhere between Leif and Björn in height, every one of them was built like a solid oak, wide and muscular. I glanced at Søren, who nodded once, unsmiling, to give me his approval.

"Welcome to the crew, guys." I beamed up at them. We needed more crew, and we found it. Skarde would be furious when he found out his gamble had backfired worse than he realized. We had certainly scored several of his best fighters, and that was going to cost him on every raid.

"The crew of what?" The tallest of the group asked, dark brown eyes crinkling around the edges as he grinned down at me. "What is your ship called?"

Leif apparently heard his question, because before I could answer he shouted, "The Valkyrie! Her name is The Valkyrie."

I turned toward him with wide, horrified eyes. Leif's bright cerulean gaze glittered, his smile absolutely mischievous.

"The Valkyrie... I like it," grunted the man. "I'm Njal. It's a pleasure to meet you, Brenna."

"The pleasure is mine, Njal." When I accepted his handshake, his massive palm engulfed mine, and I couldn't help but grin.

We were certainly on our way to claiming riches,

glory, and, most importantly, an introduction to the Jarl.

Next week, we'd set sail for our first raid. I already had a few places in mind of where we could start, but I needed to verify our location first. A quick glance skyward told me the weather would be perfect for a little reconnaissance flight: light, fluffy clouds had rolled in, mostly obscuring the sky but nothing grey or threatening.

Just perfect for soaring.

A quick conversation with Søren would tell me our planned attack routes, and then I could navigate us toward the spots that held the richest spoils. The Jarl wouldn't care if we went a little off course, so long as he benefitted from the mistake.

And I intended to make sure he benefitted richly.

The Vikings & Vengeance duet will be completed with Valkyrie Risen. Release date TBA. Make sure to join Laurel Night's newsletter to stay up to date on the latest! www.laurelnight.com/newsletter

In the meantime, enjoy this sneak preview of Wolf Shunned, book 1 in the Alpha Queen Legacy by Laurel Night.

the alpha queen legacy

KALIYA

A single droplet of sweat trailed down the side of my face, working its way from my pale blonde hairline to my clenched jaw. Hands flexed on the hilts of my blunted practice swords, fingers stretching to relieve the pressure and adjust my sweaty grip. Heart pounding, breath slow and even. Across the fighting ring, four male opponents were just collecting themselves from the heap I'd left in my wake.

Their combined scent drifted across the ring, sour with frustration. My eyes narrowed in the mid-morning sun, waiting for the last one to regain his feet. They all watched me with trepidation, perhaps hoping I was done with training for the day and they could go home to lick their wounds in peace.

No such luck.

"Again," I growled.

Emory spoke up behind me, where he remained safely outside the training area. "Kaliya, don't you think they've had enough?" His voice was gentle; suggesting, not commanding. He knew better than to challenge me.

I ignored him. Raising my swords over my head, I clanged them together and shouted, "AGAIN!"

A collective sigh rose from the males as they girded themselves for another attack. I brandished my swords at my sides, a feral grin curling my lips as I waited for them to approach. This time they rushed me as one, maybe hoping they would land a blow with so many swords flying at me simultaneously. I swirled through them like a hurricane, striking and dodging, stabbing and weaving. I struck several blows that would have killed the recipient if I wielded my lightning swords. According to the rules of engagement in the training ring, they should have stayed down, but I didn't mind if they hopped back in the fray; I'd just knock them down again.

One of the males apparently had enough of this humiliation. With a savage growl he burst from his training clothes, unleashing his wolf in an embarrassing lack of control. At over twice his human size, the mass of mottled brown fur and pearly white teeth was impressive. His ears lay flat on his head and he snarled at me, slaver dribbling from his jaw as we circled each other, my other opponents ignored.

The rest of the males immediately retreated to

safety outside the training ring. They probably assumed I'd shift in response; it wasn't an unreasonable expectation, given that's what most wolves would do when faced with such a direct challenge.

However, I wasn't in the mood to kill anyone today. My wolf remained firmly in my control.

She growled in frustration, the sound vibrating in my chest. She rarely got to come out and play, and my refusal to respond to a direct challenge tortured her wild soul. Especially since she'd have this pup bent and submitted—if not broken—in seconds.

The wolf feinted left, tongue curling and jaws snapping as he tested my reactions. His dark eyes watched me; mine never strayed, steadily holding his gaze as we circled.

When he realized I would not shift, the wolf grew cocky, charging straight at me. I vaguely heard Emory's sharp intake of breath as I crouched, leaping and twisting mid-air to land on the massive wolf's back just behind his head. Flinging my useless weapons to the ground, I wrapped my right arm tightly around his furry throat, using my left to tighten the grip and hold myself in position while he writhed beneath me.

The wolf was stuck; my legs wrapped around the barrel of his body, and my arm was cutting off his air supply. He attempted to shake me off, bucking and snarling as he ran out of oxygen. A sudden whimper escaped his throat and he collapsed on the ground, struggling to breathe. He whined loudly in surrender, but I held on until I was certain he passed out. When I felt the fur recede signaling his return to human form, I released him and stepped off his naked body. He was small and pathetic once more.

But luckily for him, still alive.

I walked away without a backward glance as the rest of the team hopped the wooden fence to check on their fallen comrade. Once they confirmed he was still breathing, the biggest one shouted angrily, "You psycho bitch! You could have killed him!"

I stooped to grab one of my practice swords, calmly wiping the flat of the blade on my leather pant leg. "He should have thought of that before he shifted during a training session and challenged a stronger wolf. He's lucky I didn't kill him."

"You're full of shit," he snorted. "I bet any of us could take you; you just don't want anyone to see your freak of a wolf. No wonder you spent so much time learning sword fighting; your wolf just isn't up for the challenge of a real male. Frigid *bitch*."

I finished collecting and cleaning my second sword, ignoring the angry snarl of my wolf. *It wouldn't help anyone to give in to his goading,* I reminded myself. Focusing on my control, I breathed in deeply and resolved to ignore the taunting.

However, I forgot that we had an audience.

A pale streak crossed my vision in the taunter's direction. *Shit.*

The sound of fist meeting face seemed to echo in the suddenly silent training arena. "You fucking apologize, pup!" Emory shouted.

Sighing, I turned just in time to see the much stronger man hit Emory with an uppercut so hard his head snapped backward, lean frame flying several feet until his unconscious body landed in the dirt.

My wolf strained at my control, and I narrowly kept her within the reins as I charged the taunter, spinning behind him and knocking the bully to his knees with a swift kick. Placing one knee on his back, I scissored his neck between my swords. "There is no honor in beating a weaker foe," I hissed. "But for you, I may make an exception. It seems you have not yet learned your lesson."

"He attacked me first!" He choked out. The training swords were blunted, so they didn't slice his flesh to ribbons. But the pressure of the steel on his neck was still uncomfortable enough to make him rethink his position. He held perfectly still, his scent tainted with the bitter tang of fear.

"He's not a challenge to you," I growled, "As you are well aware. You beat him because you *could*. That is a sign of weakness and cowardice, not strength. You're a pathetic excuse for a warrior." I withdrew my swords and the knee from his back, then gave him a sharp kick that sent him sprawling in the dirt. "Don't ask for my help again until you know your place."

Emory was just stirring when I reached him, shaking dirt and bits of straw from his wavy brown hair. He grinned when I offered him a hand up, then winced. "Ow. He didn't break my face, did he?" He rose and stretched, his lean frame half a foot taller than my five-foot-seven, before ducking his face closer to mine for inspection. The sweet, untainted scent of chocolate and cinnamon filled my senses, and I breathed him in with relief.

I lightly ran my fingers along his narrow jaw, pressing gently as I traced the sharp curve below his ear down to his adorably cleft chin and up the other side. "Nope, you're not broken. It'll swell up but you'll be fine in a few hours, thank the Ancients." I brushed my hands over his wide shoulders, helping to remove the dirt from his fall. "That was stupid, by the way," I commented mildly. "You know he's much more dominant than you, even as a pup."

Emory shrugged, unapologetically re-rolling his sleeves. "He shouldn't have spoken to you like that. You're doing him and his pathetic friends a favor; they're lucky you didn't kill them all. If you would not defend yourself, someone had to." His warm brown eyes met mine with a glint of mischief. "If your wolf wants to teach them a lesson, I could leave for a few minutes. By the time I get the healers and return, she should be about finished."

I chuckled. "As tempting as that is, it wouldn't please Alpha for me to be teaching *that* kind of lesson to his newest warriors. They're just young; they'll learn."

Emory wrapped a lean, muscular arm around my shoulders, squeezing lightly. "You're too kind, Kaliya. If it were me, I'd unleash the beast and give them all an epic beat-down. You'd only have to do it once."

"As a male, I'm sure that would work well for

you. As a female, I shouldn't be able to. It's bad enough that I've defeated nearly every male our age and up; flexing on younger wolves is just cruel."

Emory was thoughtful as we followed the wooded path back toward the village. "A younger wolf may be your only chance, Kali," he reminded me softly. He didn't finish the phrase, but we were both thinking it as we continued in silence.

A younger wolf may be my only chance to avoid expulsion from the pack. At nineteen, I only had a few more months to find a mate. Wolves had to contribute to the replenishment of society, and our prime pup-bearing years were the younger ones. We didn't live long happy lives, thanks to the beasts that stalked us at night. Something else we had to thank the Ancients for. Whether we called them night stalkers, wraiths, or just 'creatures', they were adept at keeping us constantly on the edge of extinction.

It was an unfair rule, but a rule nonetheless: if a wolf wasn't mated by their twentieth birthday, they had no place in the pack. It mostly ensured we didn't waste time finding a mate, and I only knew of one time they actually enforced it.

From the way things were going, I might be the second.

Of course, Emory had the same issue. We were born mere minutes apart, and neither of us had mates. Not that Emory was unattractive, or weak. He was tall, lean yet muscular, and objectively handsome with his sharply angled jaw, warm eyes, and lips made for kissing. He was also incredibly intelligent, if a little awkward at times. His brilliant mind was one of his finer attributes, and that was saying something. If people could choose their own mates, Emory would have been happily settled years ago.

But humans didn't choose mates; their wolves did.

Emory's issue was that his wolf struggled to find a female submissive enough for him to mate, while mine was the opposite: I had yet to find a male who could force my wolf to submit.

Mates were chosen when a male issued a mate challenge to a female and submitted her. The stronger the pairing, the stronger and more dominate the pups would be. Therefor every male tried to mate the most dominant female he could handle.

Fortunately, there was one small nod to the female in this archaic process. The male could force the Mate Challenge, but he couldn't force the mating. The female had to accept him and seal the pairing. In theory, it could be years before he earned her respect enough to mate, and he just had to wait for it.

For me, the issue was bigger. I'd already been mate challenged by most of the eligible males in the pack, and my wolf defeated them all. Since I reached mating age, the only eligible male who had yet to challenge me was the pack's despicable Beta, and I destroyed him thoroughly a few weeks before I turned fifteen. He'd spent the last five years ignoring me completely, clearly bitter about the ass-kicking he'd received as a pup. Since he was younger than me, he still had over a year to find a mate.

Whereas I was swiftly running out of time.

My thoughts turned to the upcoming Clan Gathering at the Blackwood Fortress. All five packs in our territory would come together, as they did every five years. It was a festival of sorts, but it served multiple purposes: One was to have a variety of games and tests of battle prowess. Another was to exchange information with all the other packs, find out what the wraiths in their territories had been up to, and discuss any recent issues the rest of the clan should know.

But the purpose that mattered the most to me was the chance to find a mate outside my pack. The Clan Gathering encouraged the intermingling of pack members to make stronger wolves. There was an entire arena dedicated to official challenges, and they started on the Summer Solstice, longest day of the year. Many held out hope of finding their mate at the event, if for no other reason than the chance to leave their own pack and live somewhere new.

I suspected Emory was hoping he'd find a submissive female at the Clan Gathering who was closer to his own age. Fifteen was technically mating age, and many females were more submissive when they were young. Less dominant males tended to prey on them to secure a place in the pack, which was partially why Emory was still unmated.

But they were little more than pups at that age. I couldn't imagine finding a fifteen-year-old attractive enough to mate, no matter how dominant his wolf could be. Emory felt the same way.

I was just hoping that there was one wolf among

the thousands across our territory that was dominant enough to mate me.

Surely, there had to be one.

***

Want to keep reading? Pick up Wolf Shunned on Amazon.

also by laurel night

THE ALPHA QUEEN LEGACY - COMPLETE SERIES

A SLOW-BURN REVERSE harem romance featuring a fantasy dystopian setting that has been compared to 'I Am Legend' crossed with 'The Shanarra Chronicles' and wolf shifters. Named one of Book Authority's Top Fantasy Books of 2021, and Red Feather Romance's 10 Top Adult Fantasy Romances. Available on Amazon and Kindle Unlimited.

MIDNIGHT WOLVES OF SMOKY FALLS

Moved abruptly from the streets to a plush mansion in a small town, Layla is eager to start her new life. However, she soon discovers there are more dark mysteries in this town than she could have imagined. This is a New Adult, Reverse Harem wolf shifter romance. Check out Book 1, Pack Dreams, here!

SCENT OF DECEPTION - A STANDALONE IN THE BONDS OF STEELE OMEGAVERSE

Raised to be a pampered omega, Sapphire Steele never manifested. Desperate, she accepted a lucrative proposal: Pretend to be the omega for a wealthy pack until one of the alphas receives his inheritance, then disappear with her share of the money.... But someone knows her secret... Check it out on Amazon and Kindle Unlimited.

GLAM - A STANDALONE MAFIA-LITE REVERSE HAREM ROMANCE

The hardworking daughter of two cops finally lands her dream job, only to be interrupted on her first day by three devastatingly handsome mafia brothers she recognized from college. Always out of her reach before, they're suddenly obsessed with her, and insist she become a part of their glittering world. Then, one night she witnesses first hand what happens in the back room of those shimmering parties, and how the Vargas family have ruled over Miami for decades.

Terrified, she knows with certainty that one of two things will happen: Either she becomes theirs, beholden to them and immersed in their world of wealth and privilege for the rest of her life.

Or no one will ever hear from her again. Check it out on Amazon here!

let's be friends!

THANK you so much for reading my books, it truly means the world to me that I can share these crazy ideas with you.

If you'd like to stay apprised of my upcoming projects (there are so many!) Please join my bi-weekly newsletter. You'll get exclusive sneak peeks and chances to win goodies that are only offered to my subscribers—plus you'll have the opportunity to download more of my work free right away!

So what are you waiting for?

Join my newsletter now!

about the author

Laurel Night is a long-time fan of fantasy and adventure. She's traveled the world, and currently resides in the shadow of the Smoky Mountains with her daughter.

For more about Laurel, her books, and future projects, you can find her at www.laurelnight.com, @laurelnightauthor on tiktok, or hanging around in Laurel's Night Queens, her group on Facebook.